HARLEQUIN'S SUPPORT OF BIG SISTERS

Harlequin began sponsoring Big Brothers/ Big Sisters of America and Big Brothers and Sisters of Canada in April 1988. Since then, we have become the largest single sponsor of Big Sisters Programs and related services in North America.

This fitting association between the world's largest publisher of romance fiction and a volunteer organization that assists children and youth in achieving their highest potential is a wonderfully different kind of love story for Harlequin. We are committed to assisting our young people to grow to become responsible men and women.

Brian Hickey
President and CEO

For more information, contact your local Big Brothers/Big Sisters agency.

Dear Reader,

When the opportunity arose to write a story for the Harlequin Superromance Big Brothers/Big Sisters of America series, I was thrilled because I believe in the family. It is the strongest institution in a democratic society, and I see Big Brothers/Big Sisters of America as a supporter and an extension of this institution. Throughout my life I have donated time through my church to being a "sister" to many children—quite a few of whom now have their own children.

Some have drawn the conclusion that only underprivileged children need the role models that Big Brothers/Big Sisters provides, but that is not true. All children have the basic need for love and companionship. That is why I chose to write about a privileged child who has everything except the one thing she wants most—a big sister.

Emma Frances Merritt

MAKE-BELIEVE

Emma Merritt

Harlequin Books

TORONTO • NEW YORK • LONDON
AMSTERDAM • PARIS • SYDNEY • HAMBURG
STOCKHOLM • ATHENS • TOKYO • MILAN
MADRID • WARSAW • BUDAPEST • AUCKLAND

Published November 1992

ISBN 0-373-70523-9

MAKE-BELIEVE

"Why didn't you tell me..."

There was an edge to Brant's voice. "Why didn't you say you were bringing me to my old house?"

"Look," Marcy replied, "if you don't want to drive past your house, turn around and we'll go to my office. Or you can take me home, whichever you prefer."

Brant rubbed his forehead. "It's been so long..."

"Have you never wanted to come home, Brant?" Marcy laid her hand over his.

Brant shook his head. His hands gripped the steering wheel. "No, when I left, it was for good. My home is in New York."

"If the memories are that bad, Brant, turn around."

"No, I've come this far. I might as well go all the way."

CHAPTER ONE

STRETCHED ACROSS her father's bed, nine-year-old Amy Calderon was watching television. "Did you hear that?"

"What?" Gil asked absently as he rummaged through one dresser drawer after the other until he found his socks. He tossed a couple of pairs on the bed.

Amy sighed. Her father never seemed to pay any attention to her. "Little girls can get a Big Sister if they join the program this woman's talking about."

"That's nice," her father murmured, and from the tone of his voice, Amy knew he was only half listening.

"Come and see," Amy invited.

"Not now, honey. I have too much to do, and I'm really in a rush." Gil threw open the closet door. After a few seconds of searching, he exclaimed, "What on earth has Nona done with my new tie?"

Amy slid off the bed and walked to where her father stood. She pointed. "There it is. You have so many, Nona bought you a new rack."

"Thanks, baby."

Amy wandered around the spacious room, finally stopping in front of the dresser. Catching a glimpse of her reflection in the mirror, she leaned closer to study herself. Then her gaze shifted to the reflection of her father, who moved in a circle from the chest of drawers, to the closet and to the bed, packing for his business trip to Dallas.

"I don't know what I'm going to do with my hair," she said. "It's a mess."

"It's beautiful," Gil answered, never looking up.

Amy was unhappy that her father was so preoccupied. She continued to stare at him through the mirror. Her friend Julie, who lived next door and was thirteen years old, said all men as old as her father acted like this. In fact, according to Julie, all parents behaved the same way. Amy knew her father was old—he was thirty-three—but she wished he was different. He was either away on business trips or was too busy to listen to her. She turned her attention back to her own image in the mirror and tugged at a strand of long, black hair. What else had Julie said? "Sometimes you just have to shock your family into paying attention."

Struggling to remember her friend's exact words, Amy began, "Julie's parents are going to let her have an entirely new image this summer. She said I need a new one, too. I've been thinking about hairweaving." She smiled at her reflection. "What do you think?"

"Fine, honey, whatever you want." At the same time that Gil closed the drawer, a pair of socks slipped from his hands and rolled across the thick carpet. He chased the ball, still not looking at Amy.

"Hairweaving will make my hair look thicker...and longer if I want." Without pausing, Amy picked up the brush and began to run it through her hair. "I called the beauty salon, and I can have it done for about six hundred dollars."

"You what!"

The exasperation in his voice caused Amy to drop her hand and to lift her head. She encountered her father's reflection in the mirror. He pushed his hand through his black hair—something he always did when he was irritated—and frowned at her. Now she had his attention—his full attention.

"Amelia Calderon!"

He was upset!

"I don't care what Julie does with her hair. That's her parents' problem. But I do care what you do." He paused, his brown eyes seriously regarding her.

Amy squirmed beneath the solemn gaze but said nothing.

"I have nothing against Julie," he continued, "but I don't consider her—*at age thirteen*—to be your role model."

"Well—" Amy stammered. She wasn't doing so great with this! Julie hadn't told her that her father might get angry, nor had she coached her on how to proceed if the plan didn't work. She took a deep breath and turned so that she was looking directly into her father's eyes. "It was Debbie's idea and she's fifteen, Daddy, and she knows all about these things. Julie told me so, and Debbie is beautiful."

"The Burrows girls could both look like Liz Taylor, for all I care," Gil replied, his tone less sharp, "but that doesn't give either of them the right to suggest a complete Amy Calderon make-over, and I'm most certainly not paying six hundred dollars for this hairweaving nonsense. Even if it's free, I don't want you to have someone else's hair woven into yours. When I come home, I want to recognize my little girl," he continued in that father-knows-best tone. "I love you just the way you are."

By the time he'd finished talking, his voice sounded less angry, and Amy felt better. She watched as he resumed packing for his second trip this month.

"I wish you had a job like Julie's father and didn't have to travel," she said. "Then you wouldn't have to worry about recognizing me when you returned. You'd be here with me all the time. We could do things together. And you could come to my recital."

Gil straightened and returned her gaze. His eyes darkened, and Amy hoped he was feeling a little guilty about leaving her.

"Honey—" he sounded tired "—don't start this argument again. We've been through it too many times already. You're a big girl, and you know I have a job to do."

"Daddy, can't you get someone else to take your place?" Tears gathered in her eyes. She missed her father when he was gone. True, she had Nona, the housekeeper, but Nona wasn't Mama. Mama was gone to heaven to be with God and would never come home again. When Daddy was with her, she didn't miss her mother as much.

"Amy, I've already explained why I can't."

Wiping her hand down the leg of her jeans, she lowered her head and studied the tips of her sneakers. A part of her understood what her father was saying, but another part was scared—the part that was lonely and hurt so much. Since her mother's death three years ago, she'd been afraid she would lose her father, too, and that she would be alone.

Amy felt the gentle pressure of her father's fingers squeezing her shoulder. His touch was reassuring and comforting. She loved him so. She blinked back tears but still did not raise her head. She could hardly stand it when he was unhappy with her.

"Baby—" he sat down on the bed and pulled her into the protective circle of his arms "—believe me, I'm sorry I'm going to have to miss the recital."

"It's a special one, Daddy. Mrs. Eanes is calling it April Showers Bring May Flowers, and I'm one of the May Flowers."

"I understand, sweetheart, and I want to come see you do your special May Flower dance, but I can't. I promise I'll be at the one you have in September."

"I don't care about that one." Amy twisted out of his arms, flopped down on the bed and pressed her face into the soft coverlet.

"Of course, you do," he told her. "Remember, you invited Wanda to attend it with us."

Wanda Courtland was the woman her father worked with. He had been talking about her a lot lately. Amy liked her, but she didn't want her father to become too friendly with her.

"She's *your* friend."

"She would like to be your friend, too," her father answered.

Amy decided to ignore Mrs. Courtland. "If you loved me," she said, "you wouldn't go to Dallas. You'd let somebody go for you."

"I let Robin take my assignment so I could attend your last recital, which was barely a month ago. I can't ask him to do it again. He also has a family to consider. I can't understand why your two recitals were scheduled so close together."

"Mrs. Eanes was doing it for us." Amy flipped over and gazed into his face. "She thinks we need to perform in front of an audience more often, so we won't be nervous. We needed the practice for the May Festival of Dance.''

"Baby, I know how much this means to you, but I'm sorry. I just can't cancel this trip or reassign it. It's too important."

"Maybe you can come home early," Amy suggested tentatively, turning her face up to her father.

"There's always a chance, but it's not very likely," her father replied. "I have too much to do. In order to be home last month, I asked my clients if I could rearrange my schedule to visit this month, and they agreed. But I can't change the meeting dates again, honey. If I did, I'd lose valuable clients." Gil sighed. "You're so young, I can't expect you to understand."

Out of the corner of her eye, Amy watched her father slide to the edge of the bed. He stood, walked to the open French doors and stared into the terraced garden outside his bedroom.

"Please, Daddy. This one is so important for me. I'll bet if you told Robin how important it was for you to stay here, he'd go to Dallas for you, and you wouldn't lose any of your clients," she begged. "Please, Daddy."

"No, Amy—" his voice firm, Gil turned "—I can't. If Mrs. Eanes had sent a schedule of her recitals in time, I could have set my appointments up differently, and I would be there. But as it is, I have to consider my job—which, young lady, is vitally important to both of us."

Her father's explanation didn't soften the blow of his refusal. Amy leaped up, with tears running down her cheeks. "You don't care about me. All you care about is your old job! You're always gone. This is the second time this month!"

"Amy, don't speak to me in that tone of voice," Gil said sternly. "I won't allow it."

Amy could see her father meant business. "I'm sorry," she murmured. She wiped the tears from her eyes. "It's just that I won't have anybody to go with me."

Gil returned to the bed and sat down beside her. He ran his hand through his hair. "You'll have Nona. And Julie and Debbie will be there."

"But Debbie and Julie's parents will be there, too, and they don't pay any attention to me. And Nona's only the housekeeper." Her voice lowered. "She's not like you or Mama."

"No, she's more like your grandmother or an aunt," Gil explained. "But she's loved you ever since you were a baby, and she's like family."

Snuggling up to her father, Amy said softly, "I know, but she's not an older sister. If only I had an older sister like Julie has. When her parents can't go somewhere with her, Debbie is always there to take her. Julie's never alone."

If she couldn't have her two parents, Amy would settle for an older sister. In the world of make-believe, she and her older sister loved each other and had fun together. In the world of make-believe, her older sister promised that if something happened to Daddy, she would always be there to take care of and love Amy.

"If I had an older sister like Julie, we could share a bedroom and tell our secrets to each other. She could drive me places and take me shopping at the mall. She could play with my Barbie dolls."

Gil caught Amy and hugged her tightly. "I can't give you an older sister, baby, but maybe someday I could give you a younger one."

Amy's gaze traveled to the large photograph of her mother on one of the nightstands. She remembered the way her parents had talked and laughed when her Mama was alive. Then she thought about Mrs. Courtland, and she felt twinges of jealousy.

"Maybe someday I'll get married again," he told her. "Like you, sometimes I get so lonely I can hardly stand it."

"Oh, Daddy," Amy exclaimed, "I don't want you to get married! You have me."

"We have each other," he agreed. "But sometimes that's not enough. You need a mother and I need a wife. We need a family, Amy."

"I don't need a mother," Amy muttered, her heart feeling heavy, her thoughts returning to Mrs. Courtland. "And I don't want a younger brother and sister. I want you, Daddy."

"Maybe for now," Gil said. "But soon, I won't be enough for you."

"Yes, you will," Amy assured him.

The telephone rang, and he reached for it.

Amy rolled over to grab the receiver before he did. "I'll bet it's for me. Julie's supposed to call me about the recital." She placed the receiver against her ear. "Calderon residence."

"Hello, Amy, this is Wanda Courtland."

Amy's heart sank. "Hello, Mrs. Courtland."

"Your father told me about your recital next week. I know you must be excited."

"Yes," Amy answered, running her hand idly up the coiled telephone cord, wishing it had been anyone but Mrs. Courtland on the other end.

"I'm really looking forward to seeing you perform in September. Your father tells me that you're quite a dancer. He refers to you as his prima donna."

Mrs. Courtland sounded nice, but Amy didn't want to talk with her at the moment. "Do you want to talk to Daddy?" she asked dully.

"Yes, please. And, Amy, good luck at your April recital. I know you're going to dance beautifully."

"Thank you. I'll get Daddy for you." Amy handed the telephone to her father. "It's for you. Mrs. Courtland."

Her father smiled and took the receiver. "Wanda, how nice of you to call."

Amy hadn't heard such excitement in her father's voice in a long time, and she resented this woman who made her father so happy. No one should be able to do that but her mother.

"Yes, I have the McInnis account." He listened, then said, "Of course, I'll be back in Dallas by that time. Why?" he asked.

Amy stole a look at her father's face. He was smiling, then he laughed softly. Amy's spirits plummeted. Her father liked this woman.

"The theater tomorrow? Yes, I'd love to go." He moved to the open door and, turning his back to Amy, leaned a shoulder against the jamb. "Wanda, thanks for the offer. I'd appreciate your picking me up. My plane arrives at seven."

Tears pricking her eyes, Amy scooted across the bed, messing up the cover as she moved to pick up the photograph of her mother. She wanted her mother;

she wanted to feel her mother's arms around her and her soft cheek resting on the crown of her head. How happy the three of them had been ... until her mother and the baby had died.

"The dance recital?" she heard her father say. "Yes, of course. Amy and I are looking forward to it.... No, really. *Both* Amy and I are happy that you'll be attending with us."

Her father's words broke into Amy's thoughts and she stiffened. Until now she had been willing to tolerate Wanda Courtland, but not anymore. Amy wanted a big sister; she did *not* want another woman in her father's life.

"We'll talk more about it when I'm in Dallas," Gil promised Wanda. "I'll see you in three hours."

When he replaced the receiver in the cradle, Amy tossed the photograph onto the bed. "That's why you can't come to my recital," she accused. "You're going to Dallas to meet Mrs. Courtland."

"I'll be meeting with Wanda," he confirmed as his gaze moved to the photograph, "but it's business, Amy. You know she and I work together, and we have for several years. When I first introduced you to Wanda, you seemed to like her. In fact, you were the one who invited her to attend your September dance recital." When Amy didn't respond, he prompted, "Didn't you?"

"Well, I've changed my mind."

Gil sat down on the edge of the bed again and picked up the photograph. He gazed at it for a long time before he replaced it on the night table and turned to Amy. "Honey, Mama is dead. If I could change circumstances and bring her back, I would."

Again Gil cradled Amy against his body, and she rested her cheek on his big chest. She listened to the steady rhythm of his heart. Amy wrapped her arms around her father and held him tightly, wishing she could understand.

"We've got to go on with our lives," he said, running his hand down the back of her head as he rubbed her hair. "If you'll just allow her, Wanda can be your friend. She would like to be."

Amy pushed out of his arms and glared into his face. "I don't want her for my friend, Daddy."

"Gil . . ." A small, gray-haired woman appeared at the door, wearing a white bibbed apron that covered the front of her dress. "Are you going to want to eat before your flight?"

He closed his mouth and shook his head. "I won't have time. I'm running late now. I'll eat after I get to Dallas."

Amy rushed across the room and flung herself against the housekeeper, Nona Ferguson. "He doesn't have time because he's going to Dallas to meet Wanda Courtland. He doesn't have time for me anymore, because he wants to be with her. He's going to eat dinner with her."

"Well, Gil," Nona announced, "I reckon I'm right proud of you. It's high time you started seeing other women. And you, young lady, I'm a little disappointed in you. I can't figure you behaving like this."

She tucked her fingers beneath Amy's chin and lifted her face. Aged blue eyes gazed compassionately into the child's. She smiled warmly. "Come on. Let's you and me go into the kitchen. We'll talk about this."

"There's nothing to talk about," Amy declared, resenting Nona's having taken her father's side.

"There's plenty to talk about, but we can wait until you think it's time," Nona replied, and in silence they walked along the corridor and downstairs into the large, bright kitchen that sparkled with chrome and glass and white ceramic tile. Moving into the breakfast nook, Amy plopped into one of the cushioned chairs.

"Isn't it about time for *Wheel of Fortune?*" Nona asked and picked up the remote control.

Although this was Amy's favorite show, she wasn't interested in watching it today. She slumped lower in the chair, feeling rejected. Today, for the first time, she had failed to get her way with her father—all because of *that* woman. He wasn't that interested in his work; he was flying to Dallas to be with *her.* Amy wished she had never invited Mrs. Courtland to attend the dance recital with them.

The theme song of the game show filled the room.

"I don't want to watch television." She continued to sulk.

"Don't, then, but I am." Nona went to the counter in the center of the room and began to dice the vegetables. "You're being rather hard on your father."

Amy crossed her arms over her chest and looked at the television, then at the growing pile of carrots on the cutting board. She had always been amazed at the speed with which Nona's hands, swollen by arthritis, could chop vegetables. Each swipe of the knife was in rhythm with her words.

"He's lonely," Nona said, then added gently, "One of these days you'll understand."

"He has *me,*" Amy mumbled.

"That's right. You're his child. You're very important to him and he loves you very much. But he needs grown-up friends as well, and he needs a woman his own age.''

With the edge of the knife, Nona swished the vegetables into a large bowl and carried them to the stove. Amy watched silently.

''If your father found the right woman, he would remarry and you could have brothers and sisters.''

''I don't want any little brothers or sisters, and if I can't have *my* mother, I don't want a mother.''

Never again, Amy thought. No one—absolutely no one—could take her mother's place. Certainly not that Wanda Courtland. Amy's mother had been beautiful, with black hair and brown eyes; Wanda was blue-eyed and had blond hair. She looked *nothing* like her mother!

''Amy—'' Nona spoke quietly and crossed the room to where Amy sat.

Already regretting her hastily spoken words, Amy lowered her face, but she felt Nona's gaze on the back of her head.

''Amy, look at me. I don't want to hear you talk like that.'' Nona's tone softened. ''I understand how you must miss your mother, but nothing we can do or say will bring her back. You and your father have to go on with your lives, and that's going to be hard on both of you because it means changing.''

''Yes, ma'am,'' Amy replied.

The housekeeper knelt in front of Amy and embraced her. Amy laid her cheek against Nona's breast, grateful for the comfort and love.

''I'm sorry, Nona. I didn't mean it.''

''I know, my darling.'' Nona rocked back and forth for a little while, brushing her hand down Amy's head and back in soothing strokes.

"Daddy's gonna meet Mrs. Courtland," Amy murmured. "He really likes her."

"And so do I," Nona said. "I'll admit we only saw her for a little while at the airport, but she seemed like a real nice lady. I think she'll be a good friend for your father... and for you, if you'll let her."

"She may take Daddy away from me." Amy voiced her deepest fear.

"No," Nona assured her. "Your father isn't going to allow anyone to come between you and him. Besides, I think Mrs. Courtland would be happy to share him with you. Why don't you give her a chance?" When Amy didn't answer, Nona said, "Sometimes growing up is hard, baby, but with love and help from the ones who love you, you're going to make it." She pulled back and gazed into Amy's eyes. A smile creased her wrinkled features. Cradling Amy's face in her hands, she placed a kiss on her forehead. "Now, I'd best get to my cooking or we won't have any dinner tonight."

When Nona walked away, tears still blurred Amy's vision. However, she turned her full attention to the television and to a child named Cindy Evans who was about Amy's age. She had seen the girl earlier on television in her father's room; it was another commercial about the Big Sister-Little Sister program. Amy wiped her eyes and leaned forward with interest.

The girl on television said, "When I grow up, I plan to become a Big Sister. My Big Sister is Anna Perron. She's twenty years old." With a broad smile on her face, the blond-haired child looked up at the woman beside her. "She helps me with everything I do, and I like being around her. She's always there when I need her. She's one of the best things in my life."

As the names of local schools scrolled along the bottom of the screen, Amy checked to see whether hers was listed. It was. She grinned. That meant people from Big Brothers/Big Sisters would be visiting her school during the coming week. Awesome! If she became a part of this program, she could get her Big Sister. What's more, she would get to choose who she wanted for a Big Sister. Now all she had to do was figure out how to join the program.

She heard a knock and looked up to see the door open. A freckled face framed in a riot of bright red curls peeked around the opened door. A broad smile revealed the latest style in colored braces. "Hi. Do I happen to be in time for dinner?"

"As always, Julie, your timing is perfect. Come in and close the door. I don't want the electric bill any higher than it has to be," Nona answered dryly. Muttering to herself, she continued, "It's only the first of April, but already it's warm out. We're gonna have a hot summer this year."

"Yes, ma'am."

The door slammed, and Julie's small, reed-thin figure, completely dwarfed in an oversize white T-shirt, entered the room.

"Did you tell your mama you were going to eat with us?"

"Yes, ma'am." Julie scurried over to sit down beside Amy. "Well," she inquired in a low voice, "did you talk with your dad?"

Amy nodded.

"Did you get his attention?"

Amy slowly shook her head and smiled deliberately, knowing she was whetting her friend's curiosity. "No, I have another idea, Julie." She looked at

Nona, then said in an equally low voice, "I'll tell you about it later."

The green eyes behind Julie's large, metal-rimmed glasses gleamed with interest. "I can hardly wait. This sounds interesting. Very interesting."

"It is."

Both of them watched Nona stir-fry the vegetables.

"Amy—" taking her index finger, Julie shoved her glasses higher on the bridge of her nose "—is this a real conspiracy or make-believe?"

"Wait and see."

CHAPTER TWO

"HI, KYLA, I KNOW it's after working hours, and I apologize for calling you at home," Marcy Galvan said, the receiver of her car phone pressed between her shoulder and her ear as she negotiated her green Bronco truck through the five o'clock traffic in downtown San Antonio. "I stopped by the office, but you had already gone. Your secretary said you wouldn't mind my calling you at home."

"No, of course not," the caseworker for Big Brothers/Big Sisters replied. "What do you need, Marcy?"

"I wondered if the supermarket had called you about the wieners and buns?"

"They did. Thanks for getting them donated. Thanks to you, we're going to have a hot-dog feast. This April get-together will be one of our best monthly meetings."

"I'm looking forward to it," Marcy told her, "and I'm eager to be assigned to a Little Sister. Do you have any prospects for me yet?"

Kyla laughed softly. "I'm working on it." Marcy could envision the black woman sitting behind her desk smiling, her hair combed into a chignon, large gold earrings lightly brushing against her smooth ebony cheeks. "At the moment, I don't have anyone who I feel is right for you, Marcy, but we're always taking new girls into the program. I'm sure we're going to have your Little Sister soon. We're visiting schools, and advertising on television. Anna Perron—you know, the woman I told you about who reminds me so much of you—is doing the commercial. If I hear anything before the party, I'll give you a call. Okay?''

"Great! I'll be seeing you then, if not sooner," Marcy said and rang off.

Exiting from the I-35 expressway, one of the main arteries through San Antonio, and turning left onto Commerce Street, she drove a couple of miles on the busy six-lane thoroughfare. Several streets later, she parked in front of a vacant school building—a historical landmark that she and others in the community were trying to restore. A six-foot Cyclone fence surrounded it and building materials were stacked on the grounds.

She lowered her window and emitted a soft groan as hot air rushed into the air-conditioned interior. She was tired and wished she were at home taking a shower. But after stopping by the office of Big Brothers/Big Sisters of America to meet with Kyla, she had run out of time; there had hardly been a few minutes for her hamburger and cold drink on the run.

Marcy's hard hat and leather gloves lay on the seat beside her; otherwise she was still wearing her work clothes. She loved her job and was completely dedicated to the Galvan Construction Company. The company had been in the family for generations. When her father died, Marcy had stepped into his shoes and become a full partner with her uncle. This morning her shirt and jeans had been clean; now, after a day at the site of the new Alamo Supermarket on the West Side, they were dirty and stained with perspiration.

Yet, the only change Marcy would make to her life was the addition of a loving husband and family—a large family. Because she came from a large family, she wanted one herself. Unfortunately, at present there was no loving husband on the horizon.

"Hi, Marcy! Over here!" a man shouted from the distance.

Interrupting her thoughts, she turned to see Pete Rodriguez, a man in his late forties, push away from the front wall of the school building and walk toward her vehicle. Pete was president of a group called Property Owners Development, commonly known as POD. This organization was trying to save the old neighborhood, and Pete took his responsibility very seriously. Since the Galvans had originally lived in the area, Marcy and her older brother Ethan had joined in the conservation efforts.

"I wondered if you were coming," he said, close enough now that he didn't have to shout.

"Sorry," she apologized. "We had a glitch at the site, and I had to stay late."

"No problem." Pete squinted against the glare of the afternoon sun, and a hot breeze riffled raven-black hair. A teasing light glinted in his dark eyes. "You look like you've had a rough day. You know what they say about people who can't take the heat."

"Well, you'll have to pardon my appearance." She laughed softly, enjoying their teasing banter. Pete was a hard worker and a visionary, whom she liked as a friend and admired as a colleague.

Marcy picked up her yellow hard hat and placed it on her head. Then she slid across the leather seat and looked into the rearview mirror. Her eyes were still slightly swollen from the cement dust. She continued to gaze at her reflection and at the color of her irises. She was the only girl in the family and had three older brothers, all of whom had chocolate-colored eyes. Hers were a golden brown with tiny flecks of green.

As a child she had realized her eyes were unusual because people always commented on them. It was her Irish heritage showing through the Hispanic, Papa had explained, always taking advantage of the compliment to talk about their ancestors.

Oh, well, she thought, not hers to reason why but hers to accept and be happy about—which she was. She brushed tendrils of damp black hair into the thick coil under her hat.

"It's been a scorcher today," Pete said.

"I know. I've been out in it all day."

Taking a handkerchief from his pocket, he wiped his face and the back of his neck.

"Think maybe we ought to move to Alaska? Perhaps I could be real creative in igloo construction," Marcy joked.

Pete grinned and tucked the handkerchief into his hip pocket. "Instead of a stonemason, I'd be a ice-block mason or an igloo mason?"

"I'd choose igloo mason," Marcy replied. "It sounds better. Do the buildings melt down every summer so we can rebuild them every winter? If they don't, we could find ourselves without a job after one season."

She and Pete usually kidded each other to hide their anxiety over the reclamation of Esteban Heights neighborhood and their dream of developing a literacy center. Both knew it would be a real struggle to reach their goals.

Reaching for a green file folder—one among several—Marcy opened the door and slid out of the truck, her booted feet hitting the ground with a thud. As if this were the first time she had been here, she slowly inspected the area. Houses in decay; the street pavement full of potholes; historic buildings that gave the community a sense of identity, which were being demolished to make way for what? Empty lots, soon to be overgrown with weeds. More slums. Hadn't some great philosopher once said, "Poverty begets poverty"?

Many lamented, but only a handful cared enough to do something about it; only a handful were fighting to save their neighborhood—to rid it of gangs and drug users and pushers, to cut down on crime, and to encourage education. There were so many in need—so many who could learn to help themselves—but so few who were willing to fight. Tonight the few—the POD board—were meeting.

"Did Ethan hear from Brant Holland?" Pete asked. When she nodded, he reached up and scratched his temple—a gesture he made when he was nervous. "Bad news?"

"Bad and good," Marcy answered.

She opened the folder and pulled out a check. "This is the good part." She handed the check and a letter to Pete.

"As you can see, Brant's administrative assistant, Shepherd Hayden, was generous to the project. He also wrote that Brant's itinerary is completely booked for the coming year, and there's no way he could attend the fund-raiser."

"Damn!" Pete exclaimed.

As if by unspoken consent, both walked through the gate toward the building.

"We can certainly use the money," he said, "but we need Brant here in person. We'll never be able to raise enough money to—" He broke off and shrugged, the checkered material of the Western shirt pulling tight across his shoulders. "Damn, Marcy, what are we going to do?"

By now they were standing in front of the abandoned, small, red brick building that had once housed the local elementary school. Marcy reached out and touched the cornerstone, her fingers tracing the inscription, which she read aloud. "Estella Esteban Elementary School Built In 1921 And Dedicated To The Memory Of Estella Esteban, Master Teacher." She turned to Pete. "You know, I was in the last class that attended school here."

"And in a few weeks this building—" Pete's hand swept through the air "—will be no more. Hell, Marcy, we can't lose this, or the neighborhood will lose a symbol of its identity and a vital part of its history. Sometimes I hate Justis Juarez."

Marcy felt as if a heavy weight were pressing against her heart. POD's virtual last hope had been Brant Holland, and they had counted on her brother Ethan to persuade Brant to attend the fund-raiser to save Esteban Heights and to convert the school and the adjacent lots into a literacy center and a playground.

Ethan had been the logical choice. He, like Brant Holland, was a product of the Heights. He and Brant had been friends all through their school days, parting ways only after they both graduated from university. For several years afterward Brant had kept in contact with the Galvan family, visiting them during the holidays and writing an occasional card.

Marcy's hand went to the small gold locket that hung from her neck. Brant had sent it to her for her thirteenth birthday. Becoming a teen, he had written, was a special occasion and deserved a special gift. How long ago that had been! Fifteen years, to be exact. Marcy felt even more depressed. Where had the years gone? And what did she have to show for them? A hard hat, several pairs of expensive boots and a struggling construction company from which she barely eked a living.

Well, she thought with a smile as she corrected herself, she actually had two hard hats. The little one that Brant had had specially made for her and had given to her on her sixth birthday. Her prized possession! Now it rested in a place of honor on the mantel in her bedroom, alongside an antique music box.

Pete asked, "Do you think calling Brant will help?"

"Ethan's already called, but this guy Hayden gave him no hope at all that Brant would be willing to help us. He evidently thought we were after more money and said we had been given all we were going to get from Brant. But," Marcy said reflectively, "I just have the feeling that Brant himself hasn't refused. I think Hayden refused for him. He's probably Brant's screen. You know how wealthy people protect themselves."

Pete sighed and lifted his head to gaze at the former school. "I was hoping to see a library here real soon."

"Me, too," Marcy replied. "We've made such strides. I'd hate to see us lose the building and the surrounding property now. This is where our community center should be."

Pete laughed and remarked sarcastically, "If we're depending on Brant Holland, it looks like we stand a better chance of losing it than saving it. I'll bet he's ashamed of his background and doesn't want people to know where he grew up."

Marcy forgave Pete his bitterness. Normally he wasn't so critical and judgmental, but Brant's refusal was the final blow to POD's efforts. They would never be able to get the money to buy the school and the property adjacent to it without large donations. If she thought about it long enough, she would get angry at Justis Juarez all over again. He owned the property, had set a price on it that far exceeded the market value, and refused to negotiate. His vision for redevelopment of the area did not include a community center; in fact he wanted to see all evidence of the old community eradicated.

"If only someone could get word to Brant himself," Marcy said, dropping her hand again to caress the locket. Although Brant had been away from San Antonio for years, Marcy couldn't accept that he had changed that much. "Brant wouldn't let us down, especially if he knew Justis Juarez was the one keeping the property from us."

"An old rival?" Pete questioned, and Marcy nodded. "But that's water under the bridge, Marcy. Brant may be from here, but I think he's intentionally forgotten his roots. My God, he's nearly forty and hasn't returned, that we know of, since he left years ago."

"He's thirty-six, and he's been gone eighteen years exactly," Marcy corrected.

How well she knew her facts. She had thought about little else since she had joined POD's efforts to save Esteban Heights. Every day she would walk to the pictures on the wall of her office to dust them and look at those of Brant.

He was eighteen when the last photo was taken, but somehow she was sure his appearance wouldn't have changed much. His eyes would still be blue, and his hair black, burnished to a sheen in the sunlight. She didn't even have to look at the photographs to remember what he looked like. She would never forget Brant Holland. He had always been her Prince Charming. Now he had become the one person who could save POD.

"He's so successful he doesn't even give his old friend the time of day," Pete said.

A silver Toyota sedan pulled up at the curb behind Marcy's Bronco, and the driver beeped the horn several times. Then a smiling face appeared in the window. The door opened, and Ethan Galvan climbed out.

"It's about time you got here," Marcy called to her brother.

Dressed in slacks and a sport shirt, Ethan sauntered toward her. "I suppose you've already given Pete the news?" She nodded, then he asked, "Come up with any alternatives?"

"We have none," Pete answered. "It's Brant or nothing."

"Well then, it looks like nothing," Ethan said.

"You're right, Pete," Marcy acknowledged. "But you and Ethan sound too pessimistic too soon. We haven't exercised all our options. We can't accept Hayden's answer. We're fighting for something we believe in, something we must have. We can't cave in because Brant Holland seems to have given us a no. This project means too much for us to give up."

"Surely we can do this without him," Ethan reasoned. "There must be others who will help us. What about Representatives Paul Mendez and Billy Covington?"

"I know both of them will help, and they're great," Marcy agreed. "San Antonio wouldn't be where it is today if it weren't for Paul and Billy, but neither of them came from this neighborhood. They never lived here."

Warming to her subject, she explained, "Brant did, and he's made something of himself. He can be a role model for our youngsters. We need that. And no matter what you think, no matter how battered your ego is after the letter and the telephone call to Hayden, we need more than Brant Holland's money if we're going to succeed. We need the man himself, and the contributions his presence will bring. He's respected and dynamic. His name alone will bring other contributors."

Ethan smiled at Marcy, but he continued to shake his head. "The way the situation looks now, little sister, we're going to have to settle for the money Shepherd Hayden sent and forget Brant. He's cut from different fabric altogether."

Forget Brant! That was something Marcy was not prepared to do. As a six-year-old she had idolized Brant Holland, and to an extent she still did. She believed he was the man to save Esteban Heights.

"No," she replied. "He *is* made out of the same fabric—he's just using a designer pattern. That's the very reason we need him. I'm sure that if we could communicate directly with Brant, he would come for the fund-raiser. He couldn't have changed so much during the past eighteen years. He couldn't have!"

"Ever the optimist," Ethan teased.

"The rest of the board will be arriving soon," Pete reminded them, "and we have to figure out what we're going to report. What's our next move?"

"That's it!" Marcy snapped her fingers. "Our next move is New York. We've been doing this *bassackwards*. We've been expecting him to come to us, but we're going to have to go to him."

Pete and Ethan looked at her in shocked surprise.

"In order to get Brant Holland to commit to coming to San Antonio, we'll send someone to talk to him in person. Didn't Hayden tell you that he'd be back from Europe in two weeks?" she asked her brother. When he nodded, she announced, "Well, then, I think I'm just that person."

THINKING HE HEARD someone call his name, Brant Holland surveyed the crowd of people who drank, ate and milled—had, in fact, been drinking, eating and milling for the past four hours—in his Manhattan penthouse. He wished he could be grateful to his secretary for having arranged the surprise birthday party for him, but he wasn't. Today had been a long day. He had returned early from Europe after having successfully completed the Grossmeyer Computers takeover and having initiated the papers for the purchase of Bennington Electronics.

He was exhausted by the time his plane had landed, and had wanted nothing more than to come home to a quiet evening by himself. Instead, Shepherd had met him at the airport, handing him a sheaf of papers that needed signing, and briefing him on what had transpired in his absence. Then, when they had walked into the apartment, lights had flashed on and people seemed to crawl out of the woodwork, yelling, "Surprise!" A surprise birthday party.

April 15. Dear God, the last thing he had wanted to remember was his birthday!

Coming back to the present, he realized he was mistaken. Evidently no one had called his name. He turned and started to make his way out of the room. If he couldn't be home by himself, at least he could find a little solitude in his study. He really needed some time alone.

"Brant."

This time he did hear his name. He stopped, and his gaze shifted to the fair-haired woman who pressed through the crowd toward him.

Smiling and lifting her champagne glass, his secretary said, "Happy birthday, Boss."

"Thanks, Joyce," he replied. "The party was thoughtful, but I believed I could depend on you of all people not to rub my age in."

She laughed. "Thirty-six isn't all that old!"

"Joyce Lynne," he admonished with mock severity, "do you want to get fired?"

"I love working for you, Mr. Holland, but I worry about you. I figured you needed some time off." Her eyes darkened with concern. "You're not having fun?"

"I'm tired."

"Even if you weren't tired, you wouldn't be having fun. You work entirely too hard."

Brant smiled. "You're beginning to sound like Shepherd."

"He's right, you know. You are a workaholic."

"No," he corrected softly, not wanting to hurt Joyce's feelings, "I'm just ensuring myself a very comfortable future. I grew up in poverty, and I don't intend to retire to it.''

Joyce laughed. ''The same answer you gave to Shepherd.''

''Speaking of him,'' Brant said, ''where is he?''

''He's at the office tying up some loose ends.''

Brant nodded.

''Knowing you'd like to do the same, I'll take care of the party,'' she told him, a decided twinkle in her eyes, ''and you can escape to your study for a few minutes. However, when it's time to blow out the candles, I'll come and get you.''

Brant laughed with her. ''How many?''

''Thirty-six and one to grow on.''

''I know you all accuse me of being a windbag sometimes,'' Brant teased, ''but I don't know if I have enough wind for that many candles.''

When Joyce walked away, Brant went on to his study, closing and locking the door behind him. The room was well soundproofed and after the noise of the party, the quiet was almost overpowering. Setting his glass on the desk, he walked through the French doors onto the balcony. He flexed his shoulders. God, but he was tired. He wished he could go to bed and sleep for a hundred hours straight.

He wasn't aware how long he'd stood there until he heard a knock on the study door.

''Brant,'' his administrative assistant called out. ''Hate to bother you, but you did tell me to let you know if we heard from Grovers, Inc. We did. Just received a fax from them. What do you want me to do with it?''

''Be right there,'' Brant called.

He opened the door to greet a large man in his late fifties, his white hair combed back in thick waves from his face. His suit coat was discarded, his shirt sleeves rolled up and his tie loosened.

"Hello, Shepherd. No rest for the weary?"

"Something like that." The deep, resonant voice boomed through the room as he waved the letter. "Well, congratulations are in order, Brant. Once again you outsmarted me. I didn't think Grovers, Inc. would come through. They've accepted our bid over Chalmers's, and they didn't wait until the first of the month."

"They had to accept," Brant answered. "We offered them a honey of a deal. One they couldn't possibly turn down. It was just a matter of time."

"Two weeks early," Shepherd murmured, clearly pleased with the deal. He walked to Brant's desk and laid the letter down. "I guess you could call this your birthday present."

"I guess you could," Brant replied indifferently.

"By the way," Shepherd continued, "this morning Aileen brought up some mail—some letters that have been following you around for several months. One of them I wish we had received at least a week ago." Shepherd pointed to the credenza behind Brant's desk. "I had her put them in your In basket and promised I would tell you about them."

"Anything important?" Brant asked, turning to rifle through the overloaded tray.

"Nothing as far as I could tell," Shepherd said. "I've answered all of them. You'll find a copy of my reply stapled to the original letter. Do you want me to leave while you read them?"

Brant shook his head and sat down in the leather chair behind his desk; his assistant moved across the room to sit on the sofa. Brant flipped through the stack, barely glancing at the letters and the answers. One by one they landed in his Out basket for filing. Finally he reached for the remaining one.

"That's the one I wish we had received earlier," Shepherd informed him. "We could have saved the little gal a lot of money, time and disappointment."

As Brant read, Shepherd went on, "I received two letters from the Galvans. When I received the first one, I sent a contribution in your name and informed them that you were presently in Europe and would be unable to take part in the fund-raising events during the coming year. Then I received this one."

When Brant had finished reading it, he refolded the letter and tossed it onto his desk. "Ethan and Marcy Galvan," he murmured. "It's been a long time since I've heard from them." Or even thought of them. "And there was Danny. He, Ethan and I were pals during school. Ethan became a dentist, and the last I heard of Danny he was going to law school. And Marcy—" he smiled "—she was going to be a construction worker just like me."

"I've never seen a construction worker who looked as good as she does," Shepherd remarked. "I'm just sorry that she made the trip to New York for nothing."

"She came here?" Brant straightened and his assistant nodded. "Marcy Galvan came here to New York?" Brant repeated.

Shepherd laughed softly. "Sorry, I forgot to tell you. So much has been happening the last few days. Yes, she came here to New York to your office."

"Well, I'll be damned." Brant found himself laughing, too. But he also felt strangely disappointed. "I'm sorry I missed her."

"I gave her a second donation and explained you wouldn't be returning until the middle of next week. As a footnote, Brant, let me add, she's about five-eight or five-nine, slender, with curves in all the right places, and black hair that is absolutely gorgeous. By a long shot, your little Marcy isn't so little anymore. She's all grown up."

Brant stood and walked back onto the balcony, where he stared down at the busy street below, the flickering lights. Lost in memories of Marcy, he stayed there a long time before he turned and reentered the room.

"Little Marcy Galvan," he muttered. "She was about ten years old the last time I saw her. Dear Lord, but she was a pesky little thing, all spindly legs and black braids."

Shepherd got up. "I'd say she's still pesky, or at least spunky, but the legs are anything but spindly. From what I saw of them, Brant, they're quite shapely, and she has the most unusual eyes I've ever seen."

"Yeah," Brant drawled, "her eyes were beautiful. A carryover from an Irish ancestor, her father always said."

"Not were. They are. Maybe you ought to accept their invitation, Brant. It might do you good to go back to your old stomping grounds. You need a break. You work much too hard."

Brant looked at the letter lying on the polished surface of the desk, and for a moment he thought he would like to go home; to see his old friends. To see Ethan and Danny...and Marcy. As quickly as the thought came, it passed. He had too much work to do. Besides, too many years had passed. After all this time, they no longer had anything in common. And he really had no desire to return to San Antonio—especially to Esteban Heights.

"No, I don't think so." He walked to his desk where he picked up the letter and lightly swatted it against his palm. Then he tossed it at the Out basket but missed. The letter fell to the floor and slid a distance. Shepherd moved toward it.

"I'll pick it up," Brant said. "Now, forget work for the night. Go on and have a good time. Enjoy the weekend."

"What about you, Brant?"

"I'm going to enjoy the party," he answered. "I'll be there later. I have to blow out the candles and serve the cake. Until then, I'd like to have a few minutes by myself to collect my thoughts."

Shepherd nodded and closed the door, the room again became suffused with the quietness that Brant had longed for all day. Turning off the overhead light, he moved through the muted glow cast by his desk lamp to the oak credenza against the wall and poured himself a brandy. Then he stepped onto the balcony again, sipping the liquid, letting its warmth flow through his weary body.

The years were catching up with him, and while he had a lot to show for them in terms of wealth, he longed for a family of his own. Ever since he could remember, he had wanted a wife. He thought he had found her in Glenna, but she had been as obsessed with her career as he had been with his. Glenna had never wanted to be a "doting" wife, as she had so scathingly described his requirements. It was true he had always wanted a woman who would be happy being a wife. Was it wrong of him to think like that? he wondered. Too old-fashioned?

But tonight—quite possibly as a result of Glenna's recent engagement announcement and his birthday—Brant admitted to himself that he wanted something more out of life. He truly wanted to be married and settled down. So why hadn't it happened? he wondered. There had certainly been numerous opportunities. Women found him attractive, and the fact that he was so successful probably added to his eligibility. But how long had it been since he had enjoyed the uncomplicated affection of a woman? A long time!

Shaking his head, Brant laughed at himself. He was entirely too close to middle age! It was pressing in on him from all sides and cluttering his thinking.

His glass was empty now and he was walking from the balcony into the study when the toe of his shoe caught Marcy's letter, sending it sliding farther across the floor. It stopped in the arc of desk light, which revealed Marcy's name clearly written on the lefthand corner of the envelope. Her handwriting—if it was hers—was beautiful.

He hadn't been loved or admired for himself as Marcy had adored him since he was eighteen years old. A quiet peacefulness settled over him as he remembered the raven-haired child who had tagged along behind him when he had worked part-time at Galvan Construction Company. He fondly remembered her trying to match strides with his longer gait.

"Someday," she had promised him solemnly, "I'll be able to walk just like you."

He took two steps, bent, picked up the letter and walked to his desk, where he set his glass down. Then he unfolded the paper, pressed it flat and brushed a finger across her name. Another memory came to mind—a skinny little girl running around the lumberyard, her long braids flying behind, her eyes always sparkling with mischief. He chuckled softly. He'd always had to watch his hard hat or little Marcy Galvan would be wearing it. In fact, to keep her away from his own hat, hc'd finally had one made specially for her. He wondered whatever had become of it.

Little Marcy Galvan. *Whatever became of her? What was she doing now?* Besides trying to get him to a fund-raiser in San Antonio.

Shepherd's words came back to taunt him, to stir his curiosity: "By a long shot, your little Marcy isn't so little any more. She's all grown up."

Of course, she would bc, and according to Shepherd she was a beautiful young woman. Cupping his hands behind his head, Brant leaned back in the chair. Years slipped away; memories became as vivid as reality; and he traveled back in time. A luxury he hadn't often allowed himself over the past eighteen years.

He was not a man to indulge in what might have been or in make-believe. His eyes were focused on the future.

"IT'S REALLY BEAUTIFUL, Clarice," Marcy said. Sitting in her bedroom in an antique slipper chair, she watched her sister-in-law twirl around as she modeled her new dress. "But everything you wear is. You could dress out of a discount store and look as if you spent a million dollars."

Clarice went over to the antique cheval glass and gazed at her reflection. "If you took more notice, you'd know that I do dress out of a discount house, but even so, Ethan is going to be a little upset.'' She reached up with one hand to adjust the collar. ''But it was a steal, Marcy. I couldn't pass it up. I feel so good in it.''

''You look very elegant,'' Marcy told her.

Clarice laughed and pulled the brightly colored sundress over her head. Tossing the garment onto the bed, she walked to the dresser to fluff her short curly hair about her face. ''I hope you don't mind my dropping by unexpectedly to see you.''

''No,'' Marcy answered. ''I hadn't planned to do anything tonight but read and watch television.''

''You haven't been yourself since you returned from New York. Ethan and I have missed your coming over to the house.''

''I haven't had time to go anywhere but to work since I returned from New York,'' Marcy muttered.

''You always had time before.'' Clarice slipped into her skirt and blouse. She cast an assessing gaze on her sister-in-law. ''Tell me what's wrong.''

''Nothing, really,'' Marcy replied. ''I just needed time to lick my wounds. My trip to New York was an abysmal failure.''

''Don't take it so hard. You gave it your best.''

''But that wasn't good enough. I got no further than Shepherd Hayden,'' Marcy explained.

''What kind of person was he?'' Fluffing the pillows under her head, Clarice stretched out on Marcy's bed as if it were her own. She propped herself on an elbow and rested her cheek against her palm.

''Fiftyish. Big. Reminds me of Brian Dennehy. Despite what I had imagined him to be, he's a real nice sort—but no help. All I've done is lower my bank account, which I could ill afford to begin with, because of my harebrained idea!"

"So you didn't get to talk to Brant."

As usual, Clarice spoke in a calm rational manner. The only thing she ever became passionate about was her cooking, and Marcy figured that most gourmet cooks were like that.

"Now you've got to figure out where POD is headed from here," Clarice pointed out.

"We're going to save Esteban Heights without Brant," Marcy declared.

"You're taking this too personally," Clarice chided.

"Of course, I am!" Marcy exclaimed. "POD was depending on me."

"I'm not talking about POD." Clarice sat up and brushed her hands through her hair again. "I'm talking about you."

"What do you mean?"

Clarice stood and walked to the fireplace. She picked up the tiny hard hat.

"As a child you idolized Brant," Clarice reminded, "and tagged along behind him when he worked for your father. You went to New York to see him for your own personal satisfaction as well as that of POD. Right?"

"Yes," Marcy admitted, though reluctantly. "I guess I did. I suppose that's why I'm so irritated and depressed. I felt so let down, Clarice. All my daydreams, all my speeches, all my..." Her voice trailed into silence.

"All the new dresses and shoes you bought," her sister-in-law gently added.

Marcy nodded. "I wanted to see him. I really did."

"To see if he was the hero you remember?" Clarice prompted. Then, without waiting for Marcy to comment, she added, "I really do wish you could have seen him. Maybe if you had, you'd get him out of your system. I've always believed your feelings for Brant have kept you from making a commitment to another man."

"Meaning Derrick?" Marcy asked, thinking about her ex-fiancé.

Clarice nodded. "It's such a shame you broke up with him. The two of you were a perfect couple, and he idolized you, Marcy. He would have done anything in the world for you."

Except communicate with me; except include me in important decisions that affected both our lives, Marcy thought. The family had really been distraught when she broke off her engagement, and they had never let her forget and had never accepted her explanation. They didn't understand how upset she had been when Derrick, practically on the eve of their wedding, announced that he had applied for and been granted a transfer to the Los Angeles office of his firm. Marcy could not believe her ears.

Derrick had never once discussed the transfer with her. When he'd refused to accept that she had some say in their future together—certainly in the decision on where they would live—she'd known she couldn't go through with the wedding. She had called it off. She had cared for Derrick, but she was not willing to give up Galvan Construction or San Antonio for him. Her roots were here, and here she would stay.

"Somehow, Clarice," Marcy said, refusing to rehash the past, refusing to feel guilty because she hadn't married Derrick, "I knew if I could talk with Brant, I could convince him to be a part of the fund-raiser. I thought about waiting in New York for him to return, but I didn't have the money. Besides I couldn't be away from the job for that long."

"It's going to be all right," Clarice promised. "You don't have to take the weight of the world on your shoulders, Marcy."

Marcy laughed. "I know. That's what Papa used to tell me."

"How about dinner at our house tomorrow?"

"I don't think—"

"Yes, come," Clarice urged. "I've been attending cooking classes at the Knife and Fork, and I've bought a new cookbook. I'm dying to create some absolutely delicious dishes to surprise you."

"You always do," Marcy replied dryly. She never knew what phase of self-discovery Clarice was in, but when she bought a new cookbook, Marcy knew her sister-in-law was making a change; and each phase resulted in a new diet.

"Well—" Clarice returned the hard hat to the mantel and moved to the bed to pick up her shopping bag "—I'd better get going. I just wanted to check on you and show you my new outfit."

"The dress is beautiful," Marcy said again. "You're going to be the best-dressed Galvan at the barbecue."

"If it were anyone else but Uncle Lonzo, I wouldn't wear a dress," Clarice admitted. "I'd wear my slacks, but you know how old-fashioned he is, and with him not feeling so good, well..." She left her sentence unfinished.

Marcy momentarily forgot her worries about Brant and POD. Immediately she was concerned about her uncle's health. She loved him dearly and had grown closer to him since her father had died four years ago of heart failure.

"You said he's been pretty sick?"

Clarice nodded. "Aunt Felicia sent for Danny...."

Just the mention of her cousin's name filled Marcy with apprehension. She and Danny had never seen eye-to-eye, especially about the running of the company.

"He should be here by Friday," Clarice continued.

"Oh, Lordy," Marcy groaned. "That's day after tomorrow, and all too soon. I do love *Tío*," she declared, fondly referring to her uncle by his title in Spanish as did the rest of the family. "But his son is a pain in the posterior. Every time Danny comes home, he sticks his nose in my business and wants to completely revamp Galvan Construction. He's not even a partner, but you'd think he is by the way he acts."

"Well—" Clarice shrugged her shoulders "—let him have his two cents worth."

"If it were only two cents worth, I could take it, but he wants to put in several millions' worth of pure garbage. Why, Ethan and David and Mark," she said, referring to her older brothers, "are more interested in Galvan Construction than Danny really is, and their interest is absolutely nonexistent."

Clarice laughed. "It's good to have you home, Marcy. If you're not feeling any better later, come on over and spend the night. We'd be glad to have the company."

"Thanks but no. I'll stay here."

After Clarice left, Marcy showered and put on her nightgown. She took the newspaper, climbed into bed and turned on the TV set. She had no sooner begun to read when she heard a child speaking.

"This is my Big Sister, Anna Perron."

Anna Perron! That was the name of the woman Kyla had mentioned to her the other day. The woman who reminded Kyla of Marcy, and this must be the Big Brothers/Big Sisters commercial the caseworker had described to her. Tossing the paper aside, Marcy turned her full attention to the television. The camera zoomed in on Anna Perron. Marcy could see why Kyla thought they looked alike. Both were Hispanic women with long black hair.

"For any of you who are interested in learning more about the program, representatives from Big Brothers/Big Sisters will be visiting many of the local schools during the coming week. If you want to find out if your school is among them, please read the list on the bottom of your screen right now," the announcer said.

CHAPTER THREE

LATE FRIDAY AFTERNOON, Marcy parked the Bronco in front of Galvan Construction. Her hard hat in hand, she walked into the main office. She laid the hat on the desk, shucked her gloves and stuffed them into it, then moved across the room to open the refrigerator to get a bottle of fruit juice. Leaning against the wall, she gazed out the window at the manicured front lawn and leisurely drank the cold drink. When she tossed the empty bottle into the wastepaper basket, she walked back to her desk and began to sort through the papers in her In basket.

She glanced at her watch. Even with her trip to the supermarket and the mall sites, she had plenty of time to get home and change for the Big Brother/Big Sisters monthly meeting. She was completing the last invoice when the door opened.

"Sorry. We're closed for the day," she said.

"Even to me!"

She looked up. "Danny!"

The moment she had been dreading. Her cousin's sporadic visits were annoying and generally pointless. As far as she could determine, his purpose in coming was to remind her how badly the company was doing and to insinuate that she was partially at fault because she was not an efficient manager. His visits always left her frustrated and angry. As she rose, her gaze moved from the tips of his expensive shoes, past his custom-made suit to his custom-made smile that never went beyond a curve of his lips.

"Being an attorney seems to agree with you," she commented dryly. "Or is it the Dallas climate?"

"Both," he answered.

He began to pace around the office, followed by Marcy's watchful eye. He ran his fingers over the backs of the three wing chairs she had grouped around an oak coffee table, whose top was filled with the latest trade magazines.

"The office looks the same," he remarked disapprovingly. "No matter how long it is between visits, it never changes."

"Not quite," Marcy replied, a tad defensively. "We've painted it, had the antique chairs reupholstered and the oak furniture refinished. We've even bought some new furniture, including the dispatcher's desk, a refrigerator and two new computer terminals."

Danny's gaze flicked over the new desk and the computer terminals, then came to rest on Marcy's desk. "You're still using the old one."

"Of course," she returned. "It belonged to Papa." She rubbed her hand over the solid oak.

"What you've done helps some," he conceded, "but it would make the office look better if you refurnished it completely. In fact, you should take time to renovate it entirely. Remember what I suggested the last time I was here? Use some bright and bold colors. Chrome or brass would also add a new dimension."

"Yes," Marcy acknowledged, "I remember. And as I told you then, I'll tell you now—it's a matter of opinion, and it's not *my* opinion. I happen to think having the old furnishings in here makes it look homey and comfortable. And after all, Daniel, I am the one who works here.''

''You're right,'' he said absently and began to prowl through the office again, and *prowl* was the only word Marcy could think of to describe the way her cousin moved about the room. From the moment he entered the office he acted as if he were caged in. Finally he came to a halt in front of a group of photographs on the wall.

Thumping one of them, he laughed softly. ''God, Marcy, will you look at this. I'd forgotten about this one.''

She moved to stand beside him and stared at the photograph of Danny, Brant and Ethan.

''I remember the day as clearly as if it were yesterday,'' he said. ''It was hot, and your Papa and Tío had pushed us until we were about to collapse. Work, work, work! That's all those two knew. We made a pact that day, the three of us, that we would get away from construction work—with no regrets. Ethan was going to be the dentist, I, the attorney, and Brant, the architectural engineer.''

''And y'all made it,'' Marcy finished.

''Yeah, we did,'' Danny agreed. ''I saw Ethan earlier today, and he told me about your newest crusade.''

''He called it *my crusade?*'' Marcy questioned.

Danny laughed. ''Not in those words, but he told me about your wanting to use Brant Holland to save the elementary school. Do you honestly believe Brant ever thinks about the old neighborhood?''

"There are others we've asked to help," she replied, her gaze pinned to his, "but they weren't interested. And yes, I believe he thinks about it, and I believe he cares enough to do something about saving it."

"Let's hope he does," Danny responded sarcastically. "As for me, I've told you repeatedly, I'm a busy man. I don't see what you've got to gain by saving that run-down little school. No one knows Estella Esteban ever existed and won't, no matter how many memorials you erect in the Heights or in the city. Nobody cares, Marcy!"

"I do," she answered quietly. "And despite what you think, there are others who care, too. But even if there weren't, Danny, I would still fight for it. I believe in what I'm doing."

Danny shrugged his shoulders dismissively and stepped around Marcy to gaze at another group of photographs. After studying them for a few seconds, he murmured, *"Abuelo."*

Looking at his paternal great, great-grandfather, he straightened the frames of each picture as he moved down the line of family members until he was looking at his grandfather.

"God, Marcy, but he was proud of his business."

"He had a right to be," she said, with an edge to her voice; she was still smarting from his earlier derogatory remarks. Her cousin's visits always brought out the worst in her. "Grandfather was the third generation of Galvans to work in construction, the third generation to own his own business."

"Our fathers were the fourth, and you're the fifth," Danny recited as if it were a litany.

He had an uncanny ability to make the family business sound like a lost cause.

"It's amazing how some people get in a rut and can't seem to get out," he added.

"I don't consider I'm in a rut," Marcy retorted. Leave it to Danny to construe anything he wasn't a part of as boring. "I think it's a disgrace that I'm the only child out of five who wanted to keep Galvan Construction going. And out of the five, not one of the men wanted to carry on the family business. It was left to the only woman."

Danny shrugged as if losing interest. "How's the rest of the family?" he asked.

"Fine," she replied. "But you didn't come here to small-talk. We can do that Sunday at the barbecue."

"You're right," Danny admitted. Sinking his hands into his pockets, he moved to her desk and perched on the corner. "You know Papa had some more tests run."

Marcy nodded. "Yes."

"Well, we received the results yesterday."

Marcy waited, her breath caught in her lungs.

"He's not improving. The scan showed that he's had several more small strokes, and Mama's health is failing, too. She's not going to be able to look after him by herself much longer." He drew in a deep breath. "I've convinced him to sell his interest in the business and to move to Dallas so Ruth and I can take care of him and Mama."

Marcy had known this was coming, but the knowing didn't temper the distress she felt at Danny's quiet announcement. Her Uncle Lonzo's health had been steadily deteriorating since his initial stroke eighteen months ago. Marcy, with the help of Joe Alexander, the supervisor immediately below her, had been running the company, letting her partner recuperate.

"Uncle Lonzo promised that if he ever sold out," she said, "I would have first option to buy."

"That's what he told me, and that's why I'm here," Danny informed her, then quoted his price.

Marcy stared at him in disbelief. "What!" she exclaimed. "That's too high! Does Tío know you're asking this much?"

"I realize it's high and so does Papa," Danny explained. "And as much as we both regret it, we can't go any lower."

Marcy paced the office. Only the night before, Clarice had admonished her not to take the weight of the world on her shoulders. Last night at their house, as they dined on raw sprouts and carrot juice, Ethan had repeated his wife's admonition. Now without Marcy's asking for it, the world seemed to be collapsing on top of her.

"I've just recently bought out my brothers' shares of the company," she told Danny, "and I don't have that much cash available. Besides, there's a recession, which means a lull in building."

"I wish it could be different," he said, "but the price is firm."

Marcy disliked haggling but could hold her own with the best if the outcome affected her well-being, and this did. She was prepared to plead if it was necessary. "You've got to cut me some slack. Remember, this is a family business."

He shook his head. "I can't. Ruth and I earn a good living, but Papa's medical expenses are costly. Also, he's a proud man, Marcy. He's determined not to be dependent on us for anything. I have to demand this amount for his sake, as well as ours."

"I understand," Marcy responded, her heart feeling as if it were pure lead in her chest, "but it's going to be hard to raise that much."

Again Danny shook his head. "Justis Juarez has made an offer."

Anger, like a bolt of lightning, seared through Marcy, burning her insides. She curled her hands into fists.

"Tío can't sell his interests to Justis," she declared adamantly. "The man is hell-bent on undermining the reclamation of the Heights."

"I know you don't approve of Justis or my morals, Marcy," Danny continued, "but I don't care what the man does with the company once Papa is out of it. I only care that he has the amount of money we're asking for."

Marcy stared into her cousin's cold and unyielding face for a second before she asked, "Do you think Tío would consider maintaining his partnership, and let me run the business? He would still get his half of the profits."

Danny shook his head. "No. I want him out from under the responsibility of it altogether. As long as he's a partner, he'll be worrying about it."

Marcy knew Danny was right. "Will you give me some time to come up with the financing?" she asked.

"Middle of June," he answered.

Gaping at him, Marcy could not believe her ears. Finally she blurted, "That's only two months."

"That's as long as I can wait. That's when we're going to move the folks up there."

"It may take me longer than that—it probably will."

Danny looked thoughtful, then suggested, "How about selling me the ranch?"

"La Rosa Blanca!" she exclaimed, and he nodded.

The White Rose was the Galvan ranch, located between Brackettville and Del Rio, Texas, close to the Mexican border. It was all that remained of a large Spanish land grant that had been given to the Galvan family in the late sixteenth century for service rendered to the king of Spain. Although she had never lived on the ranch, it was as much a part of her as it had been of the first Galvans to own it. Now it was a ranch in name more than fact since it stabled only six horses and contained a small cottage for the caretaker, Ernesto "Erny" Lopez.

"You can't be serious!" she exclaimed. "It's value is far greater than the company, at the moment."

"I'm serious." Danny rocked back on his heels and stared at her.

"Furthermore, you know how important it is to me," she pointed out. "And you know I love both the business and the ranch. La Rosa Blanca is all that is left of my Spanish legacy."

"Mine, too," Danny retorted.

"Oh, no!" Marcy was furious. "Uncle Lonzo sold his share of the ranch to Papa long ago. La Rosa Blanca belongs to me. When my own brothers wanted to put it on the market, I bought it from them. I own it lock, stock and barrel."

Angry that he would dare make such a suggestion and frightened that she was about to lose another part of her heritage, Marcy said, "You and my brothers are the first Galvans who took no interest in the company or our heritage. Without quibble or hesitation my brothers sold me their shares of the company. Like you, they were content to go on with their lives and careers totally unrelated to the construction industry. There's got to be some other way for me to get the money. I can't sacrifice one to save the other.''

"Then, I would suggest you get started finding the money elsewhere.''

Although Marcy had been disappointed when her brothers showed no interest in the construction company or the ranch, she knew they weren't cold and calculating, like Danny. His primary interest was always the almighty dollar. There was no way under God's blue heaven she would let him have La Rosa Blanca. The minute the ranch was his, he would put it on the market to the highest bidder, and sell to land speculators who would divide it into strips for tract housing.

"I'll cut you some slack, however." Danny's voice penetrated her thoughts. "After June 15, I'll give you first option to buy when I receive another offer.''

"If I don't have it by then?''

"You'll have a new partner.''

After Danny left, his words continued to haunt Marcy. She cleared her desk; then she walked around the office, looking at the furniture her cousin had ridiculed. Troubled, she picked up the telephone and dialed Clarice.

The minute her sister-in-law answered, Marcy said, "Danny just left, and I'm in a dither. He's selling Uncle Lonzo's interest in the business.''

"The way Danny was talking to Ethan today, we figured it was coming," Clarice returned softly. "And surely you did, too, Marcy. Uncle Lonzo has been getting weaker and weaker."

"I just kept hoping it wouldn't happen."

"Marcy, maybe it's time you gave up the business. It's barely breaking even. With your degrees in civil engineering you can get yourself a much better job."

"Thank you, but no, thank you," Marcy replied. "I'm quite happy with my job. I love the company. I just have to figure out a way to save it." She laughed bitterly. "Danny wants to trade Uncle Lonzo's half of the company for La Rosa Blanca."

"Well," Clarice remarked philosophically, "that would give you the money. I really can't think why you want that godforsaken property, anyway."

"You know good and well why," Marcy insisted.

"Okay," Clarice conceded. "But maybe this is an instance of where you can't have your cake and eat it, too. You could mortgage it."

"Can't," Marcy told her. "Have you forgotten the Texas Homestead Act."

"Not the Act," Clarice said. "I'd forgotten the ranch was your declared homestead."

"It is and it can't be mortgaged except for home improvements. So that's that." Marcy sighed.

"It's not really that bad, Marcy," Clarice pointed out. "Even if you can't own the whole company, you'll still have fifty percent."

"That's not enough. I want it all."

"Marcella Galvan, you're fiercely proud and stubborn to a fault," Clarice gently accused.

"Blame it on my Irish-Mexican heritage. But this time I have good reason. The partner will be equal and can demand his or her name be added to the business," she argued, "and will have no interest in preserving the Galvan family history. He will have no pride in a family-owned business."

"I worry about you, Marcy," Clarice said, concern evident in her voice. "I think a person should be proud of his or her heritage, but sometimes I think you go overboard. Your whole life is your projects, the company and your heritage. You've already lost one man because you refused to give them up."

Marcy sighed. She couldn't count the times her family had made this accusation!

"Marcy, no matter what happens, it won't be the end of the world," Clarice added.

Marcy glanced at the wall clock and realized the time. She said a hasty goodbye to Clarice and hung up the receiver. She was going to be late for the Big Brothers/Big Sisters meeting. She certainly had no time to go home to freshen up and change clothes.

Although she had been accepted into the Big Sister-Little Sister program, she was still waiting to be paired with a Little Sister. Maybe the caseworker would have some good news for her tonight. In the bathroom Marcy washed her face and applied fresh makeup. It was all she had time to do.

On the way to Villita Assembly Hall, a thirty-minute drive from the office, Marcy's thoughts were of her uncle's plan to sell the business. She wished she could talk with him, but she knew she couldn't. He had enough problems without her adding to them.

Downtown, as Marcy was stopped at a traffic light, she looked over the surrounding buildings. Some of them were new, modern structures. But many were beautiful reminders of bygone days when San Antonio was the queen of Spanish settlements in Texas and later, when the city was a flourishing cow town. Driving slowly enough to appreciate the city where she was born, Marcy detoured to see how the latest renovations had changed the complexion of Alamo Plaza, the large area surrounding the Alamo—the seat of Texas liberty.

Marcy was always inspired by this part of San Antonio. The River Walk, with its terraced gardens, walkways and bridges dotted with craft shops and galleries, was proof of what could be achieved when people took the time to incorporate the old with the new.

Parking the car in the lot across the street from La Villita, Marcy walked up the recently restored flagstone street toward the assembly hall. As she stood beneath one of the gnarled oak trees, she stopped a moment and looked around. She loved La Villita—the Little Village—the restoration of the original village that had been built alongside the mission now called the Alamo. Flowering bougainvillca framed nearly every building.

A cool breeze soothed her body, and she closed her eyes. The tensions of the day began to slip away. Coming here always affected her like this. Here she felt as if she had stepped back in time—her worries forgotten for the moment.

Then she heard laughter and loud talking and looked up to see several children racing into the building. She smiled, glad that she was a part of Big Brothers/Big Sisters. She looked forward to meeting the little girl who would be the sister Marcy had wanted all her life.

"Don't think you're going to get out of work this way," a woman called.

Marcy turned to see the caseworker, Kyla Jackson, moving toward the assembly hall, her arms filled with paper bags.

"Here," Marcy offered, "let me help you."

"Thanks. They're not really heavy, just cumbersome," the caseworker replied, transferring some of the burden to Marcy. "It's the buns, and more are on the way. The beans and chili are already here."

"The cold drinks?" Marcy inquired, as she fell into step with Kyla and the two made their way toward the building.

Kyla nodded. "Everything is taken care of."

"You hinted that you might have some news for me when I talked to you the other day," Marcy said.

"I do," Kyla answered. "A highly unusual and interesting case. But this isn't the time to talk about it. I would like to have some quiet time with you. How about later tonight after I've finished with my chores?"

Marcy nodded. "Where shall I put these?"

"At the end of the serving counter." Kyla pointed and moved in that direction herself.

"Can I help?" Marcy asked.

"You surely can," Kyla told her. "How about a managerial position? You can manage the hot-dog buns."

"I think I can handle that," Marcy replied.

Kyla set her bags down beside Marcy's, tied the apron around her waist and moved behind the counter. "Anybody for hot dogs?" she called out.

Laughing children scampered to be first in line.

Later, after the majority of people had been served, Marcy filled her plate. Carrying her tray to one of the tables, she sat down to eat. At the same time, she slowly gazed around at the crowd, finally focusing on a little girl of no more than nine or ten, who stood waiting in line.

The child looked up at just that moment, and her eyes locked with Marcy's. She smiled and picked up her tray, then walked across the large room. Her dark brown hair, a mass of curls, hung to her shoulders. She wore coordinated Cavardichi shirt and jeans, and white sneakers; her socks matched her shirt.

Approaching Marcy's table, she asked, "May I sit here?" When Marcy nodded, she said, "I'm Amy Calderon. I'm nine years old, and I'm here to get a Big Sister. Who are you?"

There was nothing self-conscious about Amy Calderon, Marcy observed. Obviously the little girl knew what she wanted.

"I'm Marcy Galvan. I'm twenty-eight years old, and I'm here to get a Little Sister."

Amy scrutinized Marcy for a second before she asked, "You're not married?"

Marcy shook her head.

"Good. I want a Big Sister who's not married."

The child's directness bordered on rudeness, Marcy thought.

"You're very pretty."

"Thank you," Marcy murmured.

Amy was also pretty and looked and talked like a grown-up. Judging from her clothes and jewelry, she came from an affluent family, Marcy concluded, noting the gold stud earrings that adorned each earlobe, the gold chain that hung about her neck, and the small pearl ring on her right hand.

An older woman joined them.

"Hello, I'm Nona Ferguson," she said. "Amy's baby-sitter."

"And she lives with us," Amy added.

"Hello, Ms. Ferguson," Marcy replied.

"Not Ms. Ferguson. Call me Nona, please," the older woman corrected with a twinkle in her eye. "I guess Amy has told you she's here to get a Big Sister?"

"Yes, she has."

"I did it all by myself," Amy boasted. "I saw the commercial on TV, and when they came to our school to talk to us about having Big Brothers and Big Sisters, I filled out an application. All by myself, didn't I, Nona?"

"That's right." Nona smiled indulgently at the child. "You signed up without your father or me knowing about it."

"And they wouldn't let me be a Little Sister until they talked with Daddy," Amy announced. As soon as the words were out of her mouth, she asked, "Where's the catsup? I need the catsup for my hot dog." She looked up and down the table, then slid off the bench. "I'm going to get some catsup for my hot dog, Nona."

"You're one of the Big Sisters?" the older woman asked.

"I've been accepted into the program," Marcy answered, "but I haven't been matched with a Little Sister yet."

"As Amy was telling you, her father wasn't sure he wanted her in the program to begin with, but she kept insisting. After he met and talked with some of the staff, they introduced him to several parents whose children are involved in the program. Gil was impressed and thinks it will be good for Amy to have a Big Sister.'' Nona smiled apologetically. "But I've talked enough about us. Tell me something about yourself. What do you do and how did you get involved in the program?''

As Marcy answered Nona's questions, Amy slid onto the bench and listened attentively, stopping Marcy every so often to ask something herself. By the end of the evening, Marcy and Amy were well acquainted. The little girl had a certain charm despite her precociousness.

When Marcy saw Kyla beckon, she rose and picked up her tray. "Please, excuse me. I promised my caseworker I would talk with her before I left for the night." She smiled at Amy first, then at Nona. "I'm glad to have met both of you, and I hope we get a chance to see each other again.''

"Perhaps we shall,'' Nona replied.

Amy finished her cold drink and set the glass down. "I want you for my Big Sister,'' she declared. Her gaze traveled up the line of Marcy's figure from her cowboy boots to her Western shirt. "Are you a cowgirl?''

"No, I'm a construction worker,'' she said and explained her job to Amy.

"Oh,'' Amy murmured, then changed the subject: "Do you like collecting things?

Marcy laughed. "Yes. And my mother did, too. She used to collect Depression glass.''

"What's that?'' Amy asked.

"Dishes that were made during the 1930s,'' Marcy answered. "Since Mother's death, I've continued with her collection.''

"I have a collection," Amy announced. "But it's not dishes. It's Barbie dolls. I have lots of them, don't I, Nona?"

The older woman nodded.

"Do you drive?" Amy asked.

"I do," Marcy replied, by now quite used to the child's mercurial change of topic.

"Oh, goody! I really, really would like for you to be my Big Sister. You could take me places," she went on, as if the matter were settled; then asked rather hurriedly, "Do you have a car?"

Again Marcy said, "I do."

"Super! We'll get along just fine. You can do the things for me that Julie's sister does for her."

"Just who is Julie?" Marcy inquired, getting the feeling that Amy wanted a chauffeur rather than a Big Sister.

"She's my next-door neighbor," Amy informed her. "She's thirteen years old and knows everything. You'll really like her."

"Amy," Marcy said, intrigued by the child, "if things work out and you and I are matched, I would love to be your Big Sister."

THE HALL had almost emptied; only a few people remained. Some of the caseworkers cleaned up while Marcy and Kyla sat talking at one of the tables.

"During the six years that I've been working for Big Brothers/Big Sisters," Kyla was saying, "I've never had a child quite as determined to become a part of the program as Amy is."

Marcy laughed. "I don't know her very well, but from what I saw tonight, she's one to get what she wants. If you're not careful, she'll have taken over the running of the office before long.''

Kyla joined in the laughter. "I can imagine. I'm going to have to be careful with her Big Sister. Amy has the kind of personality that makes it easy for a person to dislike her. I'll have to admit, I was a little apprehensive about admitting her to the program at first. In all my years of experience, I've never had a child from an affluent household wanting a Big Sister. But something about Amy tugged at my heart, and I met her father. After the interview, I began to understand her better. She's very lonely and frightened.''

Marcy listened as Kyla talked more about Amy, explaining that she had lost her mother and was afraid of losing her father.

When Kyla finally paused, Marcy asked, "Do you think I could be Amy's Big Sister?''

Kyla reached up to stroke her earlobe, running her fingers around the large gold hoop. "Do you want to be? Amy might not be the easiest Little Sister in the world.''

Marcy thought for a moment, then answered, "Despite her precociousness, I like Amy. But she acts and talks too much like an adult, so I'd like to teach her how to play and be part of a family. I want to give her childhood back to her.''

"Those are certainly good reasons, and I admit it sounds like a good match," Kyla acknowledged. "But, as you know, the final decision isn't up to me. When we have our staff meeting next week, I'll recommend that the two of you be matched. That's the best I can do.''

"Thanks," Marcy said. "I'd appreciate that.''

"How's the restoration of the school coming?" Kyla inquired.

"Not so good," Marcy admitted, then quietly told Kyla all that had transpired during the past month.

They were finishing their lemonade, when a woman called from the other side of the room. "Kyla, we're ready to lock up. Check to see if we've packed everything the way you wanted it."

Both Kyla and Marcy rose.

"I'll be right over," Kyla called back and grabbed the empty paper cups. "Marcy, I'll give you a call as soon as I know something."

"NONA, DO YOU THINK Marcy is pretty?" Amy asked as she dressed for bed that evening.

"Indeed, I do."

"She reminds me of Mama," Amy said.

"Well, I wouldn't go that far," Nona replied, turning down the bedcovers. "Your mother was a petite woman with—"

"I know—" Amy cut her off "—but both of them have black hair."

"True," Nona agreed.

"Do you think Mrs. Jackson will let me have Marcy for my Big Sister?"

"I don't know," Nona answered. "Remember what Mrs. Jackson told us when they accepted your application. They have to consider many things in both the Little and the Big Sister before they pair them. They have to be sure the two of you are good for each other. We have to trust their judgment, darling."

"But I like Marcy," Amy insisted. "She'll be a fun Big Sister."

"I liked her, too," Nona admitted.

"Do you think Daddy will like Marcy?" Amy questioned. She gazed intently at the housekeeper.

"I'm sure he'll like whoever the program assigns to be your Big Sister."

"Oh, Nona, I really want Marcy."

"Well, don't get your hopes up too high, so you won't be disappointed if you don't get her. Now, hop into bed."

As soon as Amy was in bed, Nona pulled the sheet up and leaned down to kiss her on the forehead.

"Good night," she murmured. "And sweet dreams."

Amy looped her arms around Nona's neck and drew her down onto the bed. "I love you, Nona."

"And I love you." Reaching out, she brushed the dark brown curls from Amy's face. Here in her own bedroom, Amy's grown-up demeanor vanished. She was a small, frightened little girl. "Would you like me to read to you?"

"Yes, please." Amy darted out of bed and over to her bookshelf. She didn't search long before she returned with an extremely worn book. "This one."

Nona could have guessed which book Amy would choose. *Heidi* was one of her favorites and this copy had belonged to her mother. Nona opened the cover and looked at the inscription as she had done so many times before.

On the bed again, and leaning against Nona's back, Amy read over her shoulder, "To Sondra with love, Mama." She paused, then declared, "I'm going to keep my mother's books forever, Nona, and when I have a little girl, I'm going to let you read to her, just like you read to me."

Nona laid the book on the nightstand and took Amy into her arms. "Yes, sweet," she murmured, "I would like to do that."

"You'll live with me forever, Nona."

"Well, I can't promise to live with you that long," Nona responded, choking back the tears. "Somewhere down the line, you're gonna find a fine young man that you'll want to marry, and then you'll have no need for Nona. Besides—" Nona laughed softly "—I'll have other things that I'm going to want to do. But I won't leave you until you're ready for me to, darling."

"Promise?"

"I promise. Now, get under the covers and I'll read until you're asleep." Having read the entire book aloud to her many times and knowing that Amy herself read and reread it and had her favorite parts, Nona asked, "Where shall I start?"

"Nona," Amy asked, without answering the question, "do you think my daddy sees Mrs. Courtland every time he's in Dallas?"

"Yes," the housekeeper replied, "I'm sure he does. After all, both of them work for the same company."

Amy sat up. "Do you think Daddy and Mrs. Courtland are dating?"

Nona lowered her head and gazed at the frayed edges of the book. Carefully she sought the right way to respond to Amy. "Your daddy and Mrs. Courtland are having business dates," Nona explained.

"That's not the same as dating?" Amy persisted.

"Well," Nona replied, "not really. Right now both of them are just friends and business acquaintances. Why do you ask? Don't you like Mrs. Courtland?"

"Yeah, I guess she's okay," Amy admitted and paused before she added, "One of my friends at school said that's the way her daddy started dating her stepmother. They worked together."

"It could happen," Nona told her, "if your father and Mrs. Courtland fall in love."

"If Daddy marries again," Amy continued, "will he have time to love me?"

"Of course, he will! What makes you say this?" Nona asked. "Has Julie been talking to you?"

"Oh, no!" Amy shook her head vehemently. "One of my other friends at school—Vanessa—she knows all about stepmothers. She has one, and she says her daddy doesn't love her anymore."

"I don't know about Vanessa's father," Nona said, "but I know your father real well. He's not the kind of man who would ever stop loving his little girl, even if he did remarry."

As she lifted her face to look at Nona, Amy's brown eyes sparkled with tears. "I love my daddy. I don't want to lose him, too."

"You won't, darling."

"Promise?"

Always when Amy needed to be convinced of something, she begged Nona to "promise"; she trusted Nona completely. Nona gazed fondly at her charge. She had been with the Calderons since Amy was a few months old and her mother had returned to her job. She was with them when Sondra died. How difficult that period had been for Amy. Too young to realize what was happening, she only knew that the baby her parents were so excited about, was making her mother sick. It was in Nona's arms that the heart-broken child had sobbed when she was told her mother and the baby had "gone to heaven." Nona hadn't lied to Amy then, and she wouldn't do it now.

"If you love him," Nona said, "and if you're willing to share him, you'll never lose him. I promise."

Yawning, Amy lay down and snuggled the back of her head into the pillow. "I'm ready for my story." She smiled. "Tonight, you pick the part to read."

Nona nodded her head and smiled, sliding her finger into one of the many well-marked pages. As she began to read, Amy's eyes closed, and her dark lashes made crescents on her cheeks. Nona read awhile longer until she was sure Amy was asleep, then shut the book and laid it on the nightstand. Leaning down, she kissed Amy again and tucked the sheet beneath her chin. She walked to the door, where she switched off the overhead light and stood for a moment, gazing through the muted glow of the night-lamp at the sleeping child.

"Good night, my little darling," she whispered. "And sweet dreams."

CHAPTER FOUR

DRESSED IN SHORTS and a shirt, Marcy was up early Sunday morning, preparing potato salad and two desserts for the barbecue. Feeling hurried because Clarice and Ethan were going to stop by to pick her up, she kept glancing at the clock. She would much rather drive herself, but no amount of argument had dissuaded Ethan. She had finally given in. She had a feeling that she was going to be the recipient of big-brother advice, whether she wanted to be or not, and Ethan had obviously decided the best place for this was a locked, moving automobile—from which she had no chance of escaping.

Briefly Marcy wondered what Clarice was bringing. Something wonderful, she hoped. Marcy was in the mood for something really decadent. Please don't let Clarice still be going through her health-food phase, she thought. A carrot cake was one thing, but an alfalfa-sprout pie would be too much. Marcy opened the refrigerator door, set the large bowl of salad inside, then proudly surveyed her lemon-cream pie and the strawberries and sauce she'd prepared to go with a shortcake.

Having finished in the kitchen, she quickly showered and changed clothes. She was standing in front of the cheval glass scrutinizing her brightly colored skirt and matching blouse when the doorbell chimed, announcing the arrival of Clarice and Ethan.

"Coming!" Marcy called out and slipped into her high-heeled sandals.

When she opened the door, Clarice exclaimed, "Marcy, you look great!"

Marcy smiled. "Every time I wear a dress you say that."

Ethan, moving past his wife, leaned over and pecked her on the cheek. "You do look great. Sometimes I think that hard hat is growing to your head. It's nice to see your hair every once in a while, to be assured that you have some." He gently tugged her ponytail. "Gorgeous hair like this needs to be hanging free, especially if you're wanting to catch yourself a guy."

"Maybe I'm not trying to catch myself a guy," Marcy retorted. Her marriage status or lack thereof always seemed to be of primary concern to her family. Every time they were around her, they mentioned it.

"Then you should," came Clarice's advice from the kitchen. "You're soon going to be too old to have children without complications. Just the other day I was reading an article—"

"I'm well aware of that, thank you," Marcy replied. "But I'm not going to marry some man just to have children. Everyone concerned deserves better than that!"

"You're right," Clarice admitted. "And I'm sorry, I didn't mean to press the panic button."

Marcy heard the refrigerator door open and knew Clarice was inspecting her goodies. She joined her sister-in-law in the kitchen.

"Oh, Marcy, this looks scrumptious. No one makes potato salad like you." Clarice closed the refrigerator door and went to the bay window, to sit down on the cushioned bench.

"Thanks," Marcy said. "What did you prepare?"

Her eyes twinkling, Clarice hedged, "Wait and see."

"Why do I have the feeling that we're going to be trying something new today?" Marcy murmured.

"Where's the picnic basket?" Ethan asked. "We need to pack your stuff and get moving if we're going to arrive by nine o'clock."

"It's in the pantry," Marcy answered. "Will you get it for me?"

Nodding, Ethan walked into the utility room off the kitchen, and Marcy heard him open a door.

"Where are my two favorite nieces?" Marcy inquired. "I have a surprise for them."

"Your *only* nieces," Clarice pointed out as she idly flipped through the magazines and the Big Brothers/ Big Sisters material that Marcy had dropped on the window seat when she came in on Friday night.

Marcy laughed. She could envision the two lively little girls—Sarah, age six, and Diane, age four—excitedly opening their presents. She always kept little gifts on hand so that when she saw the children, she could give them a surprise. She loved the two of them as if they were her own, and had already thought about the fun they would have with her Little Sister, should Marcy ever be matched.

"They insisted on spending the night with David and Josie. They wanted to 'baby-sit' their new cousin. I tried to talk them out of it, but when Josie insisted on their staying, I lost the fight," Clarice explained.

"I'm not really surprised," Marcy said. Her second eldest brother and his wife had a six-week-old baby.

"Oh, Marcy, when I hold Joshua, I get so lonesome for a baby."

"Don't you dare get any ideas," Ethan warned as he reentered the kitchen with the food basket. "If we survive the two we have, we'll be fortunate."

"Maybe the two of you should try for a boy," Marcy suggested.

Clarice looked up from the magazine and smiled at Ethan. "That's what I've been telling him. If David and Josie can do it, I don't see why we can't."

"Do you know if Mark and Tammy are coming?" Ethan asked.

Both women looked at each other and grinned. He was deliberately changing the subject. Marcy laughed softly and taunted her brother. "Ethan, this ploy isn't going to work. You know what Clarice is like once she gets a bee in her bonnet."

"I know." Ethan looked at his wife and smiled, his eyes reflecting the love he had for her. "We'll talk about it later in private," he promised. Then he opened the refrigerator and began to remove the potato salad and desserts. "I've called Mark several times but only talked to the answering machine. I wish that youngest brother of mine would be a little more considerate of the family and let us know what he's doing. I wanted to bring him my old set of golf clubs, but I refuse to load them up until I know I'm going to see him."

"I haven't talked with him since I returned from New York," Marcy said and moved to the cabinet to take out several plastic containers for her pie and strawberries and sauce, "but I'm sure he'll be there. He always shows up wherever there's free food and booze. Besides, Tammy would insist. She can't keep her hands off Joshua."

"Do you get the feeling that we're going to be having another addition to the family pretty soon?" Clarice asked rhetorically, glancing suggestively at her husband.

"If Tammy has anything to do with it, yes," Marcy agreed. "If it's Mark's decision, I'd say no. He doesn't want them to have a baby until he's through with his doctorate."

"Which is wise," Ethan remarked. "After he's established himself, they'll have plenty of time."

"I like that!" Marcy said. "Mark is thirty years old, but he has plenty of time for a family. But I—who am twenty-eight—do not have time."

Ethan grinned at her. "At least he's married, and you haven't even begun to get interested in anyone since you broke up with Derrick three years ago. You never date a guy more than three or four times. You keep yourself so busy with all your pet projects, you don't have time to fall in love."

"I allow myself plenty of time to date, and *I do date!*" Marcy exclaimed, slightly irritated with her brother. "I just haven't met a man I'd be interested in making a commitment to. And I'll have you know that I have seriously dated several men since Derrick."

"Two that I know of," Clarice interjected as she straightened the magazines on the window seat. She held up the Big Brothers/Big Sisters folder. "Have you been assigned a Little Sister yet?"

"No. But I met a most interesting little girl last night," Marcy said. As she helped Ethan pack the basket with extra plastic forks, napkins and condiments, she talked about Amy.

"She sounds delightful," Clarice remarked. "If the two of you are matched, you'll have to bring her to the house to meet the girls. In fact, if the program allows, maybe we can all do something together, like go horseback riding or spend the day at Splashtown or even go to Sea World."

"I'll check and see," Marcy answered. "I'm not really sure what her interests are. From what little I know of and about her, I think she needs to learn how to play like a little girl."

"Play isn't something that should be restricted to children," Ethan declared. "But how can you teach her something you don't do because you're spreading yourself so thin? You're always on some kind of crusade, Marcy. Always trying to save the world but never giving your own welfare a second thought."

"Crusading is what Danny accused me of yesterday," she pointed out. "Seems that you and he have been talking."

"I've been wanting to talk to you about the company for a good while," Ethan confessed. "You're barely making a living, and you're giving it all you've got. It's like an albatross around your neck. Why don't you sell out, too?"

Marcy shook her head. "I strongly resent the company's being referred to as an albatross, and furthermore, the subject of my selling it isn't even open for discussion."

"Marcy—" Clearly Ethan was armed for battle.

"If you insist on continuing with this, Ethan, I'll drive myself over to Tío's," she stated firmly. "I had to listen to Danny yesterday. That was enough. I'm not going to listen to you or anyone else who tries to convince me to sell."

"She's right," Clarice agreed. "None of you guys wanted any part in the company. You sold it without a second thought. It's hers, so let her do what she wants with it."

"I'm just trying to keep her from making a terrible mistake," Ethan argued. "Papa isn't here any longer, so it's my responsibility to look after my baby sister."

"It's my life and my mistake," Marcy said. "I'll take full responsibility for it. I want you to know you irritate me, Ethan, because you obviously have no confidence in my ability to manage the company and to make it successful."

"She's got a point," said Clarice, agreeing a second time with Marcy, and Ethan turned to glare at her. She smiled. "Now, if all the food is packed, let's be on our way. I don't want Tío to lecture us for being late."

By the time Marcy, Clarice and Ethan arrived at their uncle's house in Garden Ridge Estates, the huge backyard was full of people and laughter and happiness. Marcy always looked forward to the barbecue. It was held every year on the middle weekend of April, and was the Galvans' way of expressing their appreciation to the company's construction crews and workers.

Carrying the two baskets, Ethan strode to the long table spread with food and drinks. While Marcy and Clarice unpacked, he fished out a beer for himself from the zinc tub filled with ice and cold drinks. Opening it, he walked over to greet and chat with his aunt and uncle. Then he meandered over to the grill to talk to Mark and Danny, who were manning the barbecue.

"Marcy!" two young voices called in unison.

Marcy turned to see her nieces running toward her. Kneeling, she opened her arms and captured the two of them in an embrace. Little arms wrapped around her neck, and little fingers tangled in her hair. Smacking kisses landed on both her cheeks.

"Did you bring us a surprise?"

She nodded. "It's in your daddy's car. You can open it when you go home tonight."

With a little girl holding on to each hand, Marcy listened to their chatter as the three of them walked across the lawn to the elderly couple who sat in lawn chairs beneath the pecan tree.

"Hello, Tía, Tío."

"Marcella," Aunt Felicia greeted, as usual calling Marcy by her christened name, "it's good to see you."

Taking their delicate hands, clearly marked with strutted veins, Marcy kissed first her aunt, then her uncle. "It's good to see you both. How are you feeling?"

"Not so good," her aunt replied. "But I suppose Danny told you about it."

"A little," Marcy answered.

Sitting down at their feet, Marcy talked with her aunt and uncle for a long time. Neither of them brought up the sale of the business and Marcy didn't either. She knew the subject must be painful for Tío. To him—as it had been for his brother, Marcy's father—the company had been his life's blood, his purpose for living.

When they finally lapsed into silence, Marcy relaxed against the trunk of the tree and watched the children dart back and forth across the lawn, playing. Later she saw Joe Alexander and his wife arrive. After they had set their food on the table, Annette joined Clarice and another group of women, while Joe moved to the beer tub. Rising, Marcy walked toward him.

Joe Alexander was a tall, slender man in his mid-twenties. Marcy's farther had hired him to work at the company when he graduated from high school. Working during the day and going to college at night, Joe had recently completed his B.A. Both Marcy's father and her uncle had liked Joe. Because of his dedication and loyalty to the company, he had been promoted until he was a supervisor on the same level as Marcy and immediately below the two Galvan men. When Rubin Galvan had died, Marcy had assumed his responsibilities; Joe had done the same when Lonzo became ill. Between them, Marcy and Joe virtually ran the company.

"Marcy," Joe greeted with a big smile. "How's it going?"

"The barbecue is going great," she replied.

"But what, Marcy?" He laughed. "I recognize that tone of voice."

Marcy sighed. "Uncle Lonzo is going to retire."

Slowly the smile left Joe's face, and he lowered the beer bottle from his mouth. "What does this mean for the company?"

"Danny's going to sell Tío's half. He's given me two months to come up with the money."

"We knew it was coming," Joe reminded her.

"But I just didn't expect it this soon," Marcy admitted. "I thought I'd have longer."

"Can you get the money?" Joe asked.

"I don't know," she answered. "I'm going to give it my best."

"I wish I could help you out, Marcy," he said. "But my cash flow is low, and I'm so deep in debt I couldn't begin to swing a loan for that amount."

"Thanks, Joe, but I'll see what I can do. I just wanted you to know. I'm not going to tell the others yet," Marcy explained. "Not until I know for sure what's going to happen."

AS USUAL, LUNCH WAS a great success—everyone oohing and aahing over the different dishes, taking a bite of this and that, even packing "people" bags to take home. Afterward they lounged in the backyard, letting their meal settle.

Never one to leave a messy kitchen until later, especially when she was on the cleanup crew, Marcy had immediately begun to tidy the kitchen. She had washed, dried and put away all her aunt's dishes and stacked the others on the counter, to be claimed later by their owners.

Marcy was gathering the dish towels when the doorbell chimed several times in succession, as if the visitor were impatient. Draping the soiled linen over her arm, she walked to the door and opened it.

"Hello."

Marcy stared into the face of a stranger—a ruggedly handsome face dominated by shining black hair and blue eyes. His voice was rich and resonant.

"Hello," she said. The man looked vaguely familiar, but she couldn't place him.

"I hope I'm not disturbing you. I'm Brant Holland."

"Brant Holland!" she murmured. Her knees seemed to turn to the consistency of butter, and she felt as if she were going to melt into a puddle on the floor.

"I called Ethan's office and the answering service said I could find him here," he told her, then repeated, "I'm not intruding, am I?"

Finally regaining control of her voice, she hastened to say, "No, not at all."

"I did have to twist the answering service's arm, so to speak, to get them to divulge the information."

Marcy continued to stare. She had often imagined what the mature Brant Holland would look like and had been prepared for changes, but she hadn't reckoned on his being so devastatingly handsome. Laughter grooved the corners of his mouth, and his blue eyes twinkled. They were beautiful eyes—the color of Texas bluebonnets.

By now there was a definite look of amusement in his face. "Do you want me to wait out here while you get Ethan?"

"Oh, no," Marcy exclaimed, jolted out of her reverie.

Suddenly she was aware of how she must look, with her clothing wrinkled from playing with the children, strands of hair escaping her ponytail clasp, and damp dish towels draped over her arm. She wished her first meeting with Brant could have been under different circumstances, but fate had intervened, and now Marcy would simply have to make the best of it. She swung open the door.

"Please, come in. I'll get my brother for you."

"Your brother?" It was the man's turn to stare at her. "You did say *your* brother?"

"My brother." She was pleased to see his momentary confusion. "I'm Marcy Galvan."

Brant could only stare. Her sweetly curving lips were tinted a rich rose, and her cheeks were touched with raspberry freshness. A tiny pearl dotted each earlobe, and a gold locket hung around her neck.

"You can't be," he insisted. "She was a little girl who tagged along at my heels."

She laughed softly—a sound that was pleasant to his ear. "Who was quite a *rascal*—I believe that's the word you used to describe me—and who used to call you 'Uncle Brant' just to irritate you."

"Yes," he murmured. "I remember."

Her calling him uncle had rankled then, but not nearly as much as it would now. Brant quickly realized that he didn't feel the least bit avuncular toward her.

"It's nice to see you," she said.

Unable to look away from her eyes, he stepped into the hallway. "I can't get over your being little Marcy."

She laughed again. "Marcy, all right, but not so little."

"No," he agreed, as his gaze moved down her body, "not so little."

Shepherd Hayden's description had not done her justice. She was more than attractive; she was beautiful. Her black hair was clasped at the crown of her head, to hang in a luxurious ponytail down her back. Round, firm breasts gently contoured the floral material of her blouse. The matching skirt draped over shapely hips. Little Marcy Galvan indeed was all grown up.

"A tad under five-eight. And the heels must give me an added two inches."

"At least."

"I guess my height is the first thing some people notice about me." Her smile widened. "But I like being tall."

Her happiness was infectious; Brant felt himself returning her smile. For some odd reason that defied explanation at the moment, he wanted to assure her that he didn't mind her height.

"I like you tall, too," he answered. "When I said 'little,' I wasn't referring to your height but to your maturity."

"Height, I can talk about objectively," Marcy replied. "Now, age is quite another subject. I sometimes fear that as modern as I would like to think I am, I have retained a somewhat outdated and stereotypical attitude toward aging. Basically, I don't like to be reminded of it."

"I don't know the adult Marcy," Brant acknowledged, "but I have the feeling that you're anything but outdated and stereotypical."

"I'm glad you think that."

They lapsed into silence and stared at each other.

"I'm glad you came," she finally said. "I told Ethan you would."

I hadn't planned to, Brant thought. Memories of his childhood in the Heights were unhappy, and being away from San Antonio had helped him forget them for long periods of time. But eventually curiosity had gotten the best of him. After he had reminded himself of the more enjoyable parts of his life in San Antonio, he found he wanted to see Ethan, and Danny— and Marcy.

"Mr. Hayden said you wouldn't be back from Europe until the middle of next week."

"I closed the deal earlier than expected."

In the mirror on the far wall, he saw their reflections. They made a good-looking couple—she in her skirt, blouse and sandals, he in his boots, jeans and Western shirt. In the scoop neckline of her dress, he noticed for the second time the gold locket glinting against her flesh. It looked familiar.

"Is that the necklace I sent you?" he asked and stepped closer.

She nodded. "Yes, it is."

"For your thirteenth birthday."

"Yes," she murmured. "I'm surprised that you would remember. It was so long ago."

Brant still found it difficult to believe the beautiful woman standing in front of him was the little girl of his memories. If it were not for those unusual eyes, he might have been harder to convince. Oddly, he found himself thinking that there was a much greater age difference between eight and sixteen than there was between twenty-eight and thirty-six.

"If you'll follow me," she said, "I'll take you to Ethan and Danny. Will they be surprised!"

"The annual barbecue?" Brant stated more than asked. "I remember it well. I always looked forward to all the good food, the company and the festivities."

"We've already eaten," she told him, "but we have plenty of food left. Are you hungry?"

"No, thank you. I ate before I drove over."

He fell in step behind her as she led the way through the spacious ranch-style house. She gave a soft laugh—the same melodious sound that had stirred his senses just moments earlier.

"May I share the joke?" he asked.

They had reached the den when she stopped and turned. The golden brown eyes with green highlights sparkled with the glint of mischief he so clearly remembered. Adulthood had been good to Marcy; it had sculpted her into a beautiful woman but hadn't changed her sense of humor one iota.

"Danny and Ethan are going to be surprised. They didn't think you'd come."

"But you knew?"

"I had hoped," she correctly quietly.

Again they stared at each other for a long moment. Brant had so much he wanted to say to her, but for the first time in many years, he found that glib conversation would not suffice. While he wanted to see Ethan and Danny and to renew his friendship with them, he wanted to spend time—private time—discovering who this new mature Marcy was.

"They're—in the back," she explained.

He cleared his throat and nodded. "Would you like to dispose of those dish towels before we go out there?"

Marcy looked at him blankly, then down at her arm. She laughed again and her cheeks burned. "I'll go hang them up in the utility room, but don't go out until I return. I want to see Ethan's and Danny's faces when they see you."

Brant couldn't remember when he had last felt so lighthearted or when he had smiled so freely before. "I promise."

She walked out of the room, and Brant stood by the sofa waiting for her. When she returned, she held her hand out and he laid his in hers. Her hand was warm and seemed to pulsate with life and vigor.

"I can hardly wait," she said. She slid open the double glass doors, stepped onto the Saltillo tile patio and called, "Ethan, look who's here!"

Brant saw a man in one of the lawn chairs beneath the huge pecan tree rise, shield his eyes against the afternoon glare and stare at him and Marcy. With a puzzled expression on his face, he began to come toward them.

Brant stepped forward. "Hello, Ethan. Long time no see."

Ethan clasped the extended hand, but his face still didn't register recognition.

"Brant Holland," prompted Marcy.

"Brant! You old son of a gun!" Ethan exclaimed and playfully slapped him on the back. He turned. "Danny, come here!"

Danny appeared and greeted Brant, and the four of them talked for a few minutes before Brant said, "I'd like to see your father."

"He died four years ago," Marcy told him gently.

"I'm sorry," Brant murmured, knowing the words were inadequate to express his sorrow at hearing of Rubin Galvan's death. Now he regretted not having kept up with the family so that the sad news would have reached him in time for him to pay his last respects.

"He died peacefully in his sleep," Marcy explained. "His heart evidently just stopped beating."

"Your Uncle Lonzo?" Brant asked.

"He and Aunt Felicia are here," said Marcy, and as they walked toward the tree under which the couple was still sitting, she told him about her aunt's and uncle's health.

After Brant had greeted the elder Galvans, the four younger people sat on the grass beneath the tree, laughing as they recalled their years together at Galvan Construction. Although Marcy didn't join in the conversation as much as Ethan and Danny, Brant was continually aware of her presence.

Once when Ethan was regaling them with one of the trio's wild exploits in high school, Brant's gaze locked with hers. Slowly she smiled at him—not a flirtatious smile but a warm smile, a welcome-home smile. Marcy and Ethan had invited him back to San Antonio so he could help them raise funds for the Heights, but he knew their reason did not preclude friendship. There was warmth and love here—something he had missed.

He had been apprehensive about returning to San Antonio, and even at the last minute he had almost turned around without ringing the Galvans' doorbell. He had always believed that one couldn't go back to the past; that one couldn't return home. Now he was glad he had stayed. He felt good; he was enjoying the afternoon. It had been a long time since he had lounged on a lawn with a bottle of cold beer and a group of good friends; a long time since no one was expecting something from him or he wasn't negotiating a deal.

"It is with sadness that I am selling my half of the company," he heard Uncle Lonzo say with a shake of his head, "but I must. I am an old man, Brant."

Brant looked at Danny. "You kept your word," he said. "You're not going to keep the business?"

Danny nodded, then lifted a long-necked beer bottle to his lips and took a long drag. Swallowing, he replied, "I promised myself that once I got away from that company, I'd never return."

"What about you, Ethan?" Brant asked.

"David, Mark and I sold our interests to Marcy. Like Tío, she owns fifty percent."

Brant's gaze moved to Marcy.

"I kept my word, too," she told him. "I became the construction worker."

Just like you! The little girl's words rang in Brant's mind.

"Not exactly," Ethan corrected, with an edge to his voice. "She has her Master's degree in civil engineering."

"With minors in English and history," Marcy added impishly.

Brant watched as she stretched her legs out in front of herself. They were long and attractive.

"We don't have to ask what you're doing," Marcy teased. "If you're not in *Forbes,* you're in the tabloids."

Brant chuckled, and rose to go over to the ice tub for a beer.

"Renowned and wealthy architectural engineer in demand all over the world," she quoted. "That's the way you were described in the last article I read."

"Never believe everything you read." He returned and sat down again, "Even I can't recognize myself in most of those stories."

"I'm glad you're here, Brant," Danny said, "but did you really come back to be a part of Marcy's crusade? Do you think it's worth all her time and effort to save a three-story, red brick building that's a safety hazard?"

Again Brant looked at the woman sitting across from him. No, he honestly hadn't come because of that, he admitted to himself. He had returned home because he wanted to see old friends; he wanted to see people who had liked him before he had earned his fortune. And he had come because he was curious about Marcy.

Ignoring Danny's question, he asked her, "Exactly what is your crusade?"

"As I wrote you, the respectable and law-abiding citizens are working through POD to take back what rightfully belongs to them. They are reclaiming the Heights."

"POD?" he questioned.

"Property Owners Development," she explained. "Ethan and I are members."

"It's a lost cause," Danny remarked, rising and going after another beer. "Those people out there aren't interested in saving themselves. They want a handout."

"You're wrong," Marcy said.

Brant saw Marcy's body tense, and her eyes flashed—something he figured they probably did quite often. Marcy Galvan had always championed the underdog with passion as a child, and had sheltered every stray she found. Evidently she was still doing it.

"If we can turn that schoolhouse into a literacy center for adults, we'll teach them how to take care of themselves. Education is the key, Danny. Where would you be today if it weren't for yours? Do you think you'd be wearing designer clothes, or driving a Jaguar car, or living in a house that cost half a million dollars if it weren't for your education?"

She had pinned Danny to the wall. But Brant liked that; he always enjoyed a worthy adversary. And it had been a long time since he had found a woman who titillated his senses the way Marcy Galvan did. He also knew that if he said something to irritate her, she would round on him just as quickly.

"Not every one with an education makes it," Brant pointed out.

"No, but they have a better opportunity," countered Marcy.

"Perhaps I can give you a larger contribution," Brant suggested.

"We appreciate what you've given and will gladly accept more," Marcy replied, "but we want you, Brant. Your nice, warm body."

"Really!" Brant raised his eyebrows and gave her a quizzical look. The four of them laughed.

"Really," she echoed, her eyes sparkling with mischief. If she was embarrassed, she gave no evidence of it.

"I haven't received such an interesting proposition in a long time. It's one I have to consider."

"Great!" she enthused. "That's what I was hoping for."

"Oh, God, Marcy—" Danny spat out the words contemptuously "—what is POD trying to do? Make a name for themselves?"

"No, what we're trying to do is arouse some sense of civic responsibility in people who have been lucky and successful and who now have the resources to help others less fortunate than themselves.

Although Marcy was answering Danny, she was speaking to Brant.

"In order to help these people, we must give them hope and evidence that they, too, can succeed, and that they can do it without turning to a life of drugs and crime. We've got to show them the importance of education."

Chuckling, Brant set his bottle on the grass. "That's a very eloquent speech. You want me because I'm a product of the Heights. A poor boy makes good. Right?"

"Right."

"I was idealistic once," Brant continued, "and fought for lost causes, but not anymore. I'm rather selfish about my time and my energy because I don't have the emotional stamina for crusading. If I weren't wealthy and well-known, you and your group wouldn't want to have anything to do with me."

It was always the same story. Rather than seeing him, people saw dollar signs.

"That's not quite true," Marcy answered. "We gratefully accept help from anyone willing to give it. But in your case—being the great success that you are—you could help us immensely."

Brant leaned back against the trunk of the tree and studied Marcy. "At least your honesty is a refreshing change."

Sitting on the grass across from him, she leaned forward. The soft cotton material of her blouse pulled taut across her breasts. She stared at him for a full second before she asked, "If you weren't interested in helping, why did you come?"

"I was curious," he answered.

"I see," she said dully.

"You're disappointed because I'm not a knight in shining armor come to the rescue. I came because I was curious to see the little girl who used to tag along at my feet when I worked for Galvan Construction."

"You've seen her now. What next?"

Marcy had spirit, but she was young and idealistic—as he had been at one time. So why had he felt it necessary to disappoint her? He had hurt her feelings, but he had known, as he was speaking, what effect his words would have on her. What had prompted him to be so callous? Was he afraid—afraid of caring too much for Marcy Galvan and Esteban Heights and San Antonio? The answer was yes and it gave him pause.

It seemed to him that only he and Marcy existed at that moment. He leaned over and placed his hand over Marcy's. "I'm sorry. What I said was true, but I shouldn't have been so brutal. I've been gone from San Antonio twenty-some—"

"Eighteen years," Marcy corrected.

"I stand corrected." He wanted to brush an errant curl from her forehead. "The Heights is no longer a part of my life. In fact, Marcy, it's a part of my life that I don't want to remember. I certainly don't want to immortalize it. I'll be glad to help you save the old school financially, but I don't have the time . . . and to be honest, Marcy, I really don't want to be involved personally."

"What if I said we were saving your old house, Brant?"

"Perish the thought." Brant got up and walked away from her. He didn't stop until he stood on the bank of the small creek that ran behind the house.

He could still picture—although he didn't want to— the five-room frame house in the Heights. When he was seven years old, his mother had deserted him and his father. A long-haul truck driver, his father had never remarried and had asked his older sister to take care of Brant. His aunt and uncle had loved him, but he was the youngest of eight children; and if they were not living at poverty level, they were only a tad above it.

The only way Brant had been able to attend university was to earn his tuition. The first three years he had worked at a local construction company. The last he was fortunate enough to get an internship with an engineering firm. When he'd left for university he'd promised himself that his life would be different. And it had been. He was grateful that he'd made some money before his father and aunt died and that he'd been able to make sure they were comfortable in their old age. For the most part, his cousins had made it on their own and he seldom heard from them. But if they called or if he learned they needed financial help, he always obliged.

"The house is structurally sound," he heard Marcy saying, and knew she had followed and was standing behind him, "and we're going to save it. Of course, it doesn't warrant a historical plaque, but perhaps one day it will. The school is different."

He turned to look at her.

"It's not just any old building," she continued. "It's Estella Esteban Elementary, Brant. Where you and I both learned the three R's. One of the first elementary schools named after a Hispanic woman."

Marcy's eyes sparkled when she talked, and her voice was animated. "A wonderful woman who gave her life to the education of children, regardless of their ethnic or economic background. We've already applied for the historical plaque and we're sure of getting it. If we lose that school, Brant, we lose the symbol for the Heights and quite possibly the battle. I may be crusading—as I'm often accused of doing—but my cause is worthwhile."

"This means a lot to you, doesn't it?"

"Enough that I took a week off work and financed my own trip to New York on the chance that I'd get to see you."

"You always were a determined little cuss," Brant recalled. "Once you made up your mind, nothing on earth could change it. Somehow I don't think that trait has altered through the years."

"I would say not," Marcy admitted. She reached up and brushed the wisp of hair from her brow—a movement that drew Brant's attention to the classical structure of her features.

"Do you remember Justis Juarez?" she asked.

Brant's eyes narrowed. "Yes. He was a bully, always taking advantage of the smaller guys."

"He's still a bully," Marcy said, "and he's still taking advantage of the underdog. He's a real-estate developer now, and he owns the property that surrounds the school—property we need if we're going to build a playground for the children and a cultural center for the adults."

Brant looked at his watch, then grinned at her. "My plane leaves at three o'clock tomorrow afternoon. It's about ten minutes after three now. That means you have—let's see—about twenty-four hours, if we don't count sleep time, in which to persuade me to your way of thinking. How may hours of sleep do you require at night?"

Marcy grinned. "Eight."

"So we must deduct eight hours from the twenty-four and we have sixteen persuading hours left."

"You're going to give me all of it?" Marcy questioned.

"I am. Wasn't that what you came to New York for?"

She laughed aloud, making a warm and vibrant sound, touching cords of awareness in Brant that had been dormant for years.

"Then let's cut down on the sleep hours. I can catch up on that after you leave."

"All right. My proposition is this. We'll split the persuading hours. You choose what we do for half the time; I choose for the other half."

"But all the time is mine to persuade you?" she clarified.

"You've got it."

"I know you're the visitor, but I'd like first choice."

"Where do you want to go?" he asked.

"To the Sunken Gardens," she replied.

"Is there a special reason why we're going there first?"

"Wait and see."

Eighteen years had produced a vixen, Brant reflected. A lovely, adorable vixen. Marcy Galvan was positively one of the most provocative women he'd ever met. He wondered if she was aware of the effect she had on men—and on him in particular. Probably she was. Most beautiful women were aware of their power.

CHAPTER FIVE

AN HOUR LATER, Marcy and Brant stood on one of the arched bridges at Sunken Gardens and gazed at the waterfall splashing down the side of the old rock quarry. Once abandoned and an eyesore to the city, the area had been turned into a botanical park. It was one of Marcy's favorite spots in San Antonio.

The entire bowl of the quarry was a huge fish-pond. Nestled in it was a maze of gardens, connected by cobblestone walkways and arched bridges that wound along its floor and up and down the sides. Perennial native plants provided a flurry of color.

"It must have taken an enormous amount of work to create this," Brant said thoughtfully. The afternoon sun touched his hair, burnishing it to a blue-black sheen; his eyes were hidden by sunglasses. "I wouldn't have believed it possible. I suppose the zoo has been fixed up, as well."

"Yes."

They began to walk again, and Brant caught her hand as they descended the steps to the lowest level of the garden. Marcy realized Brant was being solicitous because the pathway was rough and she was wearing heels, but she enjoyed having her hand wrapped in the warmth and protection of his. As a child she had thought him to be the strongest man she knew. Seeing him again hadn't changed her mind; he still exuded an aura of strength.

His strength stirred more than memories. Over the years, Marcy had pushed aside her feelings for Brant, thinking they were nothing but childish adoration or puppy love, at most. Now she wasn't so sure. She was certainly attracted to him and now the feelings were those of a grown woman.

She would have to be careful not to indulge in flights of fantasy where Brant was concerned. Through the years, she had relied on memories to mentally mold him into what she wanted him to be; but reality had created another man. Brant was not the eighteen-year-old on whom she'd had a childhood crush. Years and maturity had changed him. This was the first time in eighteen years that he had returned to San Antonio. Curiosity had brought him back, and it was this same curiosity that had thrown them together.

The hours were passing swiftly and he would be leaving tomorrow afternoon. Marcy was determined to enjoy what little time they had together. She was sure nothing serious would develop from their relationship because both of them had changed; both had matured. And they were seeking different goals in life. Marcy loved her roots and wouldn't leave them for the world; Brant wanted to forget his altogether. Still, there was no reason why they couldn't enjoy each other's company.

Marcy and Brant stopped and stood in front of the waterfall. They were close enough for Marcy to feel the delicate spray against her face. As she gazed at the foliage on either side of the rushing water, she was caught up in memories. Events that had happened years ago flowed freely through her mind, much like the water that splashed down the side of the quarry. One day in particular kept returning to her thoughts. In fact, it was this memory that had spurred tonight's visit to this part of town.

"Do you remember the day Ethan and I brought you and some of my cousins to the zoo?" Brant asked.

"Yes," she murmured. "I was thinking about that."

"Is that why we came?"

She nodded, and their gazes locked for a second. Then he turned to look around the garden.

"Over there—" he pointed "—that's where you fell and scraped your knees."

"And you picked me up and carried me to the water fountain," Marcy finished, "to clean me up."

Brant chuckled softly. "You were quite a hypochondriac that day, playing your wound for all it was worth."

Marcy laughed with him. "Ice cream, candy, cold drinks."

"And free rides when you were too tired to walk," he reminded with mock severity. Laughter lines softened his facial features, and his eyes sparkled. "It was amazing how frequently your leg hurt after you fell."

"You said I weighed a ton."

"But it didn't stop me from carrying you. Even then, Marcy, you had a penchant for getting your way."

Again Marcy noticed how handsome Brant was. She looked at their hands, still entwined. As she studied his hand holding hers, she became even more aware of her attraction to him; and this attraction definitely was not that of a ten-year-old toward her eighteen-year-old idol. She had to remember they were mature now—he a man, she a woman. She gently disengaged her hand and, looking up, smiled. With a start, she realized she had compared every man she had ever dated to him—or to her childhood dreams of him—and they had all fallen short.

"Thanks for coming with me," she said.

"I wouldn't have missed it for the world."

Slowly his gaze moved over the features of her face. So intently did he look at her that Marcy felt as if he were actually touching her, caressing her. A sudden warmth spread through her body.

"This has been a good day for me," he added.

They started forward again, climbing the steep incline. Brant's hand gently rested under her elbow as he followed her until they reached the path that circled the top of the garden. They stopped inside the rock pagoda at the summit in order to have one last look at the garden below; then they turned and walked to the parking lot. When they reached his car he unlocked the door on the passenger side.

"The next stop is yours to choose," Marcy announced.

He nodded as he slid into the driver's seat of the Lincoln sedan.

"May I make one small request?" she asked.

Brant smiled, and she thought surely her heart turned a somersault in her chest.

"I left some of my blueprints at the office yesterday, and I need to look them over before morning. Would you mind dropping me by on the way home tonight?"

He shook his head. "Not at all. I'd like to go by the place myself. Now, how about an ice cream to salute old times?"

Marcy nodded and laughed softly. He made his request sound like an adventure—exciting and enticing. "Close the door. I'll show you a place near here."

Half an hour later they sat across from each other at a small round table in an ice-cream parlor on Broadway.

"Tell me more about the reclamation project," Brant suggested.

"Well, as you already know, the people in the Heights are . . ." Marcy began without preamble, always ready to talk about her pet project. As she continued, Brant listened, asking questions here and there. "We have to have money if we're going to buy the property adjacent to the school for the literacy center," she concluded. "And, of course, we want the heart of the project to be the old school."

Marcy dropped her spoon into her ice-cream dish and leaned forward to lay her hand over Brant's. She gazed into his eyes, which had turned a deep purple-blue in the artificial light—eyes that were fringed with dark eyelashes. She was suddenly so overwhelmed by an awareness of him that she almost forgot her train of thought. She forced herself back to the discussion at hand. While returning home was nostalgic and sentimental for Brant, tomorrow he would be gone. She had to guard against making his visit more than what it was. She had to keep her feet firmly on the ground.

"Please consider helping us, Brant."

"I am," he answered.

Although he admitted that he was only considering it, in her heart of hearts Marcy knew Brant was going to help them. She saw it in his eyes; she heard it in his voice.

"How about going to get your blueprints now?" he asked. "I'm curious to see the office."

She nodded and soon they were on their way.

As he drove, Brant remarked, "I'm surprised that you were the only one of the children to follow in your father's footsteps."

"You shouldn't be," she replied softly. "I always told you I would."

"So you did," he murmured. "Somehow I'd gotten the impression that you were getting your degree in arts—English and history. Construction work is a far cry from that."

"I headed in that direction," Marcy confessed, "but as Ethan told you earlier, I soon turned to civil engineering. I love construction."

Stopped at a signal light, he turned his head to look at her. "You're a beautiful woman, Marcy. I'm surprised you're not—that you've never been married."

Although her brothers had joked in front of Brant about her not being married, Brant hadn't seemed to take much notice; certainly he had made no comment. Now she was taken aback by his abrupt reference to the subject. She didn't mind, but it did momentarily disconcert her.

"Thank you," she acknowledged, feeling her face become warm beneath his open scrutiny. "But marriage is not necessarily contingent on the way one looks. Although we're living in a fast world, I'm rather old-fashioned about marriage. A lot of my friends have gotten married saying that if it doesn't work out, they can always get a divorce. That's not my philosophy. Like my parents, I want a 'forever' marriage."

"Yeah," Brant drawled. "Once I was as idealistic as you. I wanted a forever marriage, too, but I didn't get it. In case you didn't know, I'm divorced."

"I know." It had not been difficult to keep up with him through the years. As Marcy had teased him earlier, his renown meant that his name continually surfaced in the media.

The smile left Brant's lips and for a moment his eyes lost their luster. "I was idealistic when I was younger," he repeated. "I had dreams to fulfill and worlds to conquer."

"And you've done both," Marcy pointed out.

"To an extent."

"Would you like to see one of my dreams?" she asked.

"The elementary school?" he guessed.

She nodded.

"All right," he agreed and returned his attention to his driving.

"They're working on the streets, so we'll have to take a detour," she warned, and gave him the directions. "The neighborhood has changed quite a bit since you've been gone."

He nodded but was silent while they traveled for several blocks. Then he said, "I almost didn't come to San Antonio, Marcy, and even after I arrived at Lonzo's house, I had doubts about ringing the doorbell."

"Why?" she asked.

"I've always believed that a person can't return home, and in my case I've never had a desire to return. My childhood wasn't filled with happy memories. The farther away I am from the old place, the better I can forget."

Surprised at such a confession, Marcy replied, "It sounds as if you've spent the last eighteen years running from yourself." Looking at Brant's side profile, she saw his lips tighten into a grim smile.

"No—not running from myself, but creating the self I wanted to be."

Giving directions kept Marcy from making an immediate comment. "Turn right at the next street," she told him.

When the headlights illuminated the street sign, Brant braked to an abrupt stop, which threw Marcy forward before the seat belt jerked her back.

He turned to Marcy and there was an edge to his voice, "Why didn't you tell me you were bringing me to my house?"

"I didn't do it intentionally," she explained. "I told you the streets were under construction—some of them are gone altogether. This is the only way we can get to the school."

His hands gripped the steering wheel tightly.

"Look," Marcy said, unable to comprehend Brant's aversion to his childhood home, "if you don't want to drive past your old house, turn around. We'll go on over to the office." When he didn't respond, she added, "Or you can take me home. Whichever you prefer."

Brant reached up and rubbed his forehead. "I apologize," he replied in a weary voice. "I didn't mean to accuse you. It's been so long since I've been here, and suddenly to realize where I am—" He broke off.

Marcy laid her hand over his. "If the memories are that bad, Brant, turn around."

He shook his head. "No, I've come this far. I might as well go all the way."

He pressed his foot on the accelerator and the car moved slowly forward. The headlights beamed down the narrow street that formed a corridor between two rows of wooden houses. During the 1920s the houses had been pretty, white frame buildings in a middle-class neighborhood, but the growth of the city and migration of the people had changed that. Now, the neighborhood was part of the barrio or slums. Most of the homes were in decay—the lawns overrun with weeds, the fences long gone. Already some of them had been torn down, leaving trees standing on the empty lots as stark reminders of what used to be.

Brant stopped the car in front of his aunt's house and turned off the ignition.

"We've just begun repairs on it," Marcy told him.

Although not much work had yet been done on it, the house stood out from the others. The lawn was neatly mowed, the stately pecan trees pruned, and the low picket fence had been repaired and painted.

"What do you think?" Marcy asked.

Still looking at the house rather than at her he asked, "Why are you doing this?"

"This is what I was telling you about earlier. We're taking back what belongs to us. POD bought the house, and now a number of members are donating time to repair and renovate it. Members of POD also offer their services to anyone who wants to buy one of these houses and restore them."

Now he turned to look at her. "You're going to sell it?"

She shook her head and grinned. "No, we're going to keep it. Someday we may want to apply for a historical plaque." Then she added, "Actually, the property we want to buy for the playground and cultural center lies between your house and the school. Since the building was structurally sound, we decided to keep and use it. After all, it is part of the Heights' history."

Brant laughed, and the earlier tension dissipated. "You really know how to make a man feel his age, Marcy."

She laughed with him. "I'm talking about the house, not you."

"Good," he said. "I don't want you to get the two of us mixed up."

As if she could!

Their laughter quieted, but they continued to stare at each other. The streetlight dimly illuminated the interior of the car, casting their faces in shadowy relief. It seemed to Marcy that time had stopped, and she and Brant were the only people in the world.

"A week ago no one could have convinced me that today I'd be in San Antonio, visiting with old friends and looking at my childhood home." His lips curved into a slight smile. "But then you showed up in New York, and my curiosity got the better of me. I had to see you."

The words were like a caress to Marcy. "Have you never wanted to come home?" she asked, unable to comprehend not wanting to return to one's roots.

Brant shook his head. "No. When I left, it was for good. My home is New York."

"New York is beautiful," Marcy admitted, "but it's not for me. I like the wide-open spaces and laid-back living."

"You'd like New York, if you gave it a chance," Brant said. "Come up for a visit one of these days. I'll take you around and show you what a wonderful city it can be. You'd never want to live in San Antonio again."

"No way, José!" Marcy insisted. "I might love New York and have a wonderful time, but when the visit was over—and it would be only a visit—I'd be ready to head home. This is my city."

"I can understand how you feel." Brant turned on the ignition and steered the car down the street. "When I first left San Antonio for the university, I was like a fish out of water. Then I graduated and went to work for Fulbright Engineering, traveling the world over and visiting many exciting cities. But no matter what their beauty or their lure, none of them appealed to me like New York. I always returned there."

"What made you decide to establish your own company?" she asked.

Brant shrugged. "I like being my own boss, and it just sort of evolved. Promotions started coming within the company, and my reputation grew. Eventually I went out on my own."

"I really admire what you've done with your life," Marcy said. "You're the success story everybody would like to be."

Brant turned down the next street and parked in front of the school, letting the motor idle. "Success is a hollow victory if you have no one to share it with. I thought I had found that someone when I met Glenna Joyce about ten years ago."

Marcy was glad Brant was talking about himself, but as unreasonable as it was, she found herself a little jealous of the thought of another woman in his life.

His voice grew far away and nostalgic. "If I've ever seen a perfectly beautiful woman, Glenna was it. We clicked from the moment we first laid eyes on each other, our chemistries meshed. We dated a couple of years before we married and I really believed we could make it work. For the first time in my life, I was happy—completely happy. I didn't think anything could or would destroy my world. But it did. After three years, Glenna confessed that being a 'doting' wife wasn't her dream and I was in the way of her accomplishing her goal of becoming a model and actress of international acclaim. Shortly afterward, we divorced."

Marcy had mixed feelings about Brant's failed marriage. Sad that he had been so unhappy, but glad that he was free and had been free long before he came back into her life.

"Do you still love her?" Marcy asked.

"No," Brant answered without hesitation. "I think I may have loved the *idea* of her more than I loved *her*."

The confession startled Brant himself. During the past three years, he seldom, if ever, spoke of his divorce, yet here he was opening his heart and soul to Marcy, disclosing some of his deepest secrets. She was easy to talk to and to be with. She listened intently as if she were genuinely interested in what he had to say; when she spoke, her comments were reasonable and intelligent.

"I like and admire Glenna, but I don't love her," Brant repeated—the words a revelation to himself as well as to Marcy. He smiled.

Marcy returned the smile and lifted a hand to point. "Turn to the right down here."

Brant nodded. "I remember."

He drove several more blocks and parked the car in front of the red brick building that was illuminated by nightlights and surrounded by a chain-link fence.

"It's going to be as good as new when we get through with it," Marcy told him. "If we ever do. Sometimes it seems like it's taking us forever."

"You're doing a great job. I'm really proud of you," Brant said.

"Thanks," she murmured, warmed by his praise.

"Where are you holding classes now?"

"In a rented two-story house close to Our Lady of the Lake University," she replied. "We've come a long way, Brant, but we still need so much. Nearly all our furniture—that is, what little bit we have—has been donated, so you can imagine what a hodgepodge it is. The pieces are not only unmatched, most of them were worn-out long before they were given to us. We need proper bookshelves, reading tables and carrels." She shook her head. "Sometimes when I get to thinking about it, I begin to wonder if our goals aren't far greater than our ability."

"No," he assured her. "To show you how much faith I have in you and your project, I'm going to join your fund-raising."

"Oh, Brant!" Marcy exclaimed. "Thank you. For a while there, you had me wondering."

"Because of my reaction to my aunt's house?" he questioned.

Marcy nodded.

He turned in the seat and caught both her hands in his. Her fingers were long and slender, the nails clipped short—a working woman's hands.

"I'm sorry about my reaction," he said. "For a second after I realized where we were, I felt like a little boy again, vulnerable and alone." *And frightened.*

"You're not alone—ever," Marcy promised. "Not when you have friends like Ethan and me."

"Thanks," he responded, suddenly realizing that he didn't want Marcy as just a friend. He wanted their relationship to grow into something more intimate. Somehow his thought seemed to affect the very atmosphere and he became acutely aware of the intimacy they had already achieved.

"I guess . . . we'd . . . better go," she murmured. "I want to get those blueprints and call Joe before it gets too late."

Brant reluctantly allowed her to withdraw her hands from his. But it was a full second before he turned his gaze from hers. He switched on the ignition and the engine softly purred to life. He wanted this time with Marcy never to end. With her, Brant felt a wholeness he had been lacking for a long time.

They had driven awhile before Brant asked, "Is there a special man in your life, Marcy?"

"No." After a pause, she added, "There was, several years ago. We were engaged to be married, but it didn't work out."

Although he wanted to know the reason for the broken engagement, Brant didn't question her.

"Knowing that I didn't want to leave San Antonio and without discussing it with me, Derrick applied for and received a transfer to the Los Angeles office of his firm. He announced to me as a fait accompli that we would move in July, a month after we were married."

"What did the transfer mean to him?" Brant inquired. "A promotion?"

"Not an immediate one," Marcy replied, feeling a twinge of guilt. "He felt that in the long run it was the quickest and best route to one."

"Don't you think you may have been a little selfish? Surely you didn't begrudge him a chance to advance in his career?"

"Well, no," Marcy argued. "But—"

"An advance that would have meant a larger income for both of you."

Marcy paused so long, Brant didn't know if she would make a comment on his last remark or not. Eventually, however, she spoke.

"If he had talked with me first, Brant, I probably would have reacted differently. But when he made his announcement after the fact, I realized that I didn't love Derrick. I cared for him, but not enough to move away from my home. I was also angry and hurt that he would have applied for a transfer without first discussing it with me. Since Derrick thought the Los Angeles transfer was an expedient move up the corporate ladder for himself, he felt I should accept his decision and follow him blindly—something I couldn't do. I believe marriage is a commitment of trust, a partnership that's bound together by honesty and communication."

"So do I," he agreed.

They were quiet for the remainder of the drive to Galvan Construction. When Brant parked the car in front of the building, he stared at it for a moment before he spoke.

"It's basically the same. I would have expected you to do some face-lifting to it. I guess you've been too busy with the center to think about this, though."

"No, I haven't been too busy. This is the way I want it." Marcy's retort was sharp.

Marcy jerked the handle and pushed open the door. Before she could slide out, Brant caught her left hand in his and tugged her closer to him. Marcy ceased her struggle and looked into his face. Only inches away from him, her features were clearly defined in the glow of the streetlight. He could see the creamy texture of her face, the dark lashes that framed her beautiful eyes, the full, sensual lips; he could smell the light, airy fragrance of her perfume.

"I wasn't being critical of the place or you," he said gently, "so don't get prickly with me. Okay?"

"Sorry," she murmured. "I've had to fight so long, I'm automatically on the defensive where the business and my career are concerned."

"Not with me. Okay?"

He leaned closer and pressed a soft kiss to her forehead. Although he was acutely aware of her nearness, his kiss held no passion; it wasn't even a prelude to desire. It was simply a promise of friendship and support. Strands of her hair brushed against his face like a gentle caress.

"Okay," she whispered.

He pulled away from her reluctantly, then gave in to the urge he'd had all day—he tucked a renegade curl behind her ear. Like silk her hair slid through his fingers. Again he felt the intimacy between them and wondered if she was also aware of it.

"Are you ready to show me your office?" he asked with a smile in his voice.

Marcy nodded, her gaze locked with his, her expression shadowed with emotion. "I've given the inside a face-lift. I had it redecorated a few months ago."

Hand in hand they went up the sidewalk and entered the office of Galvan Construction. Marcy turned on the lights and stood there looking at Brant as his gaze slowly moved around the room. He stepped away from her.

He walked around the antique wing chairs to the group of photographs that hung on the far wall. He skimmed the ones that traced her family history but lingered on those of himself and Danny and Ethan. It seemed only yesterday the three of them were working together, sharing their dreams and goals.

"Until this weekend, I hadn't thought coming home was possible. If I hadn't experienced it, I wouldn't have believed it."

"I'm glad you're here," Marcy said.

"Because I'm going to help you with your center?"

"No—" her voice lowered "—because we're getting acquainted with each other again."

A smile slowly moved across Brant's lips. He nodded his head but said nothing. As they continued to stare at each other, the tension grew. Was he really attracted to Marcy? he wondered. Or was he inundated with memories? Was he searching through the past for something that didn't really exist?

"Do you—do you like the office?" Marcy asked, breaking the silence and the tension that stretched between them. "Or does it need a more modern touch? Danny suggested some glass or chrome or brass."

Reluctantly pushing thoughts of himself and Marcy aside, Brant turned to look around the office before he said, "I like it, and as long as the technology is the most up-to-date, the office is as modern as it needs to be."

Marcy smiled appreciatively. "I'm glad you like it."

Walking to her desk, she unlocked the top drawer and pulled out the blueprints. Then she noticed the note dangling on the horn of the brass unicorn that served as her message holder. After she read it, she turned to see three boxes stacked in the corner of the room.

"One of my employees brought some books over for the literacy center. Would you mind helping me carry them to the car? That'll save me an extra trip to the office," she explained. "I need to load them into the Bronco, so I can take them directly to the POD office without coming by here tomorrow."

"I don't mind," Brant said, but he didn't move toward the boxes. "I don't suppose you'll have time to see me tomorrow?"

"See you!" Marcy exclaimed. "I'm going to take the day off to spend with you. That's one of the reasons why I'm getting all of this together now. I'm going to take the books to the POD office and the blueprints by Joe's place early in the morning. Then I'm going to come by your hotel and get you." She laughed. "A deal's a deal, and you promised me plenty of persuading time."

"But you've already persuaded me," he reminded her softly.

"You could still change your mind," she retaliated, her voice as soft as his. "I've got to make sure you won't, so don't think you're going to welsh on your deal."

His lips again curved into a smile that Marcy found altogether pleasing. "I wouldn't dream of it."

The evening was coming to an end all too soon for Marcy. The boxes were loaded into the car, and she and Brant were headed toward her home. As he turned left off Walzem Road into Windcrest, she directed him to the garden house she leased. He parked his car in her driveway, and they quickly transferred the boxes of books to her Bronco. Then she took him inside to see her house. She was a little nervous as she unlocked the door. She really wanted him to like what he saw. It mattered what he thought of her, of her home.

"This is nice," Brant commented as he strolled through the open French doors that led from the living room into the spacious den.

"I like it." She kicked off her shoes, glad to give her feet a rest. The luxuriously thick pile of the carpet felt wonderful underfoot. Heels were a far cry from the comfort of boots. She could certainly sympathize with women who wore them every day.

Across the room, she and Brant stared at each other.

He took several steps, stopping when he stood in front of her. "I guess I'd better get going. It's pretty late."

"Please stay awhile," Marcy said. "It's been a long time, and we have a lot of catching up to do."

"Yes," he murmured, "we do."

"Would you like a glass of wine?" she suggested, and he nodded. "While I'm getting it, why don't you put an album on?"

"Any one in particular?" he asked.

She shook her head. "I like them all. So you choose."

In the kitchen Marcy first called Pete Rodriguez to tell him about the books, then Joe Alexander to let him know she would be delivering the blueprints to him early in the morning because she was taking the day off.

"How about the estimate at the Bar Diamond Ranch?" Joe asked.

"I'd forgotten about that," Marcy told him. "Could you do it for me, Joe?"

"Not tomorrow," he answered. "I'm already working two men short. If we're going to finish this job on schedule, I have to be at the site. I guess you could call Mr. Hudley and postpone doing the estimate until after tomorrow. That wouldn't be so bad."

"No," Marcy replied. "That wouldn't be right. I agreed to do the estimate, and we certainly need the work." She sighed. "I'll just have to figure something out."

Hanging up, she wondered what she was going to do. There went her day with Brant. She filled two glasses with wine and carried them into the den where classical guitar music swelled through the room. His shoes off, Brant lay on her sofa. He turned his head as she walked into the room and set his glass on the coffee table.

"It's been a long time since I've truly relaxed like this," he said. "It's so peaceful here."

Marcy sat on the floor in front of the chair across from the sofa. "I'm glad you like it."

"How did your call go? Are we on for tomorrow?" he asked.

"Not exactly," she admitted.

"You're not going to be able to take the day off?"

"I need to do an estimate on a ranch house out of San Antonio. I thought perhaps I could get Joe to do it for me, but he can't. And it's something that can't be put off."

"How about my going with you?" he suggested. "I promise I won't be in the way."

"That would be great!" Marcy exclaimed.

Time seemed to pass without them noticing. Marcy and Brant talked into the wee hours of the morning. Finally, extracting a promise from her to pick him up at eight o'clock the following morning, Brant left and she locked the door behind him.

Truthfully Marcy could say she had never enjoyed the annual company barbecue as much as she had enjoyed this one. She had known that if she could get through to Brant, he wouldn't turn down her request. He had been gone for a long time and he was a wealthy man, but his principles hadn't changed.

THE NEXT MORNING Marcy hurriedly dressed in boots, jeans and a shirt. As usual, she pulled her hair into a coil on the crown of her head, but before she secured it with pins, she had second thoughts. She released the coil and clasped her hair at the nape of her neck with a barrette so that it hung loose. As soon as she delivered the books and blueprints, she drove to the hotel where she found Brant waiting outside. He smiled and waved as she drove up and parked.

Opening the door, he heaved his luggage into the back seat and said, "I didn't know how long it would take us to look at the property, so I checked out. When we're through, we can make a sure shot to the airport. How about some breakfast before we hit the road?"

Marcy nodded. "How about Shoney's?"

After breakfast they drove to Chester Hudley's Bar Diamond Ranch located in the Hill Country, north of San Antonio. As they parked, Marcy saw Chester leaning against the trunk of a tree in the front yard. He pushed away from the tree and walked toward the Bronco.

"Howdy, Marcy." A broad smile creased the weathered face. "Glad to see you. I'd sure like to get this work done and over with. I want to get this property on the market as soon as I can."

Marcy slid out of the Bronco and shut the door. "I didn't realize you were selling the house."

"Yep." Chester rocked back on the heels of his worn boots. "I've given my best to this land. Now it's time for it to give back to me. What with the money I make on this sale, I'll have plenty for retirement."

"Are you sure you want to renovate the house before you sell it?" Marcy asked, aware, as she spoke, that she might be talking herself out of a much-needed job.

Chester nodded. "Me and the wife figured we'd have a better chance of selling it if the house looked better. Don't reckon it's right to sell a house that ain't been rightly done up, and it's been vacant for several years now. Since Winnie got sick, we've been living closer to town."

"How big is the place?" Brant asked.

"Five hundred acres," Chester replied. "It ain't all that big, but it's prime property with a decent house on it and the Comal River flowing right through it. You can't find a better piece of property for the money. Why? Are you interested?"

Brant shook his head. "Just curious."

"I sure hate to leave the place," the old man said. "I've been here all my life. Even raised my kids here. But me and the wife are getting on up in years now, and—" He paused and cleared his throat. "Well, we want to join the kids in Houston."

"Your children aren't interested in keeping this in the family?" Marcy questioned.

"Nope," Chester answered. "They're city slickers all the way. They left the country with a promise never to return except for visits, and that's the way it's been for a mighty long time."

After Chester guided Marcy and Brant through the house—a rambling one-story native-stone structure—and pointed out the repairs he wanted done, Marcy began her calculations on cost and time. As she worked at the table in the old-fashioned kitchen, Chester and Brant took a walk in the backyard. When she was finished, she stepped out on the long veranda that ran the width of the house. Brant and Chester stood beneath the swooping branches of the cypress trees that grew along the banks of the river. The sun shone through the leaves, forming a pleasing, mottled design. Marcy walked down the steps to join the two men.

"Here it is." Handing Chester the bid sheet, she went over the figures explaining the costs and the procedures she would use to do the repairs. "It's going to take at least three, maybe four weeks for us to complete the job."

"Sounds good to me," Chester responded. "When can you begin?"

"Monday, two weeks from today," Marcy told him.

Chester nodded. "Well, I reckon I'll be getting back to the wife. I don't like to leave her alone for too long at a time. Y'all can stay out here as long as you want. Just make sure you close the gate when you leave."

After Chester left, Marcy exclaimed, "Isn't it beautiful out here? So peaceful."

"It's nice," Brant replied and grinned. "But give me the city anytime."

Marcy grinned back at him. "You're a Texan, born and bred, and I'm going to be the person who brings you back to your roots."

Laughing and joking, they walked back to the Bronco and soon were headed for the airport—a trip that was over much sooner than either of them really wanted.

Marcy parked the Bronco in front of the terminal and turned to face Brant. "Thanks for everything."

He caught her hand. "I'm flying to Alaska to finish a job, and I'll be gone for about two weeks. When I return, I want to see you."

"About the fund-raiser?"

His blue eyes were dark with emotion as he shook his head. "I want to see *you*, Marcy."

"Yes," Marcy whispered and waited expectantly as his head moved closer and his lips gently touched hers.

All too quickly the kiss ended and Brant pulled his mouth from hers. "I'll call you."

"I'll be waiting."

"Marcy, if you need me for any reason, call the office. Shepherd will know how to reach me."

Grabbing his luggage, Brant slid out of the Bronco. At the door of the terminal, he turned and looked at her. Lifting his hand to his mouth, he waved her a kiss. She returned it. Then he disappeared.

Marcy pulled away from the curb and eased into the traffic, all her thoughts centered on Brant Holland. He wanted to date *her*—Marcy Galvan. Reason, however, quickly put a damper on her elation. She had teased Brant about being born and reared in Texas, but no matter how much she may have wished it to be otherwise, he had changed. He no longer considered San Antonio, or even Texas, his home. His business and home were located in New York. She had to be careful not to lose her heart without carefully weighing the consequences.

Get your head out of the clouds, a small inner voice said. *Brant just wants to date you. There's no reason for you to be thinking of commitment and marriage.*

But what if the relationship did become serious? Marcy wanted marriage—the kind her father and mother had shared, with plenty of loving and caring. And out of the marriage she wanted to have three or four children. Along with all of this, Marcy also planned to continue to work and to keep Galvan Construction in the family. But now Brant Holland had walked into her life and expressed a desire to see her when he returned from Alaska in two weeks.

Brant Holland—the man who could have his pick of the most beautiful women in the world—wanted to see Marcy again. It was a dream come true.

CHAPTER SIX

THE DAYS FOLLOWING Brant's departure were busy ones for Marcy. She spent all day Tuesday at the site of the Alamo Supermarket; Wednesday and Thursday she went from bank to bank, trying without success to get a loan to buy her uncle's half of the business. On Friday she began the rounds of high-interest finance companies—with no better luck.

She was too leveraged. That's all there was to it. No one was willing to lend her the money. Worrying about what she was going to do, and seeing no option but to give up either the ranch or the company, she walked out of San Antonio Finance Company to the Bronco.

She was so deep in thought she didn't realize she was on the expressway going to the POD office until she came to her exit. Turning off the expressway and onto Commerce Street, she drove to the rented building where POD had established the Neighborhood Reading Center.

"Hi, Lupe," Marcy said to the young girl who was shelving books when she entered the two-story frame building. "Is Pete around?"

Lupe nodded and pointed. "In his office. He's working on class assignments."

Marcy let her gaze rove around the sparsely furnished room, from Lupe's old desk to the stacked bookshelves made of cinder blocks and twelve-bytwelves, donated by various lumber companies in the city. Each shelf was painted a different color because the paint, too, had been a gift.

"I hope this means new students," she murmured.

"It does," Pete answered from the door. "Also I went over to the school district office and checked out our tutorial program with the English, Spanish and reading departments. They approved, and I've got the assignment sheets from all the individual schools for the kids who are already enrolled. Adult enrollment went up by five."

"Good," Marcy said and followed him into his office.

Although she was pleased with the news, she was unable to inject much enthusiasm into her voice. If she lost Galvan Construction, POD would lose one of its main benefactors. Her crews had volunteered hours of free labor to repair this building and others in the project.

Pete, holding papers in his hand to be filed, walked across the room to an old metal file cabinet and pulled on the top drawer. It didn't budge. He yanked on it again, harder this time, and the entire cabinet fell forward.

"Damn!" Pete gritted, dropping the papers and catching the cabinet. "I should know better by now."

Marcy scooted across the floor and gathered up the scattered papers as Pete pushed the file cabinet back in place.

"I'll be glad when we get some better furniture," Pete said.

"Don't hold your breath," Marcy said.

Taking the papers from her, Pete contemplated her face. "It's not like you to be down, especially not with

Brant helping us. Things are looking better than they ever have."

"Things aren't looking so good for me," she explained.

"What's wrong?"

Sitting in the chair in front of his desk, Marcy poured out her troubles. "I don't know where to turn next," she finished.

"I'm sorry, Marcy. I wish there was some way I could help you."

"Thanks, Pete," she said, "but I'll work it out somehow. I've got to. We've got to have this center, and it's going to take more than Brant Holland or his money to maintain it. It's going to take people like me and companies like mine."

Pete grinned. "That's my Marcy."

In the outer office Marcy heard a door open, then Lupe spoke in Spanish. "Mrs. Herrera, how nice to see you. Have you already read the books you checked out last week?"

"Yes, I have," she answered in heavily accented English. "And I am here to enroll in Marcella's English class again."

"Wonderful!" said Lupe, still speaking Spanish.

"Lupe," Mrs. Herrera said gently in English, "remember, you promised to speak English. Both of us speak the Spanish very good, but me—not so good in English."

Marcy rose and walked into the office to see the elderly woman neatly stacking books on Lupe's desk and to hear Lupe apologize in English.

"I forgot."

"Hello, Mrs. Herrera," Marcy greeted, moving toward her favorite student. "How are you doing?"

"I'm fine, thank you," the older woman replied, with a twinkle in her faded brown eyes. "And you?"

"I'm fine, thank you," Marcy responded, as if she were reciting one of her English lessons. Then she exclaimed, "You're doing so well, Mrs. Herrera! You'll soon be speaking English better than I."

Mrs. Herrera laughed. "I don't think so, Marcella. But if I do, it's because I have such a good teacher. You are *muy bien, mi hija*. Very good, my daughter."

"You're wonderful for my ego," Marcy said, hugging the woman.

"Ego?" Mrs. Herrera questioned.

After Marcy translated the word, she asked, "Have your grandchildren decided whether they want to enroll in the Spanish classes?"

"They do not want to," Mrs. Herrera answered in English, then reverted to Spanish: "It is such a shame, Marcella. Neither Manny nor Rosa want anything to do with their Spanish heritage, and they don't realize what they're losing. Their parents can speak both English and Spanish, but the children—" she shook her head "—they can understand Spanish, but they don't speak it."

"Teaching children like them to speak Spanish is one of POD's goals," Marcy explained. "In fact, we've already gotten our program approved through the school district."

Mrs. Herrera lifted a wrinkled hand and gently cupped Marcy's cheek. "You're a good girl, Marcella. I don't know what we would do without you. Now, I must get more books and go home."

As Mrs. Herrera turned her attention to the shelves of books, Marcy returned to Pete's office.

Looking up from his papers, he said, "Your basic-Spanish class is filled, and the majority of the students have Spanish surnames."

"I'm glad," Marcy replied. "But it's sad that so many of us are growing away from our heritage."

"Progress," Pete remarked. "That's what it's called." He went over to the vending machine, looked at it for a few minutes, then turned to Marcy with a grin. "Do I dare?" he asked.

Marcy laughed. "It's up to you. If it falls, remember, there's only Lupe and I to help you."

Turning, he laughed softly and pulled several quarters from his pocket. "Can I buy you a cold drink?"

"Thanks, I'd love a tomato juice," Marcy answered.

"By the way," Pete said, "I heard from Holland's office today. We're working at setting a date for the fund-raising. I don't know how to thank you, Marcy. If it hadn't been for you, he never would have agreed to do this."

Marcy and Pete talked about the fund-raising schedule as they finished off their cold drinks. Afterward she settled down to help Pete work on the reading assignments for the coming month. They were through in a couple of hours, and both Pete and Lupe left for the day, but Marcy stayed to finish shelving the books. Then she locked up and headed for home.

She retrieved her mail at the front door and walked in to see her answering-machine light flashing in double time. Flipping it on, she listened to her calls as she rifled through her mail, throwing most of it into the waste basket. Her phone calls were more interesting. There were messages from Clarice who asked the same questions: Was Marcy having any luck getting the money to buy the company? Would she like to come to dinner tonight? After Clarice's third message, Marcy heard her caseworker's voice.

"Marcy," Kyla began the recording, "it's ten o'clock on Friday morning, and I'm calling to let you know that you and Amy Calderon are a potential match. I've scheduled a meeting for Tuesday evening to introduce you to Gil Calderon, Amy's father, to complete the matching. If you have a problem with the appointment, give me a call. Otherwise, I consider it a date."

"No problem at all," Marcy exclaimed aloud, as she laid the last of the opened mail on the counter and flipped off the recorder.

She smiled. At least, some things in her life were going well.

Humming, she prepared dinner—a cucumber-and-tomato sandwich on toasted wheat bread and a glass of fresh apple juice. Afterward she went into the bedroom, took off her boots and socks and stretched out on the bed to call Clarice.

"Why didn't you call me sooner?" Clarice grumbled when she heard Marcy's voice.

"I just got home," Marcy explained. "And in answer to your questions, I haven't gotten the loan yet, and I'm not going to come to dinner. I've already eaten. Besides, I'm bushed and want to go to bed early."

"Hoping Brant might call?" Clarice guessed.

"Yes," Marcy admitted.

"Wouldn't it be wonderful if you and Brant—" Clarice began.

"Clarice," Marcy quickly interjected, "please don't make more of this than what it is. Brant is probably just curious about the little-girl-now-grown-up. This is nothing but friendship.''

Marcy certainly hoped she was wrong in her assessment of the situation, but this early in her relationship with Brant, she recognized her own vulnerability. She could handle her heart and its affairs much better without the interference of loving and caring relatives.

''I don't think so,'' Clarice drawled. ''I noticed the way he was looking at you at the barbecue. That, Marcy, was a man looking at a woman with adult-to-adult interest.''

Marcy truly wanted it to be so, but she didn't dare get her hopes all built up. Brant had certainly seemed interested but she had gone out with enough men to know that what began as a hot date could quickly fizzle out. But she didn't want to discuss this with Clarice right now. She needed some time and space to deal with it herself.

''How are the girls?''

''Changing the subject, Marcy, isn't going to change the facts.''

''Clarice—''

''Okay,'' Clarice allowed, ''so you want to hear about Sarah and Diane. Well, let me tell you—''

After a few minutes of listening to the minute details of what her nieces had done since she last saw them—Marcy was sure Clarice was punishing her—Marcy hung up. Walking to her desk, she saw a copy of the bid she had written for Chester Hudley and was reminded of her day with Brant. All they had done was drive out to the Hill Country, but being with him had made the trip an adventure. She had thoroughly enjoyed his company. She remembered the intimacy they had shared as they stood on the banks of the Comal River with the spring breeze rustling through the branches of the cypress trees.

During the days since Brant had gone, Marcy had compared her feelings for Derrick, with how she felt about Brant. Derrick had never aroused the same emotions in her that Brant did. When she was a child, she had adored Brant; and at thirteen when he'd sent her the locket for her birthday, the crush had changed to puppy love. But she had matured since then; the question was, had her feelings for Brant matured?

Her day was catching up with her and she tucked the bid into her notebook. Then she took a shower and put on her pajamas. Again she pondered what she was going to do to raise the money she needed to buy the company outright. She wasn't nearly as optimistic about getting it as she had sounded to Pete earlier and just now to Clarice. At the moment, her most promising option was the sale of the ranch. As her father would have said, she was going to have to sacrifice Peter to pay Paul.

Perhaps Danny was right. She was living in the past. She had to decide what was the most important to her—La Rosa Blanca or the company. When she thought about it, she had to admit that she seldom went down Del Rio way. True, she called Erny Lopez, her caretaker, several times a month, but she didn't get down for a visit as often.

Still it hurt to think of giving up a piece of her heritage, a piece of land that had belonged to the Galvan family since the 1700s. To sell it would be to part with a portion of her heart and soul. She would suffer the same fate if she lost half the business.

Seeing no way out of her dilemma, she switched off the overhead light in her bedroom, then went over to the fireplace and picked up the little hard hat from the mantel. She would never forget the day Brant had given it to her. She had worn it with pride.

She smiled, glad that Brant Holland had reentered her life. He had brought not just a ray of sunlight; he *was* her sun. How long it would last, Marcy didn't know; but she determined to enjoy it as long as it did.

FOR HER UPCOMING meeting with Gil Calderon on Tuesday evening, Marcy put on a straight black skirt and white silk blouse, and wore her hair pulled back into a decorative clasp. She chose as her only jewelry a black onyx necklace and earrings she had inherited from her mother.

Excited about her potential match, Marcy entered the office of Big Brothers/Big Sisters. The first person she saw was Amy, who sat across the room thumbing through a magazine.

"Hi," Marcy said.

Amy looked up, her face brightening. Tossing the magazine aside, she slid out of the chair and walked over to Marcy. "My daddy's here to meet you," she told her. "And Mrs. Jackson said that we would probably be matched. Are you happy?"

Marcy nodded and looked up to see Kyla standing in the open doorway of an inner office.

"Amy," the caseworker began, "since I'll be meeting with your father and Marcy first, I'm going to ask that you wait here. Later, I'll come to get you, and the four of us will talk. My secretary is down the hall making a few photocopies for me. She'll be returning shortly. If you need anything, she'll get it for you."

Marcy followed Kyla into the office.

"Marcy," Kyla said, closing the door, "I'd like for you to meet Gil Calderon, Amy's father."

Marcy looked at the man who sat in one of the chairs in front of Kyla's desk. Giving Marcy a friendly grin, he rose and brushed a hand through his hair. She immediately liked him. He was a tall man who looked to be in his mid-thirties. Although he was overweight, he was nice looking.

"Hello, Marcy." He shook her hand. "I'm glad to finally meet you. I've heard so much about you from Amy."

"You have a special daughter," Marcy remarked and sat down in the vacant chair next to Gil's.

He sighed, nodded and also sat down again. "I'm glad you said that. Quite a few people accuse her of being precocious."

Marcy smiled. "Well, Mr. Calderon, I'll have to admit I'm guilty of believing that about her, too. But it's that very trait that has resulted in her becoming a part of Big Sister-Little Sister program."

"I vaguely remember the afternoon she saw her first commercial advertising Big Brothers/Big Sisters," Gil replied. "But I never dreamed she would take it upon herself to apply to be a Little Sister. Still, I should have known." He leaned back in the chair and chair and crossed one leg over the other. "Amy's greatest desire has always been for the impossible. She's always wanted a big sister."

"That's the beauty of a program like this one," Kyla pointed out. "Amy can have her wish. Of course, the purpose of this meeting is to see if the two of you are comfortable with the match. First, I want to emphasize that this program is based on the premise that we provide the single-parent child with a Big Brother or Big Sister—someone whom they can pal around and have fun with—a mentor of sorts. We're striving to reinforce the concept of family.''

The caseworker looked at both of them, then began to talk about the program in general, outlining the responsibilities of each of the participants.

"Now the two of you need to learn something about each other. Remember, in order for this program to be meaningful for both the Big and the Little Sister, there must be communication between the parent and the participants. There must be honesty.'' She smiled at Marcy. "Why don't you tell us a bit about yourself.''

Since neither Marcy nor Gil was inhibited, conversation was easy. First, Marcy introduced herself and described her job. Kyla quietly withdrew from the discussion to listen and to make notes. After Marcy completed her description, Gil began to talk.

Marcy's first impression that Amy was a poor little rich girl was almost correct. Gil was an executive officer of a high-powered technological research foundation, and his area of supervision covered the entire state. This necessitated his traveling frequently and leaving Amy at home with their live-in housekeeper, Nona Ferguson. Gil's wife had died of degenerative heart disease during her second pregnancy.

"Although both Amy and I have suffered from the death of my wife,'' Gil concluded, "I believe Amy has suffered the most. When her mother was alive Amy never thought about having an older sister, but after Sondra's death, Amy became preoccupied with the idea. I never understood it. If I married again, I could give her younger brothers and sisters, but she wants an older one.''

"Well," Kyla assured, "she came to the right place. We can certainly provide her with one through our program."

"I'm glad Amy is involved with the Big Sister-Little Sister program," he said. "I think both of us will benefit from it."

"I'm glad you feel that way," Kyla replied. "Now, unless either of you has anything else to add, the meeting is concluded."

Both shook their heads.

"You're satisfied with the match?"

This time both nodded.

"Then, it's settled, and it's time for us to talk with Amy to see if she's happy with the match," Kyla announced, then added with soft laughter, "As if we have to ask her."

AFTER THE INTERVIEW with Kyla was over, Marcy suggested that Gil, Amy and she drive to the nearest Baskin-Robbins ice-cream store for something to celebrate their new "kinship." Amy chose to ride with Marcy. Wanting to stay a little longer to talk with Kyla, Gil promised to meet them shortly. Amy held Marcy's hand as they exited the building and walked to the Bronco.

"I'm so glad you're my Big Sister," Amy said, squirming into the passenger seat and securing the seat belt around her waist.

"And I'm happy to finally have a Little Sister all my own," Marcy responded. "It's something I've wanted all my life."

"Me, too," Amy agreed. "A big sister, that is. I got scared while I was sitting out there waiting. It took y'all so long, I thought maybe Mrs. Jackson had changed her mind about matching us."

Marcy pulled out of the parking lot and headed for the expressway. "I wasn't worried about it tonight," she told Amy, "but these past few days have been tough. It took her so long to get back to me, I'd begun to have my doubts, too."

"Daddy's leaving for Dallas in the morning on business," Amy announced. After a long pause, she added, "I'll bet he's going to be seeing Mrs. Courtland."

"Who's she?" Marcy asked.

"A woman he works with. I think they're dating. Vanessa says if it was just business, Mrs. Courtland wouldn't be so friendly when she called and she wouldn't make it a point to talk with me every time before she asks for Daddy."

"Vanessa?" Marcy questioned.

"A friend of mine," Amy explained. "She's in the same grade as me, and she's got a stepmother. She doesn't like her."

"Well," Marcy said, "I don't know about Vanessa and her stepmother, but I have a feeling that Mrs. Courtland is a nice person. I can't imagine your dad liking her, otherwise. She doesn't have to take the time to talk with you. Don't you think it's possible she's doing it because she likes you?"

"Do you think so?"

Marcy exited the expressway. "I do."

Amy was quiet for a short while. Then she said, "I saw Mrs. Courtland once. She met Daddy at the airport, and they flew to Dallas together."

"What did you think of her then?"

Amy shrugged. "She was okay. She has blond hair. Mama's hair was black."

Marcy glanced over at Amy, who was gazing out the window now. The last sentence she'd uttered said volumes. Marcy sensed the child's fear that she would lose her father to this woman; she felt Amy's loneliness. She remembered the way she had felt when her mother died. Although she had been an adult at the time, she'd felt as if her mother had abandoned her. She'd known better, but the knowing didn't lessen the pain.

"I could tell your father loves you very much," she stated quietly. "And he's proud of you for having joined the Big Sisters-Little Sister program."

"He is?" Amy swung her head around and gazed at Marcy. "Did he tell you that?"

"Mm-hmm." She negotiated a turn and eased the Bronco into a parking slot in front of the ice-cream parlor. Switching off the ignition, she turned in the seat so that she was facing Amy.

"Mrs. Courtland has children." Amy lowered her head and unlocked the seat belt. "Daddy's going to bring them to the house sometime and introduce them to me. Mrs. Courtland says she would like to come to see one of my dance recitals, the one I'll have in September, but—"

After a long pause, Marcy prompted, "But what?"

Amy looked at Marcy a long time before she said, "The way Daddy and Mrs. Courtland work, they probably won't be able to come to my recital. He had to miss the last one. It was in April. He says he won't make any promises about coming to the next one. That way, when business comes up that he has to take care of, he won't be going against his word."

"Doesn't Nona go with you to these things when your father is out of town?"

"Yeah," Amy admitted. "But it's not like having your family—your real family—with you." She grinned. "And, now, I have a real Big Sister. You'll come with me, won't you? You won't let me be alone, will you?"

Although Marcy understood Gil's not being able to attend all of Amy's extracurricular activities, she sensed the child's hurt and her fears. Her heart went out to Amy. "I'll come. You need to give me the date so I can pencil it in on my calendar."

"I thought my daddy was the only one who did that," Amy exclaimed.

"He's not," Marcy assured her. "If I didn't, my life would be one big mess."

"Mrs. Jackson said you'd probably take me out about once a week," Amy said.

"That's right," Marcy said.

"Are we going to count this as a week that you'll be meeting with me as my Big Sister?" Amy asked.

Following the child's thoughts, Marcy grinned. "We sure are, and tonight doesn't count as our weekly visit."

Amy smiled. "My dance lessons are on Thursday afternoon. Sometime—when you can—I'd like for you to take me. I'd like for you to meet my teacher."

"How about this Thursday?" Marcy suggested.

"Could you?"

Marcy nodded. "What time shall I pick you up?"

"At three-thirty. Right after school lets out. Oh, goody!" Then she asked, "Will we get to spend some Saturdays together?"

"Mm-hmm," Marcy answered. "I was just thinking about our taking in a movie this Saturday."

"Swell! Can I choose the movie?"

"You sure can."

"This is great," Amy said. "I love having you as my Big Sister."

"And I love being your Big Sister," Marcy told her. "But this week is different. It's our beginning, so I can spend a little more time with you. Other weeks when I will only have a few hours to spend with you, you mustn't be too disappointed."

"Okay," Amy agreed. "What time will you come get me Saturday?"

"I have some chores to do in the morning, so I'll pick you up about one o'clock."

"All right." Amy grinned.

A silver Mercedes sedan slid into the parking slot next to Marcy's.

"There's your dad," she said. "Time for us to go in and celebrate."

"You won't change your mind about Thursday night or Saturday, will you?" Amy questioned.

"No," Marcy promised, "I won't. I'll meet you at school at three-thirty on Thursday."

"DON'T YOU THINK Marcy's great?" Amy asked her father as they pulled out of the parking lot in front of the ice-cream parlor.

"Mm-hmm. I think she'll make you a good Big Sister."

"She's pretty, like Mama."

"She's pretty," Gil admitted, "but I don't think she looks like your mother."

"I'm so glad she's my Big Sister. I've asked her to come to my September dance recital."

Amy sounded defensive, and Gil cast her a quick glance.

"That's nice," he said. "You should have quite an audience for yourself. Nona, Wanda, Marcy and me."

"Mrs. Courtland is still coming?" Amy murmured.

Again Gil glanced over at her and said a little sharply, "Of course, she's coming. You invited her."

"I know. I just thought maybe she would change her mind."

"I don't think so. She's really looking forward to it," Gil said.

He was disappointed that Amy hadn't begun to warm up to Wanda. In fact, she seemed to be reluctant to talk about Wanda. The more he mentioned her, the more Amy avoided the subject. Gil was at a loss about what to do.

"I'm glad you and I are having this time together, Amy. You remember my telling you about Wanda's three children." Giving her only time to nod her head, Gil continued, "Well, I've been thinking it would be nice for all of you to meet one another and for us to be friends."

Having to negotiate traffic, he couldn't look at Amy, but he felt her gaze on him. She certainly wasn't making this easy for him.

"Are you dating her?" Amy asked.

"So far, I've only attended business functions with her," Gil answered truthfully. "But I do want to date her, Amy. I like Wanda and enjoy being with her. And I want you to like her."

"Are you—are you going to marry her?"

Gil reached out and caught Amy's hand in a firm clasp. "I'm going to take one step at a time, darling. Right now, I want to date Wanda. If we should fall in love and want to get married, I would talk to you about it first."

"Promise?" Amy whispered.

"I promise." He squeezed her hand reassuringly. "Now, how about our arranging for a time to meet with the Courtland children."

"There's three of them?" Amy questioned. "Two of them older than me, and one younger?"

"Mm-hmm," Gil answered. "Elana is the oldest— she's twelve. The two younger ones are boys. Kevin is seven and Drake is ten. I thought maybe one weekend, they could fly down and we could take them to the zoo or to Sea World. Once you get to know them, you'll really like them."

"Do they have to stay home with a baby-sitter like me because their mother travels so much?"

Gil ignored Amy's bitter undertone. "No, they stay with their grandmother. She lives with them, just like Nona lives with us. When we get home, we'll look at the calendar and set up a date, okay?"

"Okay," Amy muttered, then added, "I'm really going to have fun now that Marcy is my Big Sister. She's going to take me to my dance lesson on Thursday and to a movie on Saturday."

Deciding he had pushed the introduction of Wanda and her children as far as he needed to for the moment, Gil inquired, "Have you decided which movie you want to see?"

"Well," she replied, her voice bubbly and excited now, "I've been thinking."

SITTING UP IN BED with the pillow fluffed behind her, Marcy held a mystery novel in her hands, but tonight it didn't capture her attention. Unable to think of anything but her evening with the Calderons, she finally laid it aside. She closed her eyes, thinking of all the things she and Amy could do together. Her thoughts were interrupted by the ring of the telephone. Expecting the caller to be Clarice, she leaned over and picked up the receiver, pressing it to her ear.

"Hello."

"Hi." Brant's resonant voice flowed over the line and sent warm pleasure through Marcy's body.

"Brant," she murmured, feeling her heart skip a beat. "What a surprise!"

"I called to let you know I'll be finishing up here sooner than I anticipated. I'm going to fly directly into San Antonio on Saturday morning. I'd like to spend the day with you, ending with dinner and a movie, perhaps."

Immediately Marcy opened her mouth to accept Brant's invitation; then she remembered. "I can't. I've already made plans." She knew her refusal sounded lame.

"Plans you can't break for someone special?" he urged.

"As much as I want to, I can't," Marcy replied. "I just became a Big Sister and promised my Little Sister that I would take her to a movie on Saturday afternoon."

"That's the program where a person becomes a friend to a single-parent child?" Brant asked.

"Yes," Marcy answered and succinctly described the program. Then she told him about Amy. "I can't cancel, Brant. Saturday will be our first big day together, and it means so much to her. Even though I'd love to spend the day with you, I can't let her down. How about our doing something on Sunday?''

"All right." Brant sighed. "Keep the entire day free for me. Sunday will be *our* first big day together. It means so much to me, you can't let me down. Okay?"

"Okay," Marcy responded.

Long after Brant rang off, Marcy sat up in bed. Her book was forgotten and the television ignored. Her thoughts of Amy and the Big Sister-Little Sister program had diminished. She daydreamed about Sunday with Brant.

BRANT FINISHED his drink, then stood and walked onto the balcony. Since he'd left San Antonio, he had been preoccupied with Marcy to the exclusion of all else. Shepherd had teased him about behaving like a lovesick teenager where Marcy was concerned. And, Brant admitted, perhaps he was. He had spent only a few hours with her, but he missed her. The ring of her laughter lingered in his ears; he smelled her perfume, a light airy fragrance that reminded him of springtime in the Hill Country; he compared every woman he saw to her. None of them measured up.

He was glad he would be seeing Marcy Sunday, but he was disappointed that she'd turned him down for Saturday. He wasn't accustomed to being turned down, and he had envisioned their spending the entire weekend together. He had hoped she would be eager to be with him as he was to be with her.

He knew Big Brothers/Big Sisters was a worthy organization and admired Marcy for being a volunteer, but for a moment he'd been jealous of the little girl who came between him and Marcy. He remembered

Danny and Ethan teasing Marcy about her crusades and figured that this must be one of them.

It had been a long time since Brant had been as interested in a woman as he was in Marcy. Unlike the other women who had filled his life for the past few years, Marcy wasn't caught up in the glamour of the social world. She was refreshingly natural and unspoiled—traits that were part of the reason he found her so attractive.

The first time he married, he'd chosen a person whom he thought would be good for his image, one who would help him with his career. He had been prepared to care for her and give her everything she needed. He had not counted on a woman who wanted a career of her own more than she wanted him. This time, he would marry a woman whom he loved, one who loved him equally, one who was willing to share all of herself with him. He would allow nothing to come between them.

But Marcy, he realized, was as career-minded as Glenna, and she was involved in all those projects. She had broken one engagement because she'd refused to move from San Antonio. But she admitted that she hadn't really loved her fiancé. Perhaps if she loved the man, she would be willing to move wherever he lived. Perhaps... But he couldn't be sure.

Brant heard a door open and turned to see Shepherd Hayden entering the parlor from the second bedroom. He moved to the refrigerator from which he extracted a can of club soda.

"We've finalized the date for that fund-raising event in San Antonio," he announced. "I've marked it on your personal calendar. Your flight to San Antonio is confirmed, your bags are packed and ready. And the office furniture you ordered will be delivered at nine o'clock Friday morning." Shepherd pulled the tab from the drink. "Want one?" he asked.

Brant shook his head.

After several long swallows, Shepherd said, "You know, when I encouraged you to go to San Antonio to visit your friends, I had no idea you were going to come back with your head in the clouds."

"Is it that obvious?" Brant questioned.

"I've never seen you this preoccupied before, and her name has been cropping up in the conversation with regularity. You've met beautiful women before, but they haven't flipped you out like this one has. What does she have that the rest didn't have?" When Brant didn't answer, Shepherd went on, "I've never been a busybody, but—"

"Then don't start now!" Brant was immediately sorry for his outburst. He realized he was very much on the defensive about Marcy; he wanted no interference where she was concerned.

"You've never been one to let your emotions rule your head," Shepherd pointed out. "I hope you don't start now."

Deciding it was safer to drop the subject, Brant grinned at the older man. "What time are we meeting with Flannigan tomorrow?"

Shepherd stared at Brant for a second before he shrugged. "Ten sharp. He personally is going to give us a guided tour through the facilities."

Brant walked to the desk and flipped through some of the papers. "Shepherd, get me a copy of the feasibility study we did last year on opening branch offices."

"Sure will," the older man answered, lifting the soda can to his mouth.

"Is San Antonio included?" Brant inquired.

Shepherd lowered the bottle. "I don't know. Do I conclude from the question, that if it isn't it should be?"

"That's right, and get the results to me as soon as you can."

CHAPTER SEVEN

MARCY HAD ENJOYED taking Amy to her dance lesson last night and was looking forward to the movie tomorrow, but the day in between, this Friday—the day she had to live through now—was proving to be a bummer. At the rate things were going, at summer's end she would have a new business partner.

Although it was only ten-thirty, the day was already hot and promised to be hotter. She had been at the site of the Alamo Supermarket since six. One of the men had fallen and broken his ankle, and on Monday she had to have another crew assembled so she could start the renovations at the Hudley place. One of the equipment trucks had broken down, and she had only recently learned that some of their supplies wouldn't be delivered until next week.

Staring through her sunglasses at Joe Alexander, she waved an invoice in the air. "How could Tuftland's have gotten the shipping dates screwed up?" she demanded, her voice high-pitched with exasperation. "I filled out the order myself, and it has today as the delivery date. I told them we had to have it *no later than today.*"

"It's going to be all right, Marcy," Joe assured her. "We're running a few days ahead of schedule, and while we're waiting for the beams and the tubing, we'll finish up over here."

"We're cutting it too short," she argued. "We're losing all our built-in time, and we don't have any extra men to spare. Remember, we have to have a full crew at Hudley's Monday morning."

Joe shoved his hard hat off his face and rubbed his hand over his brow. "I was worried about that, too, and I've been giving a lot of thought about what we can do. The way I look at it, we have two options," he said. "I'll lay them both out for you, and you can see which one you like best. First, we can..."

Slowly they walked the entire site area and Marcy listened as he outlined his plan. They were standing in front of Marcy's Bronco by the time he had finished.

"What do you think?" he asked.

Marcy nodded. "Let's go with the second option and the modifications I pointed out. While you're doing this, I'll run by Tuftland's and see if I can't get the tubing delivered any sooner. I'll have to see about taking our business elsewhere, if they aren't going to be more reliable with delivery."

Slipping one of her gloves off, Marcy lifted her hard hat and brushed her hand through damp hair. Although it was only morning, her shirt was already sticking to her back.

"Anything new on your uncle's sellout?" Joe inquired.

Marcy shook her head. "I'm still looking and hoping. Are you getting uncomfortable?"

He grinned and brushed his arm against his forehead. "I'm a tad concerned," he admitted, "but not enough to be worried. I'm in for the long haul, Marcy."

"Thanks, Joe."

They talked awhile longer.

"See you later, boss," Joe finally said and sauntered back to the work area.

Marcy was about to climb into the Bronco when a car turned into the lot and parked next to her. The door opened and Brant climbed out, immaculately dressed in boots, jeans and a Western shirt. His black hair was brushed back from his face, and sunglasses covered his eyes and gave him a fascinating, piratical look.

"Hi," he greeted.

His voice sounded calm, but she felt as if she were a caldron of churning emotions.

"Hi." She hoped she didn't sound too breathy.

He walked toward her, his lips curling into a smile.

"I thought you weren't coming in until Saturday," she remarked.

"Change of plans," he explained. "Are you glad to see me?"

Marcy nodded. She really felt at a disadvantage and wondered if Brant would always catch her looking her most bedraggled.

"How'd you know I'd be here?" she asked.

"I took a chance," he replied, then added, "But I don't believe in leaving things to chance altogether, so I left a message on your phone recorder and another with Pete."

"You talked with Pete?" she murmured.

He nodded. "I started real early this morning. Before I drove over here, I stopped by the Neighborhood Reading Center and met Pete and Lupe."

"I'm impressed," she said.

"Maybe a teeny-weeny bit curious, too?" he teased.

"A lot more than teeny-weeny," she admitted.

"First of all, we've set September as the month for the fund-raiser. We want it to coincide with the beginning of school since our featured historical landmark is the school building. I've talked with the governor and mayor—"

"You did!" Marcy exclaimed, unable to contain her exuberance.

Brant laughed softly. "Both of them agreed to attend the gala event."

"Oh, Brant." Marcy sighed. "This is wonderful."

"I have another surprise for you. I thought maybe I'd take you to lunch and afterward we'd drive over and I'd show it to you."

Marcy opened her mouth to say yes; then she heard a grader grind through the debris behind her to remind her of all she had to do. Today of all days, Brant was asking her to play truant. And she wanted to.

"Really, I can't," she told him. "We're—"

"I understand," he interrupted. "But I hoped we could have today."

She heard the disappointment in his voice—the same disappointment she'd heard when she turned him down for a date on Saturday. But at the same time she heard the sincerity in his voice and knew that he did understand.

"How about tonight?"

"I have to teach class tonight."

Brant breathed in deeply and smiled tightly. His facial features also tightened. Now, Marcy was glad his eyes were hidden. She had the distinct feeling that his smile touched only his lips.

"Do you think you can sandwich me in somewhere between work, POD and Big Sisters?" he asked, plaintively.

Actually, the way things were going, Marcy didn't think it would hurt her or the company if she took off one day. She had dedicated her life to Galvan Construction for the past eight years, and what did she have to show for it? Headaches. So why not do what she really wanted to—be with Brant?

"Look," she said, "if you'll give me a couple of hours, I'll go with you. I want to go home, shower and change clothes, and I need to stop by Tuftland's to check on an order we placed."

A slow smile erased the disappointment from his countenance. "If you don't mind, I'll follow you to the house," he replied, "and wait while you bathe and change. Then I'll drive you by Tuftland's on our way to lunch."

Marcy laughed. "Tuftland's isn't on our way out."

"It is now." He moved closer so that he stood directly in front of her. "I'll do almost anything to get to be alone with you for a few hours, and I'm taking no chances on something happening to change your mind."

His words were like a fine wine, going to Marcy's head and leaving her giddy with happiness.

MARCY AND BRANT spent the day together. After she showered and changed clothes, they went to Tuftland's to check on the delivery of the supplies. Then Brant treated her to a leisurely lunch in one of the Los Patios restaurants, located on the banks of Salado Creek in a beautiful wooded preserve in north San Antonio. After they'd finished their meal, Marcy and Brant strolled the grounds. To conclude the visit, they walked to the creek and threw food to the fish. When they tired of that, Brant suggested they go to the Neighborhood Reading Center.

By four-thirty, they stood in the middle of Pete's office. Brant and Pete were grinning; Marcy was running her hand over the polished surface of Pete's new desk.

"I can't believe it!" she exclaimed for the third time. Then she ran to Brant and threw her arms around him. "Oh, Brant, this is so wonderful. You couldn't have given me a better surprise."

Blinking back the tears of happiness, she raised her face to accept his kiss.

"I like thank-yous like this," he murmured, his lips moving against hers. "Would you thank me for each individual piece of furniture?"

Pulling away from him, Marcy laughed. "When— when—? How?" She was so happy she couldn't think coherently.

"I've been thinking about it ever since you described the place to me. Since I'm part of this project, I thought I should make a worthy contribution. With my job taking me hither and yon, I can't be one of your teachers, but I can provide you with decent furniture. It's no longer hodgepodge."

"All this time and you didn't say a word."

"It wouldn't have been a surprise if I had."

"Look at this, Marcy," Pete said and moved behind his desk. He pointed to a matching vertical filing cabinet. "This one won't be falling on us."

Marcy could only smile as she slowly gazed about the room, looking again at the bookshelves, the desks the chairs. Although she had done it several times before, she walked around the office, touching each piece as if to reassure herself they were real. Then she walked through the other rooms, which were also newly furnished with shelves, reading tables and chairs, and carrels.

Pete and Brant followed her.

"We have another surprise for you," Pete informed her. "Mrs. Rogers volunteered to teach your makeup class tonight, if you'd like to have the evening off."

Marcy spun around. "You know I would."

The front door opened and Mrs. Herrera, with a large shopping bag clasped in one arm and her library books tucked under the other, walked in. She looked at Marcy and smiled. Brant quickly moved to her side, taking first the books, then the bag from her.

"Thank you," she said in her slow, accented English. "I was afraid I would drop them."

"You shouldn't be carrying such a heavy load," Brant told her.

She smiled maternally and patted him on the arm. "I did not think they were so heavy when I left the grocery store, and the day is good for a walk, no?"

"Yes, it is."

"You are a nice young man. Thank you." She turned to Marcy. "I am returning my books."

"Mrs. Herrera," Marcy began, "I want to introduce you to Brant Holland, a friend of mine and a sponsor of the Neighborhood Reading Center."

Mrs. Herrera extended her hand to Brant. "Brant Holland," she murmured. "We have heard so much about you from Marcella."

"I hope it's been good," Brant teased, glancing up at Marcy.

"Oh, yes." Mrs. Herrera nodded her head. "She likes you very much."

"I like her very much," Brant said, his gaze catching and holding Marcy's. He smiled at her.

"We are repairing the house where you used to live," the elderly woman said. "I am glad you have come home, and I am pleased to meet you."

Brant smiled. "The pleasure is all mine, Mrs. Herrera."

"Mrs. Herrera is one of my top students," Marcy commented. "When she enrolled for classes six months ago, she couldn't even *speak* English. Now she reads, writes and speaks it."

"Not very good, but I get better and better." Mrs. Herrera's eyes twinkled, then she noticed Lupe's desk. "Marcella!" she exclaimed, lapsing into Spanish. "You have new furniture!" First she walked over to the new bookshelves, then to the reading table. She laughed softly and sat down in one of the new chairs. "Now I won't have to be so careful when I sit down. The chair won't fall with me. When did you buy these?"

"They came today," Marcy answered. "Brant brought these for the center."

Mrs. Herrera walked closer to Brant and gazed intently into his face. "I am glad you are our friend...and Marcella's friend. I think you are a good man. Good for Marcella."

Marcy felt her face grow warm and hoped her cheeks weren't as red as they felt.

Looking at Marcy, Brant grinned. "Thank you, Mrs. Herrera. I agree with you."

"Now, I must go home," she announced. "I have to cook. It will soon be time for dinner. I will come back later for more books."

Brant picked up the bag of groceries. "These are too heavy for you to be carrying," he said. "Marcy and I will drive you home."

"I will carry them. I do not live so far from here," Mrs. Herrera said.

"I insist," Brant said. He looked at Marcy. "Are you ready?"

If Marcy had needed evidence that Brant had not changed altogether—something she wanted to believe with all her heart—his actions today provided that proof. He was as concerned with the literacy center as she was, and he had fallen under Mrs. Herrera's spell just as she had.

She nodded. "Let me get my things."

After they drove Mrs. Herrera home, Marcy said, "This has been a perfect day."

"It's only begun," Brant told her. "I thought if you didn't mind, we'd go to River Walk."

"I'd love to," Marcy replied. "The river is one of my favorite places. It's so relaxing. It's like stepping into another world—which it really will be for you. We've improved it so much during the past few years."

As Brant drove, Marcy described some of the many improvements that had taken place in downtown San Antonio. She guided him down Market Street to the Casa del Rio parking lot. They parked and locked the car, and walked down the flight of stairs onto the Paseo del Rio, or River Walk.

As many times as Marcy had walked along the banks of the river, she never tired of its simple beauty. This river, the lifeblood of the San Antonio River Valley, flowed through one of the most colorful and historic cities in the United States. The River Walk was a magical world that long ago had cast its spell over

Marcy. She believed that the river wove the same spell over each person who came near it. For Marcy, River Walk was a world of romance, totally separated from reality; the perfect setting for love. It was also an adventure into nostalgia.

They made their way to one of the many patio restaurants that dotted the walk and sat outside to enjoy a drink in the spring evening.

"The place really has changed," Brant observed. "Yet it seems to be timeless."

The waiter took their order, returning shortly with their drinks.

When he left, Marcy said, "You have to see the new River Center Shopping Mall. They diverted the river so that it flows through the mall. When we finish here, we'll take one of the riverboats so you can see all that's been done. The river is always beautiful, but at this time of the year it is exceptional."

"You really love this city, don't you?" Brant commented.

"Yes," Marcy replied. "I do. I can't imagine living anywhere else, Brant."

"If you loved someone, Marcy, would you consider moving?"

She smiled tentatively, knowing in her heart of hearts that this was more than mere curiosity on Brant's part. Her answer was important to both of them, and she owed both of them honesty.

"I don't know. I really don't know."

"I can see why it would be a difficult decision for you to make," Brant said. "You're involved with so many things."

Marcy lifted her margarita and sipped it. Lowering the glass, she ran her tongue over the salt on her lips. "Are you being sarcastic?"

"No," Brant replied. "It's the truth. The last time we were together you told me you admired me because I was successful, because I'd made something of myself. Well, I'm proud of you, and I'm wondering if you're not more successful than I am."

"What do you mean?"

"I'm successful in terms of monetary wealth. But I have few friends, few people whom I really care to be around. You—you're wealthy with friends. And you love what you're doing and the people you're doing it with."

Marcy laughed. "I'm not so sure whether you're complimenting me or telling me that I wear rose-colored glasses."

Folding his arms and bracing them on the table, he smiled at her. "No. I saw the way you looked at Mrs. Herrera today—the pride you felt when she spoke English. I saw the way she looked at you. The feelings you have for each other are genuine."

"I love working at the center," Marcy admitted. "I really feel I'm helping people."

Marcy and Brant continued to discuss the center and the fund-raising. Afterward they purchased a ticket and rode the boat along the river, the banks of which were covered in colorful gardens of native flowers. By the time they rounded the bend at the Hilton Palacio del Rio, twilight had fallen. The lighted pathways had turned the area into a wonderland and the music of mariachis filled the evening air.

"There must be a performance at the Arneson River Theater tonight," Marcy said, looking to her left at the semicircular bleachers that had been hewn out of the side of the hill and paved with small stones. They were filled with spectators whose eyes were fixed on the stage across the river.

To the right she saw performers in bright Spanish costumes dancing and singing to traditional Mexican songs. The swirling skirts, the stamping feet and the clicking of the castanets harmonized with the guitar music and added to the romantic atmosphere of the river.

"Let's walk a bit," Brant suggested after the boat ride. "I'm not ready to leave yet."

Catching Marcy's hand in his, they began to walk slowly in the direction of the library, moving away from the hustle and bustle. They didn't talk much, but Marcy didn't mind. The silence between them was comfortable.

Every once in a while Brant would make a comment about the river, and Marcy would respond. Past the La Mansión del Norte Hotel, the lights were dimmer and the crowds sparser. In a secluded spot under one of the trees with low, sweeping branches, they found a bench and sat down.

"Thanks for being with me tonight," he said.

"It's I who should thank you," Marcy responded. "After all, you're the one who helped me get the evening off."

"The thanks for that have to go to Pete. I just went to check on the furniture, he did the rest. He's a real friend, Marcy."

"Yes," she agreed, "he is."

"Sometimes the people I work with feel like strangers to me," Brant said. "I know their names,

I've worked with them for years. But I don't really know them, and they don't know me."

Marcy sensed the same vulnerability in Brant that she had felt the night he saw his childhood home.

"I'll never forget the night my mother left my father and me," he said, his voice low. "Dad was there, but he was hurting too badly to be of much help to me. He sat in the old platform rocker and held me against his chest, his tears falling on my face. I ended up consoling him. That night, for the first and last time, I saw my father drink himself into a stupor and fall across the bed. I couldn't sleep. I just sat there alone, staring at my father. I was very frightened."

As Brant talked, Marcy wanted to take him into her arms and to soothe him; to let him know that she cared, that he wasn't all alone.

"As I grew older, I promised myself that I would never care for anyone so much that they could hurt me as my mother had. I carefully insulated myself against loving. I would care but never love, and it worked— for a while. But it didn't lead to happiness."

"Glenna?" Marcy asked.

"Yes." He reached out and brushed a tendril of hair from her face. "I had to come back to Texas to find the woman of my dreams, and I'm afraid that any moment I'm going to wake up to find out this is all a dream, that she'll vanish and I'll never see her again."

"No," she whispered and lifted her face to his. "This is no dream."

He lowered his face and placed his lips on hers, gently brushing back and forth until her mouth opened beneath his. His hands slipped around her so that he could pull her closer to him, and the kiss deepened. Without her quite knowing how it happened, and not really caring, Marcy was in Brant's arms, responding to his kisses. And what began as friendly discovery developed into intoxicating passion.

Finally he lifted his mouth from hers. Breathing deeply, inhaling the fragrance of his after-shave, Marcy lifted her hand, touching her fingers to his skin, moving them to press against the pulse point at the base of his neck.

Brant's hand lowered, and he spread his fingers against her waist. Then Marcy felt the tips of his fingers under her breasts; they brushed higher to touch their fullness, sending wondrous sensations flowing warmly through her body.

"Marcy," Brant whispered, lowering his head fractionally until his lips once again captured hers in a fiery kiss.

His fingers gently caressed her breast, and Marcy turned more fully into his embrace, her arms enclosing him, her hands moving up and down the flexed muscles of his back.

Brant lifted his head, so that she felt his breath warm against her, and moved his hands to the top button of her shirt. One by one he began to unfasten them until the top three buttons were undone. The cool rush of air against her passion-flushed skin brought Marcy to her senses.

Raising her hand, she pulled the material together and rebuttoned her shirt.

"Marcy, if I've—" he began.

"Don't apologize," she murmured softly, placing her fingers lightly over his mouth. "I wanted your kisses. I encouraged them. I enjoyed them."

"What's wrong, then?" he asked.

"I need some time," she explained.

It was unsettling for Marcy to realize that she hadn't wanted Brant to stop with mere kisses, that she had been so caught up in the magic of his touch, his kisses, that she would have been willing to let him make love to her, quite forgetting that they were on the River Walk.

"I think it's time for us to be going," he said quietly.

"Yes."

The clasp had come loose from Marcy's hair, and it hung like a long silk curtain down her back. Brant reached out and touched it. Again he was aware how different Marcy was from the women with whom he'd been associating. She had an endearing air of naiveté about her. He gave her time to regain her composure as they slowly walked back to the car.

Brant had enjoyed the day so much he didn't want it to end. Again he found himself jealous that Marcy was going to spend the next day with her Little Sister.

As he turned off Walzem onto Windcrest, he asked, "Can I tag along with you and Amy tomorrow?" Out of the corner of his eye, he saw Marcy look at him in surprise.

"Would you like to?"

He nodded. He was desperate enough to be with her that he was willing to share time with Amy Calderon.

"We're going to see a movie, and I told Amy she could choose which one." She laughed softly. "No telling what we'll be watching."

"I don't really care," he answered and parked the car in front of her garage. When they stood on the back deck, illuminated by the soft glow of the porch light, he admitted, "I'll do almost anything to be with you, Marcy Galvan."

For a moment they stared at each other, and Brant had to exert extreme willpower to keep from kissing her again. Her lips parted, the corners of her mouth turning up in a gentle smile. The wind blew several strands of hair across her face—and swept the remaining vestiges of his willpower away.

He caught her shoulders in both hands and drew her closer; her arms slipped around him and her hands moved up and down his back. They kissed, deeply and thoroughly.

"Marcy," he murmured, "do you believe in love at first sight?"

"This isn't first sight for us."

"I knew you as a child," he said, noticing that she had avoided a direct answer to his question, "but when I saw you last Sunday, I fell in love with you as a woman."

With a hand she cupped his face in a gesture that sent pleasure through his body as she outlined his jaw, his eyebrows, his lips. He opened his mouth and captured the tips of her fingers gently between his teeth.

Yes, Virginia, she thought, *there is a Santa Clause!*

They stared deeply into each other's eyes for a long time. Finally Marcy withdrew her hand from his grasp and stepped back. Taking her key out of her purse, she unlocked the door.

As she pushed it open, she answered, "Yes, I believe in love at first sight."

WHEN HER ALARM SOUNDED the next morning, Marcy yawned and stretched; then she reached out and flicked the switch to cut off the offending buzz. Seven o'clock seemed to be arriving earlier and earlier as the days passed. Slipping out of bed, she walked into the bathroom to brush her teeth and take a bath. She was drying off when the doorbell rang. She panicked and ran into the bedroom to look at the clock. Surely that couldn't be Brant. He wasn't supposed to arrive for breakfast until eight. It was only seven-thirty now. Grabbing her robe from the back of the bathroom door, she slipped into it as she hurried to the foyer.

"I'm on my way!" she called. When she opened the door, she saw Ethan leaning against the jamb.

Grinning, he held the Saturday paper out to her. "Would you believe me if I said I just happened to be driving by?"

She took the paper from him. "I would if it weren't seven-thirty on Saturday morning and you were freshly shaven. I'd come nearer to believing Clarice sent you. I know how insatiable her curiosity is and she left no less than six messages on the recorder yesterday."

"None of which you returned." Ethan pushed past her and headed for the kitchen.

"Nope, I sure didn't. I had a busy day, and it was too late by the time I got home." Marcy followed him into the kitchen.

"Got some coffee perking?" he asked.

"Full pot," she answered.

He walked to the cabinet and reached for two cups. "Uncle Lonzo had another stroke."

"Oh, no!" she cried. "Why didn't you let me know sooner?"

"There was nothing you could do." He poured the coffee. "I've been at the hospital with him and Aunt

Felicia. David's there now. Mark will relieve him this afternoon."

"I'll go instead," Marcy offered.

"It's all right," Ethan assured her. "Didn't you tell Clarice you were taking your Little Sister to a movie today?"

"I can cancel that," Marcy replied.

"No need to," Ethan said. "We have everything under control. Danny will be here in a couple of hours."

Marcy took a swallow of the coffee. She'd been having a difficult time adjusting to all the recent changes. She felt extremely fortunate to have Amy as a Little Sister and Brant back in her life. Still, her world seemed to be crumbling in on top of her. Danny had promised her two months in which to secure finances, but since Uncle Lonzo's health was deteriorating so quickly, Marcy feared Danny would renege on his promise.

Taking another swallow of coffee Marcy set down the cup. The miniature grandmother clock chimed the half hour. "I'm going to put on some clothes," she announced.

"Don't rush on my account," Ethan told her. "I'll be shoving off in a few minutes, probably after a second cup of coffee. I just wanted to let you know about Tío."

"I need to hurry, but not on your account. Brant's coming over for breakfast." When Ethan raised his brows, Marcy glared at him. "He'll be getting here about eight."

"Exactly who are you spending the day with?" Ethan questioned, following her through the house as she made her way to her bedroom.

"Amy and Brant," Marcy replied and shut the door to her room.

She heard Ethan laugh. "I think Brant has fallen pretty hard to want to spend a day with you and your Little Sister. What movie is he going to have to endure?" He laughed again.

"Ethan," she retorted, setting her cup on the night table and shedding her robe, "I'm in no mood for your jokes this early in the morning. Drink your coffee and get going."

"No way. I think I'll wait and talk with Brant. There're a lot of things he needs to know about you, little sis."

"You can really be a pain. You know that?"

His laughter trailed into silence and Marcy figured he had returned to the kitchen. Then the doorbell rang. By the time Marcy walked into the den, she heard voices coming from outside and looked through the patio doors to see Ethan and Brant sitting on the sun deck, drinking coffee.

"Good morning," she called out.

Brant set his cup down, rose and came into the den to greet her. Ethan remained in the deck chair, his eyes narrowed in speculation.

Then Brant was in front of her, blocking out her brother. Taking her into his arms, he kissed her. She laid her cheek against his chest, listening to the steady rhythm of his heartbeat.

"I'm sorry about your uncle," he said.

"Thanks," she murmured. "I'm worried about him."

"I'm here, if you need me. *For anything.*"

Again she murmured, "Thanks."

Grateful for the strength and protection Brant provided, as well as for his promise of help, Marcy simply let him hold her. She breathed in deeply, inhaling his light after-shave. She felt cherished as she stood in his embrace, and for a moment her world changed to one simply of beauty and peace.

"Brant invited me to stay for breakfast," Ethan announced from the deck. "I think I will."

"See what you've saddled us with," Marcy whispered teasingly. Then she called to Ethan, "This is going to become a community project, each of us doing his or her share."

Among the three of them, they prepared breakfast, and soon the table was laden with pancakes, bacon, eggs and grits. As they ate, they chatted easily with each other. The subject quickly turned to Galvan Construction.

"Have you had any luck getting the money to buy Tío's interest in the company?" Ethan inquired.

Marcy shook her head.

"I didn't think you would," he commented. "You really ought to put your share up for sale."

Marcy laid her fork down and pushed back from the table. She really wasn't ready for this.

"Sorry," Ethan apologized, immediately placing his hand over hers. "I didn't mean to get you upset. I promised myself that I was going to keep my nose and my mouth out of your business."

"I'm sorry, too." She walked to the sink and rinsed out her dishes before she placed them in the dishwasher. "I don't mean to be so sensitive about the business. I just don't know what I'm going to do."

"Marcy," Ethan responded, "you know we guys would give you the money if we had it. We've talked about it, and—"

"I know," she said gratefully. "Thanks for the concern, but it's my problem, not yours."

The phone rang, and she reached for the receiver. "Galvan residence."

"Marcy," Joe Alexander said, "I wanted to let you know that whatever you said to Tuftland's yesterday did the job. They delivered the tubing this morning, and we're making up for lost time. I thought maybe that would make your weekend."

Relief surged through Marcy. One problem had resolved itself. "Thanks, Joe. It does."

"Also, I thought I'd let you know the changes I've made in the work plan for next week. First thing Monday, I'm going to..."

As Marcy listened to Joe, Ethan and Brant cleaned up the kitchen, putting the rest of the dishes in the washer. Waving to her, Ethan left, and Brant went out to the deck to wait for her.

When she hung up, she called out, "Are you ready to go?"

AMY STOOD IN THE DEN, staring out the window, watching the passing cars. She was glad Marcy was taking her to the movie, but she was a little disappointed that Marcy was bringing someone with her. Who was this Brant Holland? Amy wondered. Marcy had never said anything about him before last night.

Amy almost wished she wasn't going, but if she changed her mind now, Nona would be upset. Lately, both Nona and Daddy had changed. They didn't allow her to have her way as much as they had in the past.

A gray car pulled into the driveway. The door opened, and a tall man stepped out. Marcy got out on the other side and the two of them looked at each other over the top of the car and smiled. He walked to the front of the car and waited for her; they caught hands.

Evidently Brant Holland was Marcy's boyfriend.

Amy didn't like this new development at all, and she was going to have to do something about it. Marcy and her daddy would make a good couple. She had to figure a way to get her father interested in Marcy. If he had to have another woman in his life, Amy would rather it be Marcy than Wanda Courtland. If Marcy must have a boyfriend, it would be Amy's father—not Brant Holland.

CHAPTER EIGHT

IN THE LOBBY of the theater, Brant and Amy stood beside one of the life-size posters advertising the movie they had just seen. Marcy, her camera in hand, stood at a distance, angling this way, then that, as she focused, trying to get all three subjects in the picture.

"Marcy's pretty, isn't she?" Amy said.

"Yes," Brant replied.

"My daddy really likes her."

Brant glanced over at the child. Her smile seemed so innocent; so did the words. Yet, he sensed an undercurrent of meaning. "Really?"

"Oh, yes," she insisted. "I don't think he would have allowed me to have any other person for my Big Sister."

Brant smiled to himself. "Well, I think he's wise. If I had a little girl in this program, I would want Marcy to be her Big Sister, too. She's a wonderful person."

Amy was quiet for a second, then asked, "Are you dating her?"

"Move closer to the poster," Marcy called to them.

"You might say that," Brant answered Amy.

"I've got it!" Marcy exclaimed.

"Now, let Brant take one of you and me," Amy said.

After the three of them took turns taking photographs of one another, Brant and Marcy drove Amy home. When they arrived at her house, she jumped out of the car and raced into the house, leaving the front door open behind her.

"I'll wait here for you," Brant told Marcy.

"Come with me," she urged. "I'd like to introduce you to Gil. Nona said he would be here when we brought Amy home."

Amy's father, Brant reflected. The man who really liked Marcy. Pulling the keys out of the ignition, he opened the door and climbed out of the car. He'd like to meet this man to see if he had any competition here. Although she was only a child and Brant saw through her antics, she had placed a doubt in his mind.

"You'll like him," Marcy said. "He's nice."

"Daddy, you're home!" Amy squealed. "I've been to the movies with Marcy and Brant."

Gil walked out and smiled when he saw Marcy. "It's good to see you again."

"Hi, Gil," she greeted and caught Brant's hand, pulling him to her side. "I'd like to introduce you to Brant Holland."

"Glad to meet you." Gil shook hands with Brant. "So you went with them to the movie. What a way to date!"

Brant and Marcy laughed with him.

"Let's hope it was a good movie," Gil remarked.

"Pretty good," Brant answered. "Amy's a fine one for figuring out the plot. She could almost predict right down the line what was going to happen."

"I could, Daddy," Amy confirmed, beaming.

Smiling down at her, Gil laid his hand on her shoulder. "Won't y'all come in for a little while?" he invited.

Marcy looked at Brant, and he silently pleaded with her to say no. He wanted time with her alone; however, before she answered, Amy spoke.

"Please do, Marcy," she coaxed. "I'd like to show you my Barbie-doll collection."

"It's quite impressive, if you have time," Gil added. "She's really proud of it."

Again Marcy looked at Brant who nodded reluctantly. "All right," she agreed, following Amy into the house. "We'll come in for a little while."

"Can I get y'all a drink?" Gil asked. "We have colas, tea, coffee and beer."

"Iced tea for me," Marcy replied.

"Me, too," Amy chimed in.

"A beer for me," Brant said.

Amy caught Marcy's hand and gently tugged. "Come upstairs with me, and I'll show you my playroom."

"While they're looking at the dolls," Gil suggested, "come into the den with me, and we'll get the drinks."

Brant went with Gil, and Marcy followed Amy up the stairs to a large bedroom with a bay window. The blinds were drawn, and late-afternoon sunlight streamed into the room. A gentle spring breeze swayed the sheer white curtains, causing the hems to brush against soft pink carpet.

Marcy felt as if she had walked into a Christmas wonderland of dolls. Several large dollhouses dominated the room. Four oak chairs—child-size reproductions of turn-of-the-century furniture—were placed here and there. Most of the wall space was covered with shelves, and against one wall also stood a large white chest of drawers.

Amy walked to one of the shelves and picked up a doll that she held tenderly. It was an old one; Marcy could tell. Her blond hair wasn't nearly as glossy and thick as a new doll's, and her clothes were out of style. Amy waved to the entire shelves of dolls and accoutrements.

"These Barbies belonged to my mother. My grandmother who lived far away gave them to me before she went to heaven."

"Do you play with them?" Marcy asked, sitting in one of the small chairs.

"No, I just collect them. Nona told me to be very careful with them." She brushed the doll's hair with her palm and straightened the dress she wore. "When my mother was a little girl she used to play with this doll. Her mother even sewed clothes for it. I've got all the clothes, too. They're packed away in a Barbie suitcase." Marcy followed Amy's glance and saw the old Barbie suitcase sitting on the floor beneath the shelves.

Amy pointed to another wall of shelves. "Those are the ones I play with. I began my collection with these."

Returning her mother's doll to its place, Amy walked to a closer shelf where she removed another doll.

"This is my newest Barbie," she said. "She's 'Solo In The Spotlight' Barbie."

The doll was dressed in a slinky black gown that flounced into a thick ruffle at the knees. She wore a three-strand pearl necklace and a pearl bracelet over her black opera-length gloves. A red rose was fastened in her long, thick blond hair, and she held a sheer pink scarf in her hands. She also came with a

microphone. *So she can belt out her own sultry song!*
Marcy thought.

"Nona said this Barbie is very expensive because
she's made out of porcelain. See?" Amy handed the
doll to Marcy and rubbed the tip of her finger over
Barbie's facial features. Then she pointed to two more
dolls. "Those are Porcelain Barbies too. There're only
three of them, and I have all three." She moved across
the room. "Here's the one I got for Christmas. She's
called the 'Enchanted Evening' Barbie."

Marcy walked around the room, looking at the collection—the many Barbie dolls and her many friends,
her houses, her cars and all her accessories. No ex-
pense had been spared. Marcy could only guess that
several thousand dollars had been spent on Amy's
playroom. Marcy stood in front of a Barbie in bridal
attire.

"What's this one called?" she asked.

"'Bridal Fantasy,'" Amy replied, and went on to
tell the entire story that went with this particular Barbie. "There's a new one I'd like. She's the 'Evening
Enchantment' Barbie, with a white blouse over a light
blue long skirt. Daddy promised he'd buy her for me
next."

Marcy was fascinated by the world of Barbie and all
her accessories. In one of the Barbie houses the ele-
vator moved up and down between floors. In another—the one Amy called "the mansion"—the
appliances worked and the chandelier in the dining
room lit up.

After a while, Amy replaced her dolls and contemplated Marcy, "Did you play with Barbie dolls when
you were a little girl?"

"Some," Marcy said. "But since I have three older brothers, I mostly played with them."

"What did you play?"

"We played a lot of baseball, football, basketball and volleyball. We also fished."

"Fishing? Ugh!" Amy twitched her nose in disdain. "I don't play boys' games."

"I don't suppose sports belong to boys anymore than dolls belong to girls," Marcy remarked.

Amy grinned. "Boys don't play with dolls."

"Of course, they do," Marcy said. "My brothers collected all the G.I. Joe dolls, Jungle Jim, and the Star Trek dolls and a lot more. I can't even remember all their names now, but we still have them, they're packed up in the attic."

"Do you play ball now?" Amy asked.

Marcy nodded. "I sure do. In fact, this year I'm going to coach a softball team that's sponsored by the Neighborhood Reading Center."

Amy listened quietly as Marcy talked about the center and the group of girls who were interested in having a softball team. Marcy told her about her nieces, the oldest of whom played on her brother's team.

"We'll be playing ball all summer," Marcy finished.

"Would you take me to some of the games?" Amy asked.

"How would you like to be on the team?"

Amy stared at her for a second before she said, "But I've already told you, I don't know how to play."

"I'll teach you," Marcy said. "It's real easy, and you'll like the other children."

Amy thought a few more minutes, "But I can already read, so I can't belong to the center."

"Do you read Spanish?"

Amy laughed. "No, I can't even speak it. My daddy and mama could, but I can't."

"Then, if your daddy doesn't mind, you can join the center, and I can teach you to read and speak Spanish and to play softball."

"Wow!" Amy breathed. "I can hardly wait for school to be over. Just four more weeks." She leaped out of the chair. "When do we start?"

"Next Saturday we sign up," Marcy said.

"I'll get to spend Saturday with you?" Amy asked. Marcy nodded her head.

An excited child skipped to the door. "I'm gonna go ask Daddy if I can join."

Marcy followed Amy down the stairs, and they joined Gil and Brant in the den.

"Your tea's on the bar," Gil said. "And thank you for taking Amy to the movie. I know she enjoyed it."

"I did, Daddy," Amy said and threw herself into his arms. "And do you know what? Marcy coaches a softball team and she wants me to be on it, but I'll have to join her center and learn to read and speak Spanish. And she's gonna come get me next Saturday so I can join the team."

Brant lowered the bottle of beer from his lips and gazed at Marcy. She wondered if he disapproved.

"Hold on!" Gil laughed. "You're going so fast, I can't keep up with you."

Slowing down, Amy repeated herself, and after Marcy threw in an explanatory comment or two, he agreed to Amy's enrolling in the center and to spending next Saturday with Marcy.

"I think it's a marvelous idea," Gil declared.

"In addition to softball, we take the children on field trips during the summer," Marcy explained. "Like to Schlitterbahn, Splashtown, Natural Bridge Caverns, and Sea World. When the time comes, I'd like to take Amy along."

"I don't mind in the least," Gil told her. "But Wanda and I have been talking about taking the kids—mine and hers—to Sea World, so I'd have to know the dates you're planning for these activities." He looked down at Amy and grinned. "Of course, I have to talk to Amy about it first."

Brant set his empty bottle on the table beside the sofa and stood. Marcy could tell he was restless and wanted to leave. The doorbell rang, and Amy slid out of her father's lap and went to answer it. In a few minutes she reappeared with a red-haired girl behind her.

"Marcy," she announced, "this is my friend, Julie. Julie, this is Marcy Galvan, my Big Sister."

"Hi," Marcy said.

"Hi." Julie peered at Marcy from behind her wire-rimmed glasses.

"And this is Brant Holland," Gil added. "Marcy's friend."

"Yeah," Amy confirmed dryly.

"YOU'VE BEEN awfully quiet since we left the Calderons'," Brant observed when they reached Marcy's house and were standing in the den. "About all you've done is answer questions with a yes, a no, or a grunt."

"I've been thinking about Amy," she said.

"She's trying to match you with her father," he said.

"You've got to be kidding!"

"Not really. She knows exactly what she wants, and if you're not careful, she'll be running your life."

"Oh, Brant," Marcy exclaimed. "She's only a child who needs some attention."

"Marcy, do you realize what a commitment you made to her today? You've asked her to join the center and to become a part of your softball team. You also opened the way for her to be with you everywhere you go. Soon there won't be a minute of your life without her being around. She spent today with you. She's going to spend next Saturday with you."

"Brant, I'll be teaching at the center whether Amy's a student or not. I'll be coaching the team whether she's a member or not." She studied him for a second, then smiled and gently asked, "You couldn't be jealous, could you?"

"I could, and I am. In order to get some time with you am I going to have to join the center and the team?"

"That wouldn't be a bad idea," she answered. "We could use another coach."

"Marcy—" Brant reached out and caught her hands in his "—I know how much your program means to you, but will I always be sandwiched in between?"

"You're not sandwiched in between," Marcy assured him. "But if you're going to be part of my life, you'll have to accept me as I am."

Brant said no more, but he thought of his childhood when he and his interests had always seemed to be pushed aside for something or someone else of more importance. He was in love with Marcy and wanted time for their relationship to develop, but he didn't want to share her with the world. Where she was concerned, he was selfish. He wanted her for himself.

"Would you like a glass of wine?" Marcy offered.

Brant nodded. "While you're getting it, I need to make a phone call."

"For privacy, why don't you use the one in my bedroom," she suggested. "Down the hallway, second door to the right."

Thinking about what Brant had told her, Marcy realized again how much deeper her feelings for Brant were than those she had had for Derrick. She really hadn't been torn when choosing between Derrick and her life as it was, or between moving to Los Angeles and staying in San Antonio. She *would* be torn if she had to make that choice for Brant, and she knew she would face that choice—eventually.

In the kitchen, she opened the refrigerator and took out several apples and some cheese, slicing and placing them on a serving dish with crackers. She carried them into the den and returned to pour two glasses of wine. While she waited for Brant to conclude his call, she switched on the television and watched the news channel.

"Marcy!" Brant called out, then came into the den. "I'm surprised you still have it."

She looked up to see him holding her little hard hat. "I had to keep it," she said. "It's a memento of the man I've always adored."

Brant gazed at her intently for a long while before he continued, "As much as you adore the strays you rescue and the meganumber of causes you're fighting for?"

"More," she answered.

"I know how much this Big Sister-Little Sister program means to you, but Marcy, if you and I have a relationship—" He paused, then asked, "Are you interested in our having one? Do you want us to become involved?"

"Yes."

"Then, selfish as it sounds, I want more of your time. I don't believe in time-sharing courtships."

Marcy rose and walked over to him. "You'll have it, Brant. I promise. Just give me some time to gain Amy's confidence and to reassure her that I am her Big Sister. At the moment I believe Amy is fighting one of her biggest battles. She fears she's losing her father to Wanda Courtland and me to you."

Still holding the little hat in one hand, Brant slipped his arms around Marcy and held her tightly. "Just remember, I feel as vulnerable as the child."

Marcy pulled back and gazed at him. She was touched that he would admit his feelings so openly.

"Now that I've found you again," Brant said, "I'm afraid of losing you."

"You won't. There's enough room in my heart to love you *and* Amy." She pushed back, then reached up and with the tips of her fingers, rubbed the frown from his brow. "How about that wine?"

"First, let me put this back."

Hand in hand, Brant and Marcy went to the bedroom, and Brant returned the hard hat to its rightful position on the mantel.

"See its place of honor?" Marcy pointed out. "Right in the center of the mantel. And you have the place of honor in my heart."

Brant took her into his arms and kissed her long and thoroughly. Then they returned to the den, where they sat enjoying their wine, fruit and cheese and listening to classical music. They were relaxed and happy to be together. Brant lay back in the reclining rocker and Marcy was stretched out on the sofa.

For a long time Brant talked about his work—specifically, his latest project in Alaska. He thought of the feasibility study on branch offices he had ordered, but he didn't mention it to Marcy. It was too soon to discuss something that might never happen.

Setting his glass down, he rose from the chair and moved to the sofa to sit beside her. He took her empty glass and set it on the coffee table.

"I'm glad we're alone," he said and brushed his fingers through the hair at her temples. "Just you and me."

He lowered his head and captured her lips with his, guiding her mouth open to receive the sensual thrust of his tongue. Marcy's hands crept around his shoulders and she pulled him closer.

Brant broke the kiss and trailed his lips tenderly over her cheek. He stretched out beside her, so that the length of his hard body brushed provocatively against hers. His hands cupped her breasts, and Marcy felt them swell beneath his touch.

The longer he kissed her, the sweeter his caresses became and the more her body throbbed with need. She had felt desire before, but this was different. This time there was so much more involved.

She loved Brant Holland!

"Marcy—" Brant lifted his head and gazed into her eyes.

His were dark with desire; his breathing was heavy.

"I want to make love to you."

She reached up and brushed her hand through his hair; it was thick and wavy. "Yes," she murmured, "I know."

And she wanted him to make love to her. She had waited years for this moment.

He rose and, with his hand clasping hers, he tugged her to her feet. In the muted light that filtered from the living room into the hallway, she led him to her bedroom. He stood at the door as she walked over to the bed and switched on the lamp.

"Are you protected?" he asked.

"No, but I have protection."

Her words pleased Brant. Her answer told him that she did not indulge in casual sex; that what they were sharing was special. Marcy looked directly into his face and lifted her hands to unbutton her shirt. She pulled the material aside to reveal shapely breasts covered in frothy lace.

Her hands slid down her midriff to the waistband of her jeans. She unfastened them, slowly pushing the placket aside to shove them over her hips. She straightened and stood in front of him, clad only in her underwear.

She was more lovely than he had imagined. His body was stirring with desire as he strode the rest of the way into the room to stand beside her. He pulled the clasp from her hair causing the luxuriant black mass to cascade around her shoulders—a dramatic foil for her creamy skin.

"You're beautiful," he murmured and lowered his head to brush his lips against one shoulder. His hands slid around her waist, where her skin was smooth and warm, and he pulled her into his arms. He nuzzled his mouth against her neck, then nipped playfully along the sensitive outer edges of her lips. Finally his mouth moved completely over hers, locking her lips in a deeply passionate kiss.

She slid her palms against his chest and pushed out of his embrace. Smiling, she went to the bathroom. "I'll be back."

When Marcy returned, she was naked. The covers were turned down, and Brant, also naked, lay on her bed. She caught her breath as she looked at his lean muscular body. He pushed up on an elbow and held out his hand to her. She moved toward the bed, switching off the light before she lay down beside him.

MARCY ROSE BEFORE Brant the next morning. She stood beside the bed for a few seconds, gazing down at him. Even with his hair tousled and his face covered with beard stubble, he was handsome. His dark lashes were long and formed a thick crescent on his sun-bronzed cheeks. The sheet rode low on his body, revealing the black hair that formed a thin covering on his chest.

She wanted to touch him, but squelched the desire. Instead, she went into the bathroom and showered. She laid out a washcloth and towel, a new toothbrush and a disposable razor for him to use when he awakened. Then, putting on clean jeans and a shirt, she went to the kitchen to start a pot of coffee.

Clarice called and invited her to lunch and then to a game of tennis at the country club. When she learned that Brant was with Marcy, she invited him, too. Not making any promises other than to talk it over with Brant, Marcy rang off. Then she called the hospital and learned that her uncle was resting well and had been moved from Intensive Care to a private room.

Her aunt gave her the good news that he would probably be released in the next couple of days.

Marcy was standing on the deck, enjoying the early morning, when she heard the patio doors open. Brant was up. She felt him move to stand behind her. He slipped his arms around her waist and tugged her back against his body. He rested his chin on the top of her head.

"This is where you belong," he said. "In my arms."

She turned in the circle of his embrace and kissed him.

"You taste of toothpaste," she told him and thought how right it had felt to be in his arms first thing in the morning. "Coffee's ready. Do you want some?"

He nodded, and they returned to the kitchen where Marcy poured both of them a cup of coffee.

"What do you want for breakfast?" she asked.

"Whatever," he replied. "I'm not hard to please."

"How about waffles?"

"Sounds good. You want me to help?"

"No, thanks. I can do this just fine by myself."

"I think I'll enjoy the paper then."

While he read the newspaper, Marcy prepared the waffles and a strawberry sauce to go on them. After they ate, they cleaned up the kitchen together. They were lounging in the den, enjoying the lazy morning, when they heard a knock. Marcy walked into the foyer and opened the door.

"Danny!" she exclaimed.

"I'm sorry to come by unannounced," he began. He was unshaven, his shirt collar was unbuttoned, and his tie hung loosely about his neck. "Just before I left the hospital, Mama told me you had called and I decided to drop by."

"Come on in," she invited. "How about some coffee?"

"Sounds good to me," he answered.

"Have you eaten?"

"I'm not hungry. Coffee will do." By this time he was in the den and saw Brant sitting in the platform rocker. His jaw went slack, and he looked from Brant to Marcy. "I'm not disturbing you, am I?"

"Not at all," Marcy assured him. "We're just reading the paper. Sit down and visit with Brant. I'll get the coffee."

When she returned, Danny said, "I'll come right to the point of my visit. Marcy, I know I promised you two months in which to get the money to buy out Papa's share of the business, but we've just received an offer we can't turn our backs on."

"We?" Marcy questioned. "As in you and Tío or as in the three of us?"

"The three of us," Danny confirmed. "Colby Zacharias—"

"*The* Colby Zacharias?" Brant asked.

"The same," replied Danny. "The largest contractor in the state has made an offer for Galvan Construction. He wants the entire business and is willing to pay top dollar for it."

"Which is?"

"Double my asking price," Danny answered.

Marcy sucked air into hurting lungs. Even to her the price was tempting—but not tempting enough. "I'm going to hold you to your promise, Danny."

"Marcy—" Danny leaned toward the edge of his chair "—you can't pass this offer by. The man wants the entire company. He's willing to give you more than the company is worth. You'll have more money than you'll know what to do with."

Marcy shook her head. "If he's willing to pay more than the company is worth, then the company must be worth more, Danny. I'm not selling my shares. You had no right to indicate that I would . . . if you did."

Danny slammed his fist against the coffee table. "Damn it, Marcy! You can be so stubborn. You never have and never will listen to reason."

"Not to your kind," Marcy pointed out.

"Marcy," Brant ventured quietly, "I don't mean to interfere, but shouldn't you take some time to think about this? I believe Danny's right. This is an offer you can't throw away without thought."

Feeling momentarily deserted by Brant, she faced both men defiantly. "I don't need any time to think about the offer because I'm not selling. I may not be able to raise the money to buy Tío's share, but I won't give up mine. Galvan Construction is mine—at least, half mine—and I'm keeping it!"

By the time Danny left, Marcy was seething. She paced the floor.

"Marcy," Brant said, "you're not being disloyal to your family or your heritage if you sell the company. There comes a time when you have to make such decisions. With your education and experience, you would have no difficulty getting another job, and you wouldn't be saddled with a company to run."

Marcy looked at him with incredulity. "I know I can get another job, but that's what it would be, Brant. Just a job. I thought that surely you, of all people, would understand that I'm not *saddled* with the company. I want it because I love it. This is my life."

Moving close to her, he took her into his arms and pressed her cheek against his chest. Seeing how passionately she felt about the subject, Brant said no more, but he was concerned. Only hours ago he and Marcy had admitted to wanting more than friendship and memories. They were developing a relationship. But, in the face of her argument with Danny and her determination to keep the company, Brant wondered how deeply their involvement could become. He had thought that if she made a commitment of love to him, she might be willing to give up her commitments here. It wasn't as if she would be giving them up forever; she could easily become involved in similar work and programs wherever she lived.

If Galvan Construction was her life, was there any room for him?

There were two options open to him. One, that they break up, which was totally unacceptable. Now that Brant had found Marcy, he didn't want to lose her. The other option was to move his office to San Antonio. Was it feasible? He still didn't know, but he had to find out. If it was, could he do it? Could he come back to the city he had sworn he would never live in again?

"Brant," Marcy said, not lifting her face from his chest, "you do understand, don't you?"

"Yes." The strange part was that he really did. In the past he had been as driven as she was now; his company had been his primary concern, his identity.

"Thanks," she murmured.

Dropping the subject for the moment, he cupped her cheek with his hand. "What are we going to do with the rest of this beautiful day?"

She lifted her head and smiled. "If you like exotic meals, we could have lunch with Ethan and Clarice, and later play tennis at the country club."

"I like, but I need to go by the hotel and change clothes," he told her, before his lips closed over hers in a kiss.

MARCY REMAINED at the house while Brant went to his hotel. By the time he returned, she had changed into olive-colored slacks and a matching silk blouse, and her hair hung in a French braid. Makeup enhanced her eyes and their long lashes.

"Sorry I'm late," he said, "but I had to call Shepherd about a client I have to meet with next week, and it took longer than I anticipated." He tucked his sunglasses into his shirt pocket.

"You'll be leaving tomorrow?" Marcy asked.

He nodded. "I'm expected in New York."

"How long will you be gone?" she questioned—the knowledge of his leaving in the morning was already taking some of the pleasure out of the day.

"At least two weeks. Maybe longer. But I promise I'll be back."

"As soon as you can."

"I wish you could come with me. I hate to be away from you even for a day."

"That would be nice," she admitted, "but there's no way. I'm already working short crews, and I have to start the repairs on Hudley's place tomorrow." She walked to the counter where she had placed her necklace when Brant rang the doorbell. Moving to the mirror that hung over an antique table, she fastened the gold chain around her neck.

"You look pretty in that olive color," Brant said, and she looked at his reflection in the mirror. "It complements your eyes."

"Thanks," she replied. "You look pretty good, too."

"Thank you. I thought slacks and a casual shirt would be more fitting for lunch than what I was wearing. Are you ready to go?"

"Yes, and Clarice is chomping at the bit for us to get there. She's been calling every ten or fifteen minutes." She laughed. "I don't know if you're ready for my family or not."

"I'm ready, but first this."

She was in his embrace, and he captured her lips in a long kiss.

"I hope you don't think it presumptuous of me," he murmured, "but I checked out of the hotel and brought my luggage with me. I counted on staying the night with you."

"I wouldn't have it any other way," she told him. "In fact, I'll give you a key to the house." Then she guided his lips to hers again.

The phone rang.

"Shall we get it?" he asked.

"No, it's probably Clarice. The recorder will pick it up. If it's important, we can return the call later. I think what we're doing right now is more important... much more important."

"Me, too."

THAT EVENING, after an enjoyable day at the country club, Marcy, Brant and four-year-old Diane battled Ethan, Clarice and six-year-old Sarah in a game of Uno. When the last hand was played, Diane was already asleep on the floor beside Marcy, and Sarah was jubilant because she had won.

Clarice rose. "That's it, Sarah. Time for bed."

"Aww, Mama," the child argued, "let's play one more game."

Clarice shook her head. "You have school in the morning. You need your rest."

"Only four more weeks," Sarah pointed out. "Then we have summer vacation."

Clarice raised her eyebrows in mock horror. "Vacation for whom?" she murmured, and the others laughed with her. "Softball organization at the center starts next weekend."

"Which reminds me," Marcy interjected, "Amy Calderon, my Little Sister, would like to enroll in Spanish classes at the center and wants to be on the softball team."

"I didn't know you had a little sister, Aunt Marcy," Sarah said, her eyes clouding with confusion. She nestled closer to Marcy.

"She's not my little sister like your daddy is my brother," Marcy explained. "She's a little girl who has only one parent, and she wants her own Big Sister, like what you are to Diane."

"Will I get to meet Amy?" the child asked.

"You sure will. Next week, when we sign up for teams. In fact, if your parents don't mind, I'll take you with me when I pick up Amy, and we'll ride to the center together."

"Oh, goody!" Sarah squealed. "Can I, Mama?"

Clarice nodded. "Now tell everybody good-night. We're going to bed."

"And so are we," Brant remarked.

Clarice and Ethan both gave Marcy a knowing smile.

CHAPTER NINE

BEFORE BRANT LEFT the next morning, Marcy gave him a key to the house. Then she called Joe and asked him to meet her at the office. She wanted him to know that Danny had a prospective buyer for her uncle's share and that she wasn't the buyer.

"Who?" Joe questioned when she told him.

"Colby Zacharias."

Joe let out a soft whistle.

"I'm holding Danny to his promise to give me until June 15 to come up with the money to buy the shares myself," Marcy said. "But the prospects of my doing it are slim to none. Because this affects you and your position in the company, I wanted you to know."

"Thanks, Marcy," Joe replied. "But as I told you before, I think I'll just weather it out. I have faith that you'll find a way."

Marcy smiled, wishing she had the same confidence in herself. "I'm going to have to let the workers know soon. I have no idea how having a new partner will affect them. Maybe not at all. Maybe drastically."

After Marcy left Joe, she drove to the Hill Country to Chester Hudley's place. During the day she was plagued with her worries about the future of the company. One of the problems was that she didn't trust Danny to abide by the terms of their verbal contract.

When she arrived home at nine o'clock that evening and listened to her recorder, she learned that she'd missed two calls from Brant. She was disappointed. Although he had spent only the weekend with her and had been gone just hours, she found the house strangely quiet and empty. Exhausted from her long day, she took a leisurely bath, then crawled into bed and was asleep almost as soon as her head hit the pillow.

Early the next morning, as she was drinking her first cup of coffee and reading the paper, the phone rang.

"Hi," Brant said. "I'm on my way to a meeting, so I only have a few minutes, but I wanted to call to let you know I miss you."

Marcy was thrilled by the sound of his voice. Just hearing it lifted her flagging spirits.

"I'll be back as soon as I can. I wish I could give you a specific date, but I can't."

They talked a little longer, then rang off.

The following week was full of long workdays, but they were fulfilling days. Marcy found it personally satisfying to work on Chester Hudley's house; once the project was under way, it kept her from dwelling on her problems. She loved the Hill Country and had always wanted a home out here. It was far enough out to be considered country living, and close enough to the amenities of town to be suburban.

By Friday, repairs and renovations were going smoothly, and Marcy found she had time to start worrying again about saving Galvan Construction. Each passing day brought her closer to the deadline and saw her further away from getting the necessary financing. Danny had called her twice, first pleading with her, then demanding that she accept the offer from Zacharias.

Even knowing she had been turned down by all the major banking institutions and finance companies in San Antonio, Marcy refused to consider the offer. She had even pushed her pride aside and asked Danny to allow her to make monthly payments. This he had refused outright. Because his father was going to need specialized care in a private nursing home, Danny claimed, they needed the money in one lump sum, and they needed it sooner than later. He accused Marcy of being selfish and of having no concern for her uncle.

Marcy had one other option left to her—sell La Rosa Blanca. The thought brought a rush of conflicting emotions. Her brothers had never understood her love for the ranch property. To them it was a barren tract of land in the desert area of west Texas; it's only value was sentimental.

Marcy wanted to see La Rosa Blanca again. She wanted to ride her horse, Bluebonnet, across the land and feel the wind whipping against her face, to feel the warmth of the sun against her skin.

She had always dreamed of having enough money to convert La Rosa Blanca into a real working ranch, but that dream seemed to be fading with the years as the company demanded all her energy and money.

"Marcy—"

Startled, Marcy turned to look at the painter who stood beside her. Dressed in white, paint-splattered overalls, he held a wet brush in one hand, a bucket of paint in the other. His billed cap, also white, was cocked at an angle on his head.

"Sorry to disturb you," he apologized, "but I did call you several times."

"It's okay, Randy," she said. "I was deep in thought."

"As if I couldn't tell," he responded dryly and held out the bucket. "This is the pewter color I was telling you about. Unlike the other one, it's neutral, and maintains it's natural color with age. I have samples of it and the other colors lying over here. Do you want to see them before we order?"

"Yes." Marcy followed him into the backyard to look at the different samples. After making her choices, she returned to the kitchen and opened the refrigerator for a bottle of apple juice. As she drank the chilled drink, she was tempted to call Clarice to discuss her troubles. But she didn't. She knew her sister-in-law only too well. Clarice would no sooner hang up the phone, than she'd call Ethan, who, in turn, would send out an SOS to David and Mark to come to the rescue of their baby sister. Much as she loved her brothers, Marcy wanted to handle this situation on her own.

Marcy called it a day at about eight o'clock that evening. When she arrived home, there were several messages from Clarice; none from Brant. After Marcy returned Clarice's call and phoned Amy to confirm what time she'd pick her up in the morning for softball sign-up and practice, she fell into bed.

It seemed to her that all she did lately was work, bathe, change clothes, sleep and worry. She worried so much and so well, she should soon have it down to a fine art. She was getting so used to her routine that if excitement and adventure came her way, she probably wouldn't recognize them.

Talking with Brant always lifted her spirits, no matter what they discussed. With a resolution to call him first thing in the morning, she went to sleep immediately.

When the alarm clock sounded early the next morning, she was still tired and sleepy. She reached out, turned it off, and slept on, not waking until nearly nine o'clock. Realizing how late she had slept, she jumped out of bed and quickly dialed Brant's home number. Much to her surprise, his secretary answered and explained they were working at his place to finish a contract. Brant was in conference and could not be disturbed.

"May I take a message?" the secretary asked.

No, Marcy thought. *I want to talk to him now.* But she said, "Please have him call me tonight. I'll be at the center all day."

Marcy called the center, then Clarice and finally Amy, to let them know she had overslept and would be late—a first for her. She dressed hurriedly and ate her breakfast. Pushing aside her disappointment over not being able to talk with Brant and her worries about raising the money to buy the company, she resolved to have a wonderful day—a tall order, but one she was determined to fill.

MARCY, ALONG WITH several other adults, stood in the empty field as Pete Rodriguez and Lupe organized the parents and children and worked on the softball rosters. At the moment, Ethan and Sarah were in line and having an involved discussion with Pete. Marcy walked up to where they stood.

"I don't want to be on Daddy's team," Sarah insisted. "I want to be on Marcy's."

Giving up the argument, Pete looked at Ethan who sighed.

Moving closer to the men and speaking in an undertone so that Sarah couldn't hear, Marcy said, "Make the change. It'll be good for her and Amy. Sarah's a little jealous of Amy right now."

Ethan pushed back his cap. "Okay," he agreed. "Fewer problems for me."

Once the team assignments were made, Pete talked to the groups about their upcoming competitions with teams sponsored by other organizations in town and gave the parents a tentative schedule of game dates. Then they separated into teams, each team having a den mother as well as a coach.

"We'll begin practicing here at the center's baseball field," Marcy said, "every Wednesday afternoon as soon as school is out. It's your responsibility to get here and to get home. The center provides the bats, balls and bases, and has the uniforms. See Mr. Rodriguez later about them, and he'll explain how you get one issued to you."

Many of the parents could afford to buy the uniforms, but others couldn't; therefore Marcy and Pete had worked out a system whereby the children could pay for them in trade, by doing odd jobs around the center.

"We have some extra gloves at the center. Not enough to go round, so it will be first come, first served. But it's up to each player to get her own glove. Remember, official practice sessions and games will start the first week after school is out. That's three weeks from next Wednesday. Practices are on Wednesday, games on Saturday. Until then, Mr. Rodriguez will put up a weekly schedule for players who want to practice sooner. These preseason practices will be on Saturdays. Today I'm going to see how much each of you knows about the game, so I'll know where to put you. Those who have never played before, please stand over here."

Self-consciously, Amy rose and moved to Marcy's side to be joined by several other girls.

Marcy turned to the others. "Mr. Rodriguez and Mr. Galvan will work with the rest of you. I'm going to work with the girls from all the teams who haven't played softball before."

Taking her group aside, Marcy explained the basic rules of the game. She demonstrated the correct way to hold the bat and hit the ball and to throw and to catch. Then she lined them up and told them it was their turn. They laughed good-naturedly at one another when they couldn't catch the ball, when they swung the bat through the air, missing the ball completely, and when they pitched a ball that plopped to the ground well short of home base.

Two hours later, Amy stood in front of home plate for the last time. So far she had not hit one ball.

"Okay, Amy!" Marcy called out. "Watch the ball!"

Marcy threw the ball and it flew right over home plate at Amy's waist. Amy swung, and her bat struck the ball to send it bumping lamely into right field.

"I did it!" Amy shouted. She dropped the bat and ran to where Marcy stood, throwing her arms around her. "I did it, Marcy. I hit the ball!"

"And you hit a good one," Marcy said, hugging Amy.

The child lifted her face. "Am I going to be a good softball player like you?"

"You might be better than me."

"You really think so?" Amy asked.

"You'll have to put in lots of practice."

"I will," Amy responded. "I'll get Daddy and Nona to help me."

When practice was over for the day, Marcy left Amy playing with Sarah and walked to where Clarice stood.

"Do you mind if the girls ride with me to take Amy home? I thought we'd stop to get a hamburger and a drink along the way."

"I wish they could. They'd love it," Clarice replied. "But they have a birthday party to go to. We're going to be rushed as it is."

Pushing his cap back, Ethan walked up. "Marcy, do you mind if Clarice and I skip out early? We—"

"I know," Marcy told him. "Clarice explained. And no, I don't mind. I'll help Pete pack things up."

"Sarah! Diane!" Ethan called. "Come on. We've got to go. Remember Anna's birthday party?"

Diane came running from one direction, Amy and Sarah, holding hands, came from another. Amy walked Sarah to the car.

"I wish you could stay," Amy said.

"Me, too," Sarah answered. "You're my friend."

"I'll see you again real soon," Amy promised. "Maybe at softball practice."

Sarah nodded. "And maybe one day you could come to my house to play."

"Yeah," Amy drawled, "maybe I could. I'll ask Nona and my daddy."

"We could play with my dolls," Sarah offered. "I have the Cabbage Patch dolls. Some of them are porcelim."

"Porcelain," Clarice corrected.

Sarah nodded. "I have them, too."

"Do you have any Barbies?" Amy asked. When Sarah nodded her head again, Amy's eyes lit up. "I do, too. Julie won't play with me because she's too old."

"I'm not," Sarah declared. "I like to play dolls."

"I hate to break this up, girls," Clarice interjected, "but we've really got to be going. Into the car, Sarah."

The children waved and yelled goodbye to one another while Clarice settled Sarah and Diane into the back seat, making sure their safety belts were fastened. As the car pulled away, the three of them waved to each other, and when they were out of sight, Amy rushed back to where Marcy stood.

"I'm so glad you brought me here today," she said. "I've really had fun. Sarah wants me to come visit her. We're going to play dolls. She has Cabbage Patch and Barbie dolls."

"That's nice," said Marcy. "If you'll remind me, I'll mention this to Nona when we get to your house. Then she can talk to your father about it."

"I like Sarah," Amy continued, and then called off the names of several of the girls on the softball team. "I like them, too. They were lots of fun." After a slight pause, she stated, "Julie doesn't play dolls with me. She's too old for them, she says."

"Then it's good for you to have other friends, as well," Marcy told her.

Amy nodded her head. "I like it out here, Marcy, and I'm going to like the Spanish classes, too. It's not going to be like real school at all, is it?"

"Not exactly," Marcy agreed. "What about helping me get this equipment packed up, so Pete can return it to the center?"

"All right." By the time the words were out of Amy's mouth, she had picked up the cardboard box and was dragging it behind her, throwing the bases into it as she walked the diamond.

"Thanks, Amy," Pete said when all the equipment was boxed up. "You're a real good helper. I'm sure glad you decided to join the softball team."

"Thank you, Mr. Rodriguez." Amy gave a smile that spanned her face.

Pete smiled back, then looked at Marcy. "I'll take it from here."

Marcy took Amy for a hamburger, French fries and a cold drink. As they ate, Amy laughed and talked about her day.

"And I had fun helping gather up the equipment," she remarked. "Mr. Rodriguez said I was a real helper."

"You are," Marcy replied. "And I'd like to ask your help for something else."

"What?" Amy asked, pulling a swallow of cold drink through her straw.

"I want you to be as good a helper to your father as you were for Mr. Rodriguez and me."

"How?"

"Your father is going through a hard time, learning to live without your mother. But he's let you have me as a Big Sister, and look how willing he is to share you with me and with all the other people at the center. I want you to do the same for him."

Amy lowered her head and kicked her foot back and forth, hitting the leg of the chair with the toe of her sneakers. "Mrs. Courtland," she said.

"Mrs. Courtland," Marcy confirmed. "According to your father, she's a nice woman who wants very much to meet you."

"Daddy wants her and her children to come to San Antonio one weekend and for all of us to go to Sea World."

"That would be nice," Marcy told her. "You would enjoy it. And it'll give you a chance to make more friends."

Amy raised her head. "Would you come with me?"

"No. That's a time for you to spend with your father and his friends. Later, when you know the Courtlands better, maybe all of us could do something together."

"Something really special?"

"Yes. Do you have something in mind?" Marcy asked.

Amy popped a French fry into her mouth, chewed slowly and swallowed. "I've always wanted to own a horse, and Daddy promised to buy me one, but he never seems to have the time."

"Having a horse isn't as easy as having Barbie dolls," Marcy pointed out. "I have six of them, so I know."

"You do!" Amy's eyes were shining with excitement. "What are their names and what do they look like?"

"My favorite ones are named Bluebonnet and Daisy," Marcy replied, then described the two mares.

"Where do you keep them? Here in San Antonio?"

"On a ranch between Brackettville and Del Rio."

"Could we go there one day, Marcy? Please. I'd love to see a real ranch with real horses."

"If your father gives his permission," Marcy said, "I'll take you there. A friend of mine, Erny Lopez, lives in the house and takes care of the horses and land."

"When can we go? Huh, Marcy?"

"Maybe weekend after next," Marcy answered. The mention of the ranch brought to the forefront her worries and the real reason she needed to visit it so soon.

"When we get home, will you tell Nona that you've invited me to spend the day at your ranch?" Amy asked. "Also tell her that if Mrs. Courtland wants to, she and her children can go with us. Will you, Marcy?"

Marcy nodded.

Amy ate another bite of her hamburger and washed it down with a swallow of her cold drink. "If my Daddy marries again," she announced, "he may want to have more children."

"That's a possibility," Marcy admitted. "Does it bother you?"

"Yes. I don't want any little brothers or sisters."

"Why?" Marcy inquired.

"My mama died because of my little brother," she explained. "And if my daddy marries again, my new mother might want babies, and she might die, too."

"I don't think so. Having babies is a very natural thing. What happened to your mama hardly ever happens and it's not likely to happen again."

Amy regarded her solemnly for a while. "You really think so?"

"I do."

Suddenly it became clear why Amy had wanted a big sister rather than a younger one. Maybe the child didn't resent Wanda Courtland so much as she was afraid to love her for fear of losing her as she had lost her mother. Marcy promised herself that she would speak to Nona and Gil about this and let them discuss it with Amy.

"If you're through eating, we'll be on our way," Marcy said.

Amy nodded, and the two of them quickly cleaned up their table and dropped the trash in the receptacle as they walked out of the restaurant. When they reached Amy's house, Marcy told Nona about Sarah's invitation for Amy to come play with her and also that she, Marcy, would like to take Amy to her ranch in Brackettville the weekend after next. Nona promised to discuss it with Gil and to get back with an answer as soon as she could.

As Marcy drove to the house, she was glad to be by herself. She had enjoyed her day with Amy, but she missed Brant. She wanted to talk with him—not that she had anything in particular to say. She just wanted to hear his voice again, to hear his laughter.

BRANT SAT BEHIND his desk in the office of his penthouse in Manhattan. Across from him was Shepherd Hayden. On Brant's desk between them lay a bound portfolio containing the feasibility study; Shepherd held a similar one in his hands.

"So there you have it," the administrative assistant said. "We had to pay them a hefty sum for a rush job, but when Brant Calloway Holland speaks, the world listens and obeys."

"I think we can dispense with the sarcasm, Shepherd," Brant remarked.

Rubbing the back of his neck, he stood and walked around the room. He was tired. He had been going from "can" to "can't" since he had arrived back in New York. Earlier, Shepherd had described him as a man dogged by the hounds of hell, and that's exactly the way Brant felt. He simply wanted to get back to Marcy.

He looked at his desk clock. Eight o'clock. He needed to call her. She would be waiting for it. The silence in the office was broken by the fax that came in. Shepherd rose and moved to the machine, tearing the pages off, one by one, and skimming them before he handed them to Brant.

"Here are the figures on Galvan Construction that you asked for."

Brant took the report and began to read. When he was through, he handed it to Shepherd, who also read it.

"Not an acquisition that someone like Colby Zacharias would make," Brant mused. "Shepherd, I want you to run a check on him. Find out everything you can about him and his company. I want to know why he's interested in offering two or three times what the company is worth."

"Anything else?" Shepherd asked.

"I want a complete dossier on the Estella Esteban Elementary School and adjacent property."

When Shepherd finished writing, he laid his pen and notebook on the desk. "Brant, you've really got me worried," he said. "I've grown accustomed to you being a workaholic. I've accepted that you're not a person to delegate—you want to hold the reins in your hands at all times in all places. But in all the years I've been working with you, I've never seen you act this way. All this talk about opening a branch office in San Antonio. This investigation into Galvan Construction and Colby Zacharias. A complete dossier on this property in a barrio in San Antonio. Maybe your involvement with this woman is a nostalgic whim that's going to fade shortly."

Brant shook his head. "My feelings for Marcy aren't a nostalgic whim," he declared. "And I've never made it a secret that I want to open more branch offices."

"No, you haven't," Shepherd agreed. "But you weren't interested in San Antonio as a possible location for a branch office until you became involved with the Galvan woman. She's at the bottom of this change in you."

Slowly Brant admitted, "Yes, she is."

Shepherd stood, gathered his papers and stuffed them in his briefcase. "If you open a branch in San Antonio, what will it mean to me?"

"I won't ask you to take charge of it, since your roots are here," Brant explained. "I'll leave you here—if you like."

"I like," Shepherd answered. "You'll be going to San Antonio?"

Brant shrugged and sighed wearily. "I don't know, Shepherd. I haven't seen the study yet."

"I hope you think long and hard about this before you make a decision about opening an office in San Antonio or moving there yourself."

Long after Shepherd had gone, Brant paced the office, thinking. He hadn't mentioned to Marcy that he was even thinking of opening a branch in San Antonio; that he had been thinking of ways for her to keep her company; or that he was really getting involved in the literacy center.

Even if the feasibility study proved that the opening of an office in San Antonio was a realistic option, he didn't know whether he'd actually do it. It would be a very difficult decision.

Clearly, for the first time in many years, he was allowing his emotions to affect his business. And that unsettled him. He had always been in control and had built his life and his financial empire that way.

When the clock chimed the half hour, he realized that time was getting away from him. He returned to the desk and dialed Marcy's number.

"Hello," she answered.

"Hello."

"Brant. I'd about given you up."

"I've been in meetings ever since I got here," he explained. "I've been working long hours, so I could get the job finished and return to you."

"Does this mean that you'll be here sooner?" she asked.

"I'm flying out Wednesday," he informed her. "I'll be in San Antonio about noon."

"I wish I could pick you up," Marcy said, "but I can't. I'm still working shorthanded."

"Don't worry about it," he told her. "I'll be at the house waiting for you when you get home." The word *home* sounded wonderful to him, the concept even better. He was beginning to feel as if his home was with Marcy. "I'll even have your dinner waiting for you."

"A bucket of fried chicken?" she teased. "Or a pizza?"

He chuckled softly. "For that, Marcy Galvan, you'll just have to wait and see."

They laughed, then he inquired, "How's the Hudley place looking?"

"Great," Marcy replied. "If I had the money, I'd buy the place. I'd love to decorate it."

"I didn't know you were interested in interior decorating," he remarked.

"For myself," she qualified. "And I can envision myself living on the Hudley place. Every day at noon, I'd take my lunch and go sit on the riverbank to eat."

"Is it the same without me?" he questioned, remembering the day they had stood beneath the rustling leaves of the cypress trees.

"No," Marcy murmured. "I'll be glad when you come home."

"I will, too," he answered.

After he hung up the telephone, he went out to the balcony and looked down on the busy street below. He heard the hustle and bustle; he saw the bright lights. The excitement and the pace of the city was so much a part of him. He was a real New Yorker. How would he feel if he gave it up?

Marcy had told him he was "a Texan born and bred," and that she intended to be the one to bring him back to his roots. Maybe his roots *were* in San Antonio; for sure, his heart was.

TUESDAY EVENING Marcy sat in the Big Brothers/Big Sisters office for her meeting with Kyla. The caseworker pushed her glasses up on the bridge of her nose, opened her notebook and began to flip through the pages.

"How are things going with Amy?" she inquired.

"Good, I think," Marcy answered and counted off the visits she and Amy had shared.

"Sounds very good to me," Kyla commented, writing in her file. She laid her pen down and looked up, smiling at Marcy. "You and she have gotten off to a running start."

"I don't know if we're running yet," Marcy admitted, "but we're moving along, and our relationship has been anything but boring." Marcy laughed and described in detail her trip to the movie with Brant and Amy. "Brant thinks Amy is trying to match me with her father."

"Is the situation getting out of hand?"

"No."

The caseworker nodded and leaned back in her chair. "Just don't let it interfere with your relationship with Brant."

"I'm not. In fact, I'm more concerned about something else," Marcy said, relating Amy's conversation with her on Saturday. "She's not so much opposed to Wanda as she is afraid that if her father remarries, her new mother might die during pregnancy. That's the reason why Amy was so insistent on having an older sister rather than a younger one."

As Marcy talked, Kyla made notes.

"I wanted to discuss this with Gil myself, but felt that I should talk it over with you first," Marcy continued.

"I think you should tell Gil about it," Kyla agreed. "When I talk with him, I'll also mention it." Again she picked up her file and thumbed through the pages. She jotted down more notes, then remarked, "I can see that your role as a Big Sister is expanding, Marcy. You're going to play a part in helping Amy accept that her little brother didn't kill her mother and that her father has a right to have a woman in his life."

"And I'll have to make her understand that that woman in his life is not me," Marcy declared.

"YES, SIRREE," Chester Hudley said, walking through the house. "You're doing a fine job, Marcy. This old place is beginning to look like new. Why, when Winnie sees this, I'll just bet she's gonna want to move back in."

"Thank you, Mr. Hudley," Marcy replied, and the two of them moved onto the back veranda and gazed out across the lawn. The spring day was peaceful—the sun shining and a gentle breeze blowing, rustling through the leaves of the cypress trees along the river. "I can understand why the two of you love this place so much. This is only my second week, and I'm already in love with it."

"Well, then," Chester responded, his weathered face creasing into an easy, friendly smile, "you can just have it. I'll be mighty happy to sell it to you."

Marcy returned the smile. "If I had the money, I would have taken you up on your offer before now."

"That young feller you brought out here with you when you did the estimate seemed kinda interested," he commented. "I wondered if he might be interested in buying."

"I don't think so," Marcy answered. "He's not from here. He lives in New York."

"Didn't seem like a Yankee to me," Chester mused, rubbing his hand over his chin.

Marcy laughed. "Well, he's not really. He was born here. He just migrated up north."

Chester leaned his shoulder against the porch column and gazed at her, his eyes narrowing speculatively. "These old eyes of mine sorta thought he had him a young filly down here."

Having grown fond of Chester during the week and two days that she had been working on his house, Marcy didn't mind his probing into the status of her relationship with Brant. "We're dating," she admitted. "But it's nothing serious."

"Yet," Chester added quietly.

"Yet," she agreed.

Chester pushed away from the post and walked to the back door. "Well, if'en he should be interested in buying a house and land out here, convince him this is the buy for him."

"I will," Marcy promised.

His hand on the door handle, Chester turned. "Pardon an old man's inquisitiveness," he said, "but how do the two of you court when he lives in New York and you live down here?"

Marcy did forgive Chester his curiosity. "He flies here to be with me," she explained.

"And you're telling me that ain't serious?" He shook his grizzled head. "When are you gonna see him again?"

"He's flying in today," she replied and looked at her watch. "In fact, he should already be in San Antonio." She smiled, remembering Brant's promise to have dinner prepared for her when she got home.

"Why don't one of you move to where the other lives and make it easier on yourself?" Chester asked.

"I'm sure that's a point we're going to have to discuss pretty soon, Mr. Hudley," Marcy agreed. *A point that neither of us is flexible on,* she reflected.

"Reckon I'll be moseying on," Chester said. "You know how to reach me if you need me."

The remainder of the day seemed to drag by, and all Marcy could think about was Brant. She called her house several times but received no answer, and she didn't leave a message for Brant to call her.

Since she had worked the crew long hours last week, she felt comfortable in slowing down now. They were a little ahead of schedule and could afford some slack.

At five o'clock, after the crew left, she locked up the house. On her way in, she dialed her number again to hear Brant answer.

"Hi," she said, "I was just checking."

"I'm here," he confirmed with a smile in his voice.

"And dinner?" she inquired.

"It's here, too."

"Did you buy it already prepared, or did you cook it?"

"Oh, no. I'm not saying a word about it. You'll just have to wait until you get home to see."

The miles couldn't pass quickly enough for Marcy. Filled with anticipation, she finally pulled into her garage and switched off the ignition. She bounded out of the Bronco and rushed into the house to be welcomed by Brant's open arms. As he embraced her, she lifted her face and their lips came together in a long, satisfying kiss.

Several kisses later, she laid her cheek against his shoulder. "I missed you so much, Brant. This past week has seemed like years."

"I know," he agreed. "I could hardly wait to see you again."

Then Marcy sniffed and she sniffed again. "I smell a roast." She pulled back and looked at him. "You're cooking a roast!"

"All by my little lonesome," he admitted. "Of course, it's modest by Clarice's standards, but I never developed my culinary talents beyond basic meat and potatoes."

"I'm a potato-and-meat woman."

"At least we have something in common," he pointed out. "Why don't you take a shower and change clothes real quick, and we'll have a drink before dinner."

"Sounds good to me."

Later, when Marcy walked into the den, Brant handed her a glass of wine, and the two of them went out to the deck to enjoy the evening. At Marcy's instigation Brant discussed his latest contracts, then asked about her work. She repeated her recent conversation with Hudley.

"If it's all right with you," he suggested, "I may drive out there tomorrow and have lunch with you."

"I'd love it. We can drive into town—"

"No," he said. "Let's have a picnic by the river."

"All right. Are you going to surprise me again?"

He grinned. "Of course. Whatever is left over tonight will be our lunch tomorrow."

"Leftovers?" she exclaimed.

"Well—" he said "—I'll see what I can do."

Planning the picnic lunch, they set the table and ate dinner. Afterward they sat on the sofa together, watching television.

"Do you want me to stay with you?" Brant asked.

"Yes." She paused, then asked, "For how long?"
"Through the weekend."
Four glorious days! she thought.

CHAPTER TEN

THE FOUR DAYS WITH Brant sped by much too quickly. Sunday morning Marcy wakened first and lay quietly so as not to disturb him. At least she would be left with many wonderful memories of their time together—the picnic on the river at Chester Hudley's place on Wednesday; staying home on Thursday and Friday nights, talking and getting to know each other; touring the Alamo with Amy and Sarah and playing softball on Saturday; and having dinner with Clarice and Ethan afterwards.

"Good morning," Brant said.

"Good morning." She turned her head on the pillow and reached out to brush a strand of hair from his forehead.

"What are you thinking so deeply about?" he asked.

"Us."

"What about us?"

The stubble of his beard, as intensely black as his hair, gave him the mystique of a pirate.

"You're not even gone, yet I'm missing you," she confessed. "Although I've lived on memories of you for the past eighteen years, they're no longer enough, no longer satisfying." She placed her palm against the curve of his cheek. "I want you with me."

Brant clasped his hand over hers. "What do you think we should do about it?" he asked.

"I don't know," Marcy murmured, having struggled with this question for the past three days. "Truly, I don't."

He pushed himself up and fluffed the pillows behind him. Leaning back, he pulled Marcy into his arms, so that her head rested against his chest. "Whatever the answer, we can't continue this long-distance courtship."

"I know."

They lay in silence for several minutes.

Then Brant spoke softly. "I love you, Marcy."

She laid her hand against his chest, feeling the steady beat of his heart. Without raising her head, she echoed his words: "I love you."

He tucked his fingers beneath her chin and lifted her face for his kiss—a sweet, warm kiss.

"When I first saw you at the company picnic," he said, "you told me you were an old-fashioned woman who wanted a forever marriage."

"Yes."

"I want a forever marriage, Marcy." He caught her shoulders and turned her so that they were looking into each other's faces. "I know we haven't dated that long, Marcy. I know this is rather sudden, but I want to marry you."

"We haven't resolved our problems. How can we talk about marriage?"

"Well, as I see it, one of us is going to have to move." His blue eyes searched hers intently. "Surely you've given this possibility some thought, Marcy. Has marriage to me never entered your mind?"

"Ever since we started seeing one another," she confessed. "And I've loved you longer. But...I don't know that I'm ready to make the sacrifice of giving up my life here to follow you to New York. Even if I were, Brant, I don't know that I could be happy there."

Brant's eyes darkened to a deep blue. Marcy could see that the admission hurt him as much as it did her. She eased out of his arms and got up. Gathering her wrap from the end of the bed, she slipped it on.

"Brant, have you thought about moving here and working out of San Antonio?"

"Yes," he admitted, as he got got out of bed, too, and headed toward the bathroom. "I went so far as to have a feasibility study done on San Antonio as a prospective city for a new branch office for Holland Enterprises."

Marcy quickly turned to face him, her cotton wrap swirling about her ankles. Her hopes rose. "And?"

"The study isn't completed yet, but so far, San Antonio isn't high on the list of probable sites." He turned on the tap and brushed his teeth. After he rinsed them, he went to the door. "I've always had the feeling that I came in second to your causes and your strays."

"That's not true, Brant, and you know it," Marcy countered. "It's just not easy to change your life when you've spent twenty-eight years establishing it."

"You could give up your crusades here, and become involved in social work wherever. Surely it would be easier for you to move than it would be for me to move my office."

"It's not just social work, Brant," Marcy explained. "Here I'm working with my people. If I left, what would I do with the company?"

"You could sell it. The way I see it—the same way Danny and Ethan do—is that it's more a liability than an asset. With the money Colby Zacharias is offering to pay you and Lonzo, the two of you would be quite well-off."

Marcy didn't reply. Part of what he was saying made sense, but Marcy was sure she could make the company profitable if she were given a little more time. She walked to the window and stared out. Then she felt him behind her. His warm breath touched her skin, and his hands caught her shoulders. His mouth softly brushed against the back of her neck.

"Honey, take some time off and come stay with me in New York. You haven't give me or the city a fair chance. You're saying you wouldn't be happy, but you don't know for sure."

Marcy leaned against Brant, savoring his strength, wanting to remain in his arms forever.

He continued: "Without any sense of compromise, you're asking me to move. You're assuming the move would be easier for me to make than for you. For either of us, it will be a sacrifice. But we've got to give ourselves a chance."

"Yes," Marcy agreed, "we do." Her heart was lighter than it had been only moments ago. She turned in his embrace and put her arms around him, hugging him tightly. "We'll find a way, won't we, Brant?"

"Yes," he murmured. "Do you have someone trustworthy you could leave in charge?"

She nodded her head, her cheek brushing against his chest. "Joe Alexander. You may have seen him at the picnic. He went to work for the company when Papa was alive, and he's worked under Papa and Uncle Lonzo. He's my right-hand man."

"When do you think you can make the trip?"

"I'm not sure. I'll have to talk it over with Joe, and study our schedule and work load." She gently pushed out of his embrace but kept her hands on his waist. Looking into his eyes, she said, "No matter what decision I make, Brant—whether I go with you to New York or whether I stay here—I want to keep the company, and I want to own all of it."

Returning her intent gaze, he declared, "All right, then. I'll buy the company for you."

"Why would you do that? You don't think the company is worth much, do you?"

His answer was slow in coming. "The business is worth it to me because I love you," he replied.

"I appreciate the offer," she said slowly, "but if you did that, I'd feel as if *you* owned the company and not I. And you would, too. It wouldn't be long before you'd be telling me how to run it."

Brant smiled grimly. "You're right. I probably would." He was quiet for a few seconds, then questioned, "So if I don't give you the money, what are you going to do? How are you going to buy the company?"

"I could sell the ranch."

"Sell La Rosa Blanca? You'd sell the ranch for the company?"

"It seems to be my only choice," she told him. "I wish you really understood me, Brant. Because you have no strong feelings about your heritage, you can't understand mine. Just because you walked away and left it, doesn't mean that I can. Yes, my options are limited, and any one I take involves consequences that are painful." She paused, then asked, "Would you consider making me a loan of the money?"

"No," he answered gently with a sad expression in his eyes. "I'll buy it for you, but I won't lend you the money."

"You'd rather I be beholden to you?" she inquired.

"I think you'd feel more beholden to me if I loaned you the money. And I don't want to add another worry to your heavy load. You're leveraged as it is. Another loan would spread you too thin, Marcy."

Marcy was right back to square one—not knowing what to do or where to turn. Talking as much to herself as to him, she argued, "It's through Galvan Construction that I'm helping my people retain pride in themselves rebuilding their slum-ridden areas. They need to know somebody cares. They don't want or need to be given money. They don't want charity. They want to provide for themselves through their own individual efforts."

She took a step toward him. "They don't accept, spend or want money from the government. My people want and need someone to have faith in them and to work beside them to get things done."

"I agree with you," Brant responded evenly. "I'm not against any of your goals, but you're letting your pride stand in the way of your common sense. You can still contribute to your people as half owner of Galvan Construction or as no owner at all. It's you, Marcy, not the company, who is the contributor."

Marcy smiled sadly at him. "It's my problem. I'll work it out."

"No," Brant disagreed. "It's our problem. We're no longer talking about *your* future or *my* future as though they were separate. We're talking about *our* future. We'll work this out *together*."

"All . . . right."

"Now," he suggested, "let's go get a cup of coffee. I could use some."

Together they went into the kitchen and Marcy put the coffee on.

"What would you like for breakfast?" she asked.

"Nothing. I'll have coffee when it's made." He walked down the hallway and opened the front door, returning shortly with the Sunday paper. "How did you get the money to buy out your brother's interest in the company?" he asked.

"A personal loan in addition to the money I received from the house in town that I sold."

"So you've already had to sell part of your heritage," he pointed out.

Marcy searched his expression, but saw no sarcasm or teasing; just interest. He was serious about their working together for their future. "No. Papa bought it about fifteen years ago. It was much too big for one person, and after Papa's death, I had no desire to remain there. I had no second thoughts about getting rid of it."

"Marcy, you'll have more than second thoughts if you get rid of La Rosa Blanca. It's been in your family far too long. And, barring a miracle, there is no way you can get the money to buy out your uncle. To keep the business in the family—or at least, in the almost-family—I'm going to top the offer made by Zacharias and buy your uncle's half."

"You're going to buy Tío's half?"

"I am if Danny will sell to me," he declared and paused as if expecting her to protest.

She questioned, "No strings attached?"

"One," he replied.

"What?"

"You'll provide me with a complete dossier of the company, along with your immediate and long-range objectives. Between us we'll agree on a date by which we will have reached these goals. If by the projected date, we're falling short of them—and I mean the least bit short of them—and see no way of meeting them, you'll agree to sell the company."

Marcy contemplated this; then pronounced, "Agreed."

"I also promise I won't change the name of the company and I'll leave the running of it totally in your capable hands. If you choose to marry me and come to New York to live, you'll be the one to find a competent person to manage the company in your absence."

She nodded, then poured them a cup of coffee. Brant took his and went into the bedroom to pack. When he returned to the den, he set his suitcase beside the door.

"If it's all right with you, I'll be back next weekend?" he half asked.

"I've promised Amy that I would take her to the ranch," Marcy said tentatively, prepared for his scowl of disapproval. But it didn't come. Relieved that regular sessions of softball practice had not yet begun so that it hadn't interfered with this weekend, Marcy explained, "We're going down on Friday. We should be finished with Hudley's house on Thursday."

"Where will you be staying?"

"At Fort Clark Springs," she answered.

Still without speaking a word of disapproval, he told her, "I'll join you there."

When Brant left that afternoon, Marcy was feeling more desolate than she had felt in a long time. Even his promise to buy her uncle's half of the business didn't reassure her or make her happy. Her plan to visit New York was even less reassuring. Yet, if they wanted a future together, one of them would have to make a sacrifice.

A little later that afternoon, Marcy called Clarice to discuss the possibility of her visiting Brant in New York.

"Oh, Marcy!" Clarice squealed, shouting out the news to Ethan. "Does this mean the two of you are serious?"

"Yes," Marcy replied. "We're definitely serious."

By this time Ethan was on the extension, wanting to know the details.

"I don't have any details yet," Marcy answered. "Brant and I only talked about it this morning."

"Are you going to marry him?" Ethan asked bluntly.

"I don't know what we're going to do." Marcy sighed. She loved her brother dearly, but he did exasperate her at times. And this was one of those times. "Right now, we're searching for a solution that both of us can live with. I'm agreeing to a trip to New York to see how I'll fare in the big city."

"You can do it," Clarice said, then added, "Please, don't talk yourself out if, Marcy."

"I'm not," Marcy said—and meant it.

She loved Brant and wanted to marry him. If they were going to find a solution to their dilemma, she was going to have to give as much as he had given. She was going to have to fight for their happiness as diligently as she was fighting for her company.

"I'm going to call Joe and talk to him about our work load and the scheduling. Then I'll have some details to discuss with you."

She wanted to tell them about Brant's plans to buy Lonzo's half of the company, but she was afraid that one or the other of them might inadvertently discuss it with Danny before Brant was ready to act. After hanging up, Marcy called Joe, told him of her plan to make a trip to New York, and arranged to meet with him at the office early the next morning. When she went to bed that night, she was feeling better about things. She and Brant were working together to create a future for themselves.

"MARCY, I THINK that with a little rearranging, we can do it," Joe said.

They sat on either side of her desk with a monthly calender spread between them, on which the names of their projects were mounted as small, movable tiles.

"Here," Marcy suggested, shifting one of the tiles. "We can switch the McGregor job over here."

"And put the Swenson here." Joe slid another over. "Actually, that's better because it gives us more time for the Mission Park project."

After an hour or so, both of them sat back and silently surveyed their work.

"We can do it," Joe announced. "We'll miss you, but we can hold the fort while you're gone."

She smiled tightly. "Maybe that's what I'm afraid of, Joe—that you can do without me."

Joe grinned and held his hands up, palms out. "Whoa, now! I didn't say we could do without you indefinitely. We're only talking about two or three weeks, aren't we?"

Marcy nodded.

"It'll be good for you," he assured her. "You work too hard. You need to take some time off, and a trip to New York might just fit the bill."

"Joe, before Tío decided to sell out, you told me you had some ideas about updating the company. Do you want to discuss them now?"

He smiled grimly. "Maybe we ought to wait, Marcy, to see what's going to happen."

"No. I want to know what they are. I think we should proceed as if nothing had changed."

"All right." Joe agreed. "We need to change the way we do our dispatching. What we're doing isn't wrong, but it's not as efficient as it could be. I've been working on a plan that would cut down on lost time between jobs."

Marcy listened to Joe describe his plan, and as he talked, she realized he had the same vision for the company that she and Papa had, the same dedication.

"If you're agreeable to giving it a whirl, I could supervise the dispatcher until we got the bugs worked out," he offered.

"I like it," she declared. "It sounds like something Papa would have initiated. You remind me a lot of him."

"I liked your father," Joe said. "He taught me things I never could have learned in books. He gave me on-job training that I'll never forget."

For a while the two of them sat and reminisced about the past.

"How are the prospects looking for you buying your uncle's interest?"

"I'm working on something," Marcy told him, "but it's a little too soon for me to be talking about it. As soon as I know something for sure, I'll tell you."

Marcy deliberately refrained from telling Joe about Brant. If Brant bought it, the news would be good. But if he didn't, then no hopes would have to be dashed.

Joe stood. "I wish I had the money. I'd buy it."

"You'd make a good partner," she replied.

"I think so. Well, I'd better head for the site."

"Joe, please hang in a little longer."

"I am. As I told you the other day, we've weathered worse storms than this one. You can count on your New York vacation." He smiled. "How's the Hudley job doing?"

"We should be finished by Thursday," Marcy informed him. "I told the guys that I would be working out of the office through Wednesday. Thursday I'll give it the final check."

FRIDAY MARCY AND AMY headed for the ranch, arriving at La Rosa Blanca late in the afternoon. Marcy parked the Bronco in front of the small cottage, opened her door and climbed out. She loved West Texas. The stark ruggedness of the landscape had always intrigued her, and she had marveled at it's barren and desert beauty.

Hearing the screen door of the house creak as it opened, she looked up. A weathered old man with a sweat-stained Stetson pulled low over his face, came onto the porch. He carried a rifle in the crook of his arm.

"Hello, Erny, it's me!" Marcy called. Amy rounded the Bronco and came to stand beside Marcy.

"He has a gun," she whispered. "You don't think he'll shoot us, do you?"

Marcy laughed. "No. He lives out here alone, and he's just being cautious."

Amy moved closer to Marcy and clasped her hand tightly.

Raising his hand to shield his eyes against the afternoon glare, Erny squinted at them. Then he took several steps that brought him to the edge of the porch. Finally a slow smile curled his lips. "What brings you out this way, Marcy?"

Holding on to Amy's hand, Marcy went through the gate and up to the porch where Erny stood. "I wanted to bring Amy Calderon out here to meet you," she said, explaining her role in the Big Sister-Little Sister program and introducing Amy to Erny. "Amy's always wanted to own a horse, so I thought the two of us would do some riding. I'd like to ride Bluebonnet. I thought Amy could try Daisy."

Erny leaned his rifle against the house, then pulled his hat farther down on his face. "Reckon I could have them little ladies saddled right quick like for you," he replied. "Are you planning to stay the night?"

Marcy nodded.

"At the fort?" he asked.

"Yes."

"I don't want you girls out too late," he warned. "Out here the terrain looks pretty much the same, and I wouldn't want y'all lost. I'd eventually find y'all, but it might take me a long time."

"We won't be out late," Marcy promised.

She and Amy followed Erny to the stables, where Amy hit him with a barrage of questions as he saddled her mount. Marcy worked on Bluebonnet herself.

Half an hour later, she and Amy slowly rode cross-country over the rugged West Texas terrain. She felt great pride as she looked at the land that had belonged to the first Galvans who came to the New World. Unlike many of the Spanish families who had land grants from the crown, the Galvans had managed to hold on to the majority of theirs, cutting down on its size only out of choice. Marcy's Spanish heritage was still tangible. It was here, now.

Marcy halted Bluebonnet at Galvan Creek and dismounted. After helping Amy down from her horse, she knelt at the creek's edge and picked up a handful of the soft, moist dirt. This was her land; she felt as if she were one with it.

"It's beautiful out here," Amy commented as the evening breeze ruffled her hair.

Marcy rose, tossed the soil aside and brushed her palm down the leg of her jeans. "Yes," she murmured.

"I've never been to a place like this before," Amy said and reached out to catch Marcy's hand. "Thank you for bringing me. This is one of the best times I've ever had."

Marcy was caught up in the beauty and the historical significance of the place. Delighted that Amy appreciated it, Marcy squeezed her hand. "I'm glad you like it. Now, we'd better get back or Erny will be worried."

MARCY DROVE TO THE Visitor's Center in Fort Clark Springs, a retirement community located directly across Interstate 90 from Brackettville, Texas.

Amy squirmed in the seat. "This used to be a real fort?"

"That's right," Marcy answered. "It was built in the mid-1850s."

"And soldiers fought here?" Amy asked.

"Mm-hmm. Tomorrow we'll go the museum, and you can learn all about Fort Clark's history." Marcy pointed to two long, two-story buildings constructed of stone. Each building had porches that extended the length of both floors. "Those—were barracks that have been converted into a hotel. That's where we'll be staying."

"Oh, goody!" Amy exclaimed. "Get us an upstairs room, Marcy. Look! A golf course."

Marcy glanced to her left. "It's a golf course now, but when the fort was first built, this was the parade ground." Parking in the front of the Visitor's Center, she added, "Tomorrow we'll tour the grounds too, and I'll show you where John Wayne stayed when he was filming *The Alamo*. And if we have time, we'll drive over to the Alamo Village to see the movie set."

"That's where they make movies?" Amy questioned.

"That's right. Now, let's go check in."

Marcy registered, then asked the attendant, "Are there any messages for me?"

The young woman moved to the desk and shuffled through some papers that were strewn about. "Nope," she replied.

Marcy expected a message of some kind from Brant. She hadn't heard from him since he'd left on Sunday. After all, he had promised to meet her at the fort. Had he decided not to come? she wondered. Hiding her disappointment, she turned to Amy.

"Well, I guess it's time for you and me to have dinner. I'm famished. Are you?"

"Yes," Amy answered. "I'm starved." Before Marcy could say anything, she skipped out of the building.

They walked over to another historical building—once the officers' mess, now the Las Moras Inn and a favorite restaurant of the locals of Fort Clark Springs and Bracketville. After they had eaten, they returned to the car, retrieved their luggage and climbed the stairs to their second-story room.

Soon they had bathed and changed into their pajamas. Marcy slid gratefully between the sheets on her bed. When she had decided to drive up here several weeks ago, she had been contemplating selling the ranch. Now, she didn't have to consider that option. And even if Brant hadn't said anything about buying Tío's half of the business, Marcy knew she could never sell the ranch.

Amy sat up for a while, flipping from one television station to another. Finally when she found nothing she wanted to watch, she switched it and the lamp off. The glow of the streetlights filtered through the drapes into the room.

After a long time, Amy asked, "Marcy, are you asleep?"

"No."

"I can't sleep, either."

"Why?"

"I've been thinking about what you said to me the other day," the child began.

Marcy waited quietly.

"And I want Daddy to have friends, but I—I—"

When Amy said nothing more, Marcy prompted, "You what?"

"I don't want him to like Mrs. Courtland. The way he talks about her, I can tell she's more than a friend."

"We talked about that possibility the other day," Marcy reminded.

Amy flipped on her side, making the bed squeak as she moved. "Marcy, do you like Daddy?"

"Yes."

"A whole lot?"

"A lot," Marcy replied, although she was suspicious of the direction in which the conversation was heading.

"Good," Amy declared. She flopped over on the bed again. "You're the one I want for my mother. Not Mrs. Courtland. All we have to do—"

"We're not going to do anything," Marcy said quietly. "Your daddy and I like each other as friends. That's all."

"Couldn't you love him just a little bit?" Amy persisted.

"No," Marcy answered. "And he doesn't love me. And, Amy, you shouldn't jump to the conclusion that your father is going to marry Wanda."

"He likes her. I can tell." Amy slipped out of her bed and ran to Marcy. "You're the one I love. I want you to be my new mother. If you and Daddy try, you could love each other."

"No, I can't," Marcy told her. "I love someone else."

"Brant?"

"Yes."

"I like my daddy better than Brant. You don't think you could ever love my daddy for your husband?"

"No," Marcy repeated. "But I promise, no matter whom your father marries, I'll be your Big Sister as long as you want me."

"Promise me?" Amy whispered.

"Promise."

Long after Amy was asleep, Marcy lay awake in the adjacent bed. She still couldn't sleep. She finally rose, put on her wrap and walked out onto the balcony. The night was beautiful. A full, silver moon was centered in a midnight-blue sky that glittered with millions of stars. Sitting in the porch swing that was suspended from the ceiling, she rocked back and forth. She was very disappointed and concerned that she hadn't yet heard from Brant.

Nor had she heard from Danny. She was curious to know of any new developments regarding the sale of Lonzo's share of the company.

Marcy also wanted to let Brant know that she had cleared the way for the New York trip in the middle of the summer. She thought of Amy and felt a twinge of guilt. She hadn't yet given her the news. But there was plenty of time.

CHAPTER ELEVEN

MARCY GOT AMY UP early because she had promised Gil that Amy would call him by nine that morning. As the two made their way to the telephone in the Visitor's Center, Amy grumbled.

"Why don't the rooms have telephones?" she asked.

"Because most people are trying to get away from the everyday worries of life," Marcy explained.

"Well, I don't like it," Amy declared. "Wouldn't it be easier if people could have a telephone in their room? That way, they wouldn't have to get up, get dressed and walked way down here. I don't like some of this old-fashioned stuff, Marcy."

"I hear you," Marcy said. "Loud and clear, and I agree."

When they entered the building, the young girl who had been working when they registered last evening, stepped out of the back room. She saw them and smiled.

"Good morning." She walked to the desk to pick up a slip of paper, which she waved in the air. "I'm sure glad you came in, Miss Galvan. Your message came in late last night, and I haven't had time to get it to you."

"Thank you," Marcy replied and took the note, quickly reading the message. *I'll be in Fort Clark*

Springs sometime Saturday morning. See you then. Love, Brant.

Folding the note and slipping it into the pocket of her jeans, Marcy asked. "Where's there a telephone we can use? Amy needs to call her father."

Before the girl could answer, Amy opened her purse and withdrew her wallet. She extracted a small plastic card and laid it on the counter. "I have a calling card all my own," she announced.

The girl nodded and pointed to a telephone on the counter. "In that case, you can use this one."

Amy put through the call and soon was talking with her father, describing everything she had seen and done since she and Marcy had arrived. To give the child some privacy, Marcy walked across the room and stared out the front window. Eventually Amy called to her.

"Daddy wants to talk to you."

Marcy turned to see Amy holding her hand over the mouthpiece of the telephone.

When she was closer, Amy said, "Daddy wants me to come home because Mrs. Courtland and her kids are flying in from Dallas today." Her eyes filled with tears. "Please, don't let Mrs. Courtland mess up our weekend, Marcy. Please don't."

"I'll talk with your father," Marcy consented. "But he's the one who calls the shots, Amy. Not me."

When she took the receiver, Amy slowly walked off, her head hung low.

"Hello, Gil."

"Hi, Marcy," he answered. "I just told Amy that Wanda and her children are flying in today. It's an unexpected visit, but I'd like for Amy to meet them.

I'm not quite sure how to handle it, though. She's pretty upset at the idea of having to come home.''

Marcy turned to look at the disheartened little girl who had curled up in a corner of the sofa, an elbow propped on the armrest, her chin cupped in her hand.

Quickly forming an idea, Marcy proposed, "Gil, is it possible for you to bring Wanda and her children out here?"

"To Fort Clark Springs?" he asked in surprise.

"This is neutral territory," Marcy explained, and lowered her voice so Amy couldn't overhear. "If I have to bring Amy back to San Antonio sooner than I promised and you agreed to, she won't be receptive to Wanda at all."

Gil sighed. "I don't know if she'll ever be receptive, Marcy. I've done everything I know to prepare her, but she refuses to cooperate. I finally decided the best way was to plunge in."

"Trust me on this one, Gil. Bringing the Courtlands here will not only put you on Amy's good side, it will give you a definite advantage with Wanda's kids, they'll love it out here. I'll take them horseback riding, and they can swim in the Olympic-size pool to their hearts' content. You and Wanda can even take them to the Alamo Village. Also, there may be other advantages—while the children are getting better acquainted, you and Wanda will have some time to yourselves."

The line was silent as Gil thought it over. Finally he decided, "I guess we could make the trip. I'm meeting Wanda at the airport at ten-thirty. It takes about three hours to get there, doesn't it?"

"Yes."

"Then I figure we'll be there between two and three."

"I'll make reservations for you," Marcy offered.

"Three rooms," Gil instructed. "One for me, one for Wanda, her daughter and hopefully Amy, and one for the boys."

After Gil rang off, Marcy stood there for a moment, feeling quite pleased with herself. She had handled the situation efficiently. She had established a wonderful meeting place for the Calderons and Courtlands, and with their coming she would have plenty of free time to spend with Brant. Marcy reserved three rooms for Gil and one for Brant.

"Wow!" the registration clerk exclaimed. "You have a whole bunch coming in. What is this? A family reunion?"

Marcy laughed and replied, "Of sorts." She turned from the desk and looked at Amy who was still curled up in the corner of the sofa. Marcy hoped this wouldn't set the tone for the day. When she reached the child, she said, "Let's get some breakfast, then later we'll go swimming."

"I'm not going to have to go home?" Amy's face brightened.

"No, your father didn't want to mess up your weekend. But he did want you to meet the Courtlands, so he's bringing them down here."

"I don't want 'em to come," Amy said.

"Don't you remember the other day after softball practice, we decided that this might be just the place for all of us to be together?"

"I changed my mind."

Marcy squatted in front of Amy and caught her by the shoulders. "They're coming, and you're going to behave like a good girl. If you give yourself a chance, you'll like Wanda and the kids."

"I don't think so."

"Amelia Calderon!"

Amy giggled. "That's the first time you've called me by my full name. You sound just like Nona."

Marcy laughed with her. "Promise me."

"Promise," Amy agreed.

Marcy rose, and caught Amy's hand, and the two of them walked outside into the bright sunshiny day. After they'd had breakfast at the Las Moras Inn they went for a short walk before returning to their room where they changed into their bathing suits. Then, with their swimming gear packed in a small plastic bag that Amy carried, they found their way to the swimming pool that was fed with natural spring water.

Marcy swam until she was tired, then climbed out of the pool. She quickly located a thick patch of grass close to one of the pecan trees and far away from the frolicking swimmers. There she stretched out on her towel and relaxed. Amy, having made friends with other children her age, still cavorted in the water, under the careful scrutiny of the lifeguard.

The sun felt good to Marcy and for a few minutes she was able to push her troubled thoughts aside. She dozed lightly, but awakened when she heard a loud peal of laughter from the children. She sat up and watched Amy, who was entertaining the crowd as she dived into the pool. At the same time, Marcy glimpsed to see a familiar figure, wearing swimming trunks, striding in her direction.

She felt as if her heart had stopped. She had never seen him in trunks before, and he was devastatingly handsome—utterly masculine. True, she had seen him naked, but that was in intimate circumstances. Wearing only the one scant garment that covered a portion of his lower body and accented his muscular chest and sinewy legs, he was blatantly sexy.

The summer breeze ruffled his hair, and dark glasses covered his eyes, adding to the aura of sensuality. Slung over one shoulder was a large beach towel, a tip of it brushing against his chest. His lips slowly curled into a smile.

"Hi," he said.

Marcy's gaze slid down his sun-bronzed body until she was looking at the feet planted in the grass beside her. Slowly she returned her gaze up the length of him until she was again looking into his face.

"Hi," she echoed.

He spread the towel beside her and sat down, then leaned over and touched his mouth to hers in a brief kiss. Barely lifting his lips from hers, he whispered. "Glad to see me?"

"Yes," she whispered back. "And if we were someplace private, I'd show you exactly how much I've missed you."

"You'll have the opportunity later," he promised. "I took the liberty of changing our rooms."

"Oh?"

"That was the only way we could get rooms next to each other, and that's as far away from you as I want to be."

"You may be even closer than that," Marcy said, explaining that Gil and the Courtlands were on their way. "If Gil has his way, Amy will be sharing a room with Wanda and her daughter."

"I'd like that, but I'm not pinning my hopes on it," Brant replied. "I have more confidence in Amy's getting her way than in Gil's getting his. I can't see Amy sleeping in anyone's room but yours. But no matter. At least, this may mean that you and I have the earlier part of the evening to ourselves."

"I would think so." Marcy glanced at the pool and saw Amy playing in the water. She waved to her.

"Good." Cupping his hands behind his head, Brant stretched out beside her and closed his eyes. "I called Danny the other day and asked him for all the specs on his father's interest."

"You're really going to buy Tío's half?" Marcy murmured.

"If Danny will sell to me."

"What was Danny's reaction?" she asked.

"Surprised! For a high-powered attorney who should be able to handle himself under any circumstances, he stammered and stuttered a great deal. But he promised to send me the specs that I requested."

"It's not like Danny to lose his composure," Marcy observed.

"I didn't think so, either," Brant admitted. "I kept wondering about his reaction and about the reason why Colby Zacharias was interested in your company. I wanted to find out what it was, so I had Shepherd run check on Colby's holdings. We discovered he has a silent partner—an influential and wealthy silent partner. Justis Juarez."

"No!" Marcy exclaimed. "So Juarez is behind the buy out! Knowing I wouldn't sell to him, he went through Zacharias. I wonder if Danny knows."

"I don't know."

"If he did," Marcy pointed out, "he wouldn't care."

"I agree with you," Brant replied.

"I've had a rather revealing week myself," Marcy commented, turning over on her stomach and propping herself up on her elbows. "Joe and I found several weeks during the summer when I can be free to be in New York with you."

A slow smile curved his lips. "You won't regret this."

"No, I won't," she told him. "I'm looking forward to it."

Drying her hair with her towel, Amy came running up to interrupt the conversation. "Hi, Brant, when did you get here?"

"About an hour ago," he said.

"Are you here for the weekend?"

He nodded.

Amy rolled her eyes. "The whole world is going to be here."

"Seems like it," Brant agreed.

"I'm hungry," Amy announced.

"Well, then, let's go get something to eat," Brant suggested. "But first, we should change clothes."

Amy scampered around, gathering up her towel and swimming gear, while Brant picked up his and Marcy's towels and draped them over his arm.

"Marcy, when I was swimming," Amy remembered, "I heard there's going to be a dance at Las Moras Inn tonight. Are you and Brant going?"

"This is the first I've heard about it," Marcy responded. "But it sounds like a good idea don't you think so, Brant?"

"I DON'T KNOW WHEN I'VE felt this nervous before." Wanda glanced at Gil, who was slowing the van to turn into the entrance of Fort Clark Springs. "I'm so apprehensive my palms are clammy. What if she doesn't like me?''

"She will," he promised.

Wanda's oldest child, Elana, was sitting behind her with a small cassette recorder in her hand, its earphones plugged in. The two boys, buckled safely into the back seat, were playing a game.

Gil caught Wanda's hand in his and squeezed. "I wish I could make it easier for you," he added, giving her a quick glance, "but I can't."

"It's been months since I first met her, Gil, but she hasn't softened at all."

"Did you talk with your mother about it?" he asked.

Wanda nodded. "That's the nice thing about Bebe being my stepmother—she can give me some pointers. She said I was reaping what I'd sown."

Gil laughed. "You gave her a hard time?"

"I did. I guess that's why I can understand Amy's feelings. I was an only child and, like Amy, never had to share myself or those I loved with anyone else. I certainly didn't want to share my father with another woman. I was very lucky Bebe thought I was worth loving and Daddy worth fighting me for. She's just like a biological mother to me. I don't know what I'd do without her."

Gil was just as nervous about the meeting with Amy as Wanda, but he said nothing. Wanda was counting on his support, and he wanted to give it to her. He had loved his wife very much and after she died, he had thought his own life would end, too. There had been times when he had hoped it would. But it hadn't. He had survived—for himself and for Amy.

Now, after three years, he had found another woman whom he loved; perhaps differently from the way he had loved Sondra, but he loved Wanda deeply and passionately, and wanted to marry her. He prayed that Amy would like her; it would make his decision easier and the marriage could occur sooner. But, even if he had to move more slowly, he intended to marry Wanda.

Gil stopped at the guard station and applied for a visitor's permit. When the decal was affixed to his windshield, he drove to the barracks-turned-hotel and parked. He saw Amy standing on the upstairs porch. Opening the door, he got out of the van and waved.

"Hi, sweetheart."

Amy waved back and gave him a limp smile. Then Marcy and Brant came to stand behind her, waving also.

Wanda opened the door, climbed out, and looked up into the small face that peered over the upstairs railing. "Hello, Amy."

"Hello, Mrs. Courtland." Amy made no effort to join her father and Wanda.

"Hi, Wanda," Marcy called out. "I'm Marcy Galvan, Amy's Big Sister, and this is Brant Holland."

"Marcy's Big Boyfriend," Brant joked.

Wanda laughed as Marcy pulled a face and playfully slapped Brant's shoulder.

Then the side door of the van opened, and Wanda's children got out. By this time Marcy, Brant and Amy had descended the stairs to join Gil and Wanda on the sidewalk in front of the barracks hotel.

"These are my three children," Wanda said. She pointed to her daughter. "This is Elana, my twelve-year-old."

Her earphones hanging around her neck, Elana smiled at Marcy and Brant, revealing colored braces. "Hi."

"This is Drake, my ten-year-old," Wanda continued. "And Kevin, the—"

"Baby," Drake teased.

"I'm not a baby, either." Kevin made a face and swatted a strand of straight brown hair out of his face. "I'm seven years old."

"He's certainly not a baby," Wanda agreed with Kevin. "He's just the youngest."

Kevin nodded his head in satisfaction.

"This is my daughter, Amy, who's nine," Gil responded and reached for Amy, but she clung to Marcy.

Without saying anything to draw more attention to Amy's behavior, Marcy gently removed Amy's arms from around her and pushed the child toward her father. Gil forced himself to smile and act as if nothing were amiss.

"Did you get the rooms for us, Marcy?"

"Sure did." She pointed to the other barracks. "To get your rooms closer together, I had to accept rooms in that building."

"That's fine," Gil replied. "I'll get the luggage out."

"I'll help you," Brant offered.

"Wanda," Marcy inquired, "have you eaten?"

"Yes, we stopped on the way up here. The children were hungry." She added, "I'll go get our rooms set up."

Catching Amy's hand, Gil said, "You can come with us, Amy. I'd like for you to get to know the Courtlands better."

Amy went, but she dragged her feet and looked longingly over her shoulder at Marcy.

"Things aren't going to go smoothly," Brant told Marcy when they were out of hearing distance. "I had your Little Sis pegged right from the beginning."

"This is her first time seeing her father with another woman," Marcy defended.

And when Gil returned shortly, he reported, "Well, Marcy, you said this was neutral ground, an excellent place for me to bring Wanda and her children to meet Amy. But right now, I think I'm in the middle of a war zone. Amy's about to explode and Wanda to burst into tears."

"Let's ride over to Alamo Village," Brant proposed. "At least the children will be entertained while they're getting acquainted, and they'll have plenty of room to expend some of their energy."

Marcy agreed.

"I guess so," Gil responded tentatively. "It'll be a little tight, but we can all ride in the van."

The afternoon was tense for everyone. Amy rejected all Wanda's overtures. She pressed her small frame against Marcy and would not budge from her side. It seemed as if she were determined not to have a good time and to make sure no one else did, either.

Embarrassed by Amy's behavior and sympathetic to Wanda's apparent discomfort, Marcy finally took Amy aside. "Amy, you're going to have to shape up. This isn't the kind of behavior I expect from my Little Sister."

"They're messing up my trip."

"No," Marcy argued. "You're doing that all on your own. You can have as much fun as you want. It's up to you."

In part Amy responded to Marcy's admonition. She stopped clinging to Marcy, but she continued to shun Wanda. When Wanda walked into a building, Amy would walk out. By the time they arrived at the cantina where they stopped for a cold drink and to see the country-and-western show, Gil had lost patience with Amy. He made her sit between him and Wanda.

"I'd rather sit by Marcy." She moved to the other table.

"Amy—" Gil's voice was tight with frustration.

Wanda laid a hand over his. "Don't reprimand her in public. Too much coercion so soon can result in her hating and resenting me. Give her some time, Gil."

He had known this first meeting between Amy and Wanda would be difficult, but he hadn't envisioned it being like this. It disappointed him to see Amy react so badly.

"We have fifteen minutes before the show begins," Wanda said to him. "I want to buy Bebe a gift while we're here at Alamo Village. I think I'll go look through the gift shop now." She looked at Amy. "Would you like to go with me?"

"Who's Bebe?" Amy asked, without answering Wanda's question.

"She's my stepmother."

Amy contemplated her for a second before she inquired, "How long have you had a stepmother?"

"Since I was eight," Wanda replied. "I was a year younger than you when my father remarried."

"Do you like Bebe?" Amy questioned.

"Yes, and I also love her."

"More than your mother?"

"No. She and my mother are two different people, and I feel differently about each of them. Why don't you come with me?'' Wanda suggested. "I'll tell you all about Bebe and me.''

Amy continued to study Wanda for a moment before she nodded her head and rose. Gil could not suppress a smile of relief. Together Amy and Wanda left the cantina and walked across the dirt street to the gift shop. Wanda opened the door, and they entered.

"My mother was killed in an automobile accident,'' Wanda began. "Like you, I had no brothers or sisters, and for a few years after my mother died, it was only Daddy and me.''

"Like me and Daddy?''

"Exactly like you and your father," Wanda confirmed. "One day as we were eating breakfast, my father told me he was lonely without my mother. He had met a woman and wanted to start dating her.''

At that Amy moved away from Wanda to the other side of the store. Wanda hoped she hadn't pushed Amy too fast. She continued to look at souvenirs. Finally Amy returned.

"What are you going to buy?'' she asked.

"Bebe collects key rings,'' Wanda said. "I always try to find her an unusual one when I go somewhere. Why? Have you found something you think she would like?''

"No, I just wondered.'' Amy wandered around again and a few moments later, called out, "Here they are, Mrs. Courtland.''

Wanda joined Amy but didn't continue her story. She searched through the rings, hoping she could find one Bebe did not have.

"Most of these are about Texas and the Alamo and Alamo Village,'' Amy said. "Do you think Bebe would like them?''

"Here's one." Wanda pulled it off the pegged rack. "What do you think of it?"

Amy took the rectangular-shaped metal and held it in her palm, studying it. It was white enamel with bluebonnets painted on it on one side; the words Alamo Village were inscribed on the other.

"Does she use the key rings," Amy questioned, "or just look at them?"

"If she really takes a fancy to one, she'll use it, but mostly she collects them. One year for Christmas, my father had a special cabinet built for her so she could display her favorites." Wanda smiled fondly as she remembered. "That Christmas Daddy and I shopped for two special rings for her. Bebe was so pleased, she cried when she opened the gift."

"Where does she keep the cabinet?" Amy asked.

"In the living room," Wanda answered, then said to the saleswoman, "I'll take this one."

"Where does Bebe live?"

"In Dallas, not far from me," Wanda explained. "When you and your father come to visit me, I'll introduce you to her."

"All my grandmothers are in heaven," Amy stated.

Wanda smiled. "Then Bebe can be your sort-of-grandmother."

Amy grinned. "I'd like that."

"You'll like Bebe," Wanda told her. "She's a special lady. When my father and she first started dating, she sat me down and we had a long talk. She told me that no one could ever take my mother's place. She said if my father and she fell in love and married, she wouldn't try to be my mother. She did promise, however, to be the very best stepmother in the world. She said we would make lot of mistakes, but as long as we loved and forgave one another, we could make our family work.''

''Did you believe her?'

''No. I was distrustful at first. I figured she was out to take my father away from me. But soon I learned that their marriage included me. Bebe loved me enough to want to be my stepmother. In fact, right after she and my father started dating, she and I decided what I should call her. She didn't want me to call her by her first name, Belinda, nor did she want me to call her Mrs. Griffin. Between the two of us we came up with a special name for her—Bebe.''

After Wanda and Amy had left the gift shop, Amy questioned bluntly, ''Are you and my father dating?''

''Not exactly, since most of our time together is spent taking care of business. But we'd like to,'' Wanda said. ''That's one reason why we wanted all of us to meet and get to know one another. I also wanted to let you see how much I like your father.''

''Are you going to marry him?''

''I don't know,'' Wanda replied choosing her words carefully. ''It's possible. Both of us want a chance to find out if we're in love and really want to get married.''

''My father loved my mother,'' Amy declared.

''Yes, I'm sure he did, but our hearts are big enough that we can love more than one person.''

WHEN AMY AND WANDA returned, the tension seemed to have eased. Amy was friendlier to the woman, and the remainder of their trip went smoothly. By late afternoon, they returned to the fort. Marcy and Brant, wanting to be by themselves, asked

Gil to let them out at the Visitor's Center. Amy seemed content to stay with her father. "See you later," she said to Marcy, waving as the van pulled away.

"While we're here," Brant told her, "I'll call Shepherd and see if he's heard from Danny. I'm rather curious."

"Me, too," Marcy replied. "I want to know that Colby Zacharias isn't my new partner."

"Do you think Danny would sell before the deadline he gave you?"

Marcy nodded. She wished she didn't have such a low opinion of her cousin, but she did.

She and Brant entered the Visitor's Center, and Marcy sat down on the sofa while he went to place his call at the public phone.

"Sorry to bother you on a Saturday afternoon," Brant began when Shepherd Hayden answered the phone, "but I was wondering if you had heard from Danny Galvan on the construction company?"

"Yes, I did," Shepherd confirmed, and spent the next few minutes comparing the dossier Danny had sent them with the one they had already acquired.

"Call and make an offer," Brant instructed. "Use your own judgment about the starting range, but keep it within the figures we discussed the other day."

"I get the feeling that he's not too keen on selling to you," Shepherd warned. "Not that he's said anything outright."

"I got that feeling myself," Brant admitted. "But I still want you to make an offer. Start with the figure I gave you—the one he quoted to Marcy—then go on up to my ceiling."

"Considering this report," Shepherd questioned, "do you think that's a wise move, Brant? Why not let this Zacharias have it?"

"Because I want it," Brant answered shortly.

"This is too risky," Shepherd cautioned. "We don't usually touch companies like this."

Shepherd had a right to be concerned; it wasn't like Brant to engage in such high-risk undertakings.

"Brant, you're not letting your emotions override your judgment, are you?"

"Yes, Shepherd," Brant confessed. "This time it's heart over head, but my head is in full agreement with my heart."

"Whatever you say," was Shepherd's dry comment.

"Tell him I want an answer by Saturday after next. I'd like it sooner, but certainly no later."

"Do you want anything else on a Saturday afternoon?"

"What about the dossier on the Estella Esteban school?"

"I haven't received it yet."

"Call me when you get the information."

"You got it."

Reverting to business that directly affected the running of Holland Enterprises, the two men talked for a while before Brant rang off. Then he went over to Marcy, who was looking at the schedule of events posted on the bulletin board.

"Amy was right," she said. "There's a dance at the Las Moras Inn tonight. Would you like to go?"

"Is that the most exciting activity at the fort tonight?"

When she nodded, they grinned at each other, and he said, "Then it's a dancing we'll go, Miss Galvan."

Hand in hand, they walked the short distance from the Visitor's Center to the hotel rooms while Brant repeated the part of his conversation with Shepherd that dealt with the buying of Galvan Construction.

When Marcy opened the door to her room she found Gil standing there, glaring at Amy. Wanda stood to the side. Both of the adults looked to be at their wit's end. Amy ran to Marcy.

"I don't want to sleep with Wanda and Elana. I don't know them."

"Amelia Calderon," Gil said impatiently, "I have been most lenient with you today, and you've behaved like a spoiled brat. You've treated Wanda and her children badly. Now, you are going to sleep in the room with Wanda and Elana."

"Gil—" Wanda began, but Gil waved a silencing hand at her.

"Pack your clothes, Amy."

Marcy was glad that Gil had taken charge.

"I don't want to go, Daddy." Tears flowed down her cheeks. "I came here with Marcy, and I want to stay with her."

"Amy—" Wanda went over to the child and put her hands on Amy's shoulder "—if you want to spend the night in Marcy's room and your father will let you, it's all right with me. I understand."

Amy shrugged Wanda's hand from her shoulder. She glared at her father, then at Wanda. "I don't like you." She looked at Brant. "I don't like you, either. Y'all want to take Daddy and Marcy away from me. I wish Daddy had never met you, Mrs. Courtland, and I wish Marcy had never met you, Brant."

"Amy!" Gil shouted.

She turned to her father. "Daddy, why can't you love Marcy? I'd like to have her for my stepmother."

Marcy felt Amy's pain. The child didn't mean what she was saying; she was hurting and fighting desperately to keep her life from changing. But this was a matter for her father to deal with.

"Gil, Wanda," she told them, "I'm going to leave the three of you alone. I'll take a few of my things I need to get ready for the dance tonight. If you want me, I'll be in Brant's room."

"No, Marcy." Amy clung to her. "Don't leave me. Tell Daddy you want me to stay with you. Don't let them take me away from you."

"Amy—" Marcy gently removed the child's arm from around her and knelt so that she was at eye level with her "—I love you, but I can't come between you and your father. Right now, you and he have some problems to straighten out. I'll always be here for you as your Big Sister."

Gil caught Amy in his arms and held her. "Thanks, Marcy."

Marcy hurriedly packed her small cosmetic bag with underwear, stockings and cosmetics. Then she grabbed the dress she planned to wear to the dance and she and Brant walked next door to his room.

She should have felt good; certainly she had fewer worries. Brant was going to buy the other half of Galvan Construction, and she had let Amy know that she was going to be no more than Amy's Big Sister. But she was concerned about the child.

Marcy had the feeling that as soon as Amy grew to know Wanda and Elana, her needs would change. Marcy, as Big Sister, would still be an important person in Amy's life, but the focus of their relationship would alter. Marcy had anticipated this change. She and Amy had become really close and nothing would change that. Marcy was sure that she and Amy would have many fun times in the future.

"Don't worry about Amy," Brant reassured. "Gil and Wanda will take care of her."

"I know," Marcy replied. "I just wish change was easier to handle. I know it's good—even necessary and inevitable—yet it hurts."

Drawing her to him Brant held her in a tight embrace. "I'm glad we're alone," he said. "I've been wanting to hold you all day."

Marcy raised her face and he lowered his. Their lips touched tentatively at first, then more fully as the kiss deepened with desire. He moved his hands down her back and tugged the shirt from her jeans, then slipped his palms beneath the material to touch her warm, smooth skin.

Marcy moaned softly and felt her body tighten with need. She pressed against the hard length of Brant's physique, anticipating the merging of their passion, their becoming one.

"Marcy," he murmured as he strewed tiny kisses across her face, "I love you."

His hands slid between their bodies, and she felt his fingers unbuttoned her blouse. She moved away slightly, pulling the shirt off her shoulders and letting it fall to the floor at their feet.

Brant stepped back to gaze at her. In the shaft of sunlight that made its way through the crack between the drapes, she seemed to be surrounded by a golden aura and looked almost ethereal. She moved toward him.

Then all talk ceased as they created their own magical world and made wondrous love to each other.

LATER WHEN BRANT and Marcy left his room on their way to the dance, they saw no sign of Gil, Amy or the Courtlands. Enjoying the cool of the evening, they walked to Las Moras Inn, where they spent the evening dancing to golden oldies from the previous decade.

While returning to their rooms, Brant described his plans for the future and asked how she felt about turning the actual running of the company over to Joe Alexander so she could travel with Brant.

She didn't answer immediately. Instead she suggested "Let's walk awhile. We need to talk, and I'd like to ensure our privacy. I have no idea what we're going to find when we return to our rooms."

Brant caught her hand in his, and they retraced their steps, passing by Las Moras Inn and moving on toward the pool. They sat down on one of the benches beneath the dipping boughs of a pecan tree to enjoy the solitude. Moonlight made dancing reflections on the surface of the water and filtered through the thick foliage, dappling a design like silver lace on the ground around them.

"Brant," Marcy began, "I think I've loved you all my life, and when you told me you feel the same way about me, I was the happiest person alive."

"Why do I have a feeling there's a but to this?" he asked.

"I'm very happy," Marcy explained. "But I also have grave concerns. Sometimes love is not enough to bind people together in marriage."

"You don't think our love is great enough?" he questioned.

"I hope it is," she answered, "but I'm not sure. Both of us say we're willing to give ourselves time and that we're trying to see things from each other's perspectives, but are we really? I sometimes think we're just going through the *motions* of a compromise and I begin to doubt that either of us is really willing to do that."

Brant started to say something, but Marcy rushed on.

"Of course, it hasn't come to that yet. I still owe you and New York a visit. But deep down I have the feeling that each of us expects the other to make the compromise."

Brant took her hands in his and held them. "Sweetheart, I believe in our love enough to know that we'll make the right choices. Like you, I'm not sure what that choice will be, but we'll make it—together. And I assure you, we're doing more than going through the motions of compromise. We're searching for happiness, we're creating our future."

"I don't want to go into marriage with the idea that it can end in divorce if we don't make it," Marcy declared. "I really am an old-fashioned woman, Brant. I want a marriage that's going to last, and I want all the little things that go along with it—children and a home. And I want the opportunity to choose whether I work solely at home or away from home."

"I agree with you," he said, then asked. "Does my having been divorced worry you? Is it causing you to have second thoughts?"

She shook her head. "No. I just want to make sure that both of us are working from the same understanding and on the same foundation."

"We are," he assured her.

Rising, they kissed, then turned back in the direction of the hotel. They continued to talk about their plans for the future.

"I want four children," Marcy stated.

"I'll settle for two, but I'm more than willing to negotiate on more," Brant replied. "That's a decision that can be made after we see how we handle the first two. Don't you think?"

"It's negotiable unless we should have two sets of twins the first two pregnancies or a set of quadruplets the first time!"

Their conversation was light, enlivened with laughter. When they had reached onto the upstairs porch of the hotel, they saw Wanda and Gil sitting close together in the swing.

"How was your evening?" Wanda inquired.

"Delightful," Marcy answered. "How's Amy?"

"Actually, she's doing quite well," Wanda told them. "After you left, Gil had a long talk with her, and she grudgingly moved in with Elana and me. Then when she discovered that Elana also had a Barbie-doll collection, she instantly warmed. They talked dolls all evening, then they discovered a movie on television that both of them wanted to see, and things smoothed out."

"Of course, this is only the beginning," Gil cautioned. "But I think we've successfully jumped our first major hurdle."

The four of them continued to chat until late. Finally, however, they said their good-nights.

Brant was awake long after Marcy had gone to sleep. Easing out of bed so as not to waken her, he slipped into his jeans and walked onto the porch. Moonlight spilled over him, illuminating the porch and its furniture with a silver sheen.

Although he and Marcy were in agreement about what they wanted from the future and from their involvement, he was worried. She had her doubts about their working things out so that they could get married, and he was afraid of losing her—of losing her before she ever really became his.

He was extremely vulnerable when it came to Marcy. From the time he was a small child, from the time his mother abandoned his father and him, Brant had never allowed anyone to get close enough to influence his feelings—not even Glenna, whom he had once believed he loved. As a child, he had promised himself, that he would never allow anyone to hurt him as his mother had.

When he graduated from university, he began his pursuit of wealth and the security he believed it afforded. Now he had found something money could not buy and could not guarantee—love.

He had struggled with himself during the past week, thinking about buying the half interest in Marcy's company. Saying he would do it was easier than accomplishing it. But tonight, he had confessed to Shepherd that he was buying the company for Marcy. Although as Shepherd pointed out, it was a chancy undertaking, Brant didn't regret his decision. He had thought long and hard about buying Lonzo's half of the construction company. If he didn't buy it, he knew that Marcy would likely lose her shares—if not sooner, then little by little. All he had to do was wait.

But no matter what he wanted personally for Marcy and himself, he didn't want Marcy to lose her company. He wanted her to choose to be a part of his life because it was what she *desired*. He wanted no circumstance to force her into marriage with him. She must come to him of her own free will.

She had indicated tonight that she didn't feel that either one of them would be willing to make a compromise. At times, he felt that way also.

A cloud covered the moon, momentarily dousing the brilliant light. Brant returned to the room and locked the door. Easing into bed, he cupped his body to Marcy's and held her close.

He would not lose her!

CHAPTER TWELVE

THE NEXT MORNING Marcy and Brant went to Las Moras Inn for breakfast. As they approached the breakfast buffet, Gil called out and waved to them.

"Join us," he invited. "There's room for two more."

After Marcy and Brant selected their food, they sat at the table beside Amy. Kevin was describing the horror movie Drake and he had watched, and everyone else was listening.

"And then the creature went back into the swampt—"

"Swamp," Elana corrected.

"Into the *swampt.*" Kevin glared at her. "He stopped and turned around, waved, then disappeared, and the movie ended."

"Kevin," Wanda said gently, "that was a good summary of the movie, but you did mispronounce the word *swamp.* It doesn't have a *t,* on the end of it."

"I know, Mother." He filled his mouth with food and chewed.

"Then pronounce it correctly the next time."

"Yes, ma'am."

"What are the two of you planning for today?" Gil asked.

"We're going to do some horseback riding before we head for home," Marcy replied.

"Oh, Marcy!" Amy exclaimed. "May I go with you? I'd like to see Daisy again, and this time I'll bring something for her to eat?"

"Sugar," Kevin piped up. "I saw them feed a horse some sugar cubes in a movie once. The cowboy let the horse eat the sugar out of one hand while he rubbed the horse's neck with his other hand. He was waiting for a gold shipment from—"

Wanda laid a hand on Kevin. "We don't need the summary of another movie. One was enough."

"Ah, Mother." He grinned, took a bite of biscuit and slid back in the chair.

Marcy smiled at both of the children. "I'm sure Daisy would rather have sugar cubes, but Erny frowns on feeding our animals sweets, so she'll have to settle for carrots."

"Will you take me with you?" Amy asked a second time.

"Not this morning," Marcy replied.

Clearly Amy was disappointed, but Marcy didn't change her mind or her answer. This was a day she intended to spend with Brant, giving her full attention to him. He had been wonderful about traveling all this distance to be with her and about sharing the weekend not only with Amy but with the entire Calderon-Courtland clan.

Brant laid his hand over hers. Leaning close to her ear, he whispered, "If you're doing this just for me, thanks. But I don't mind if she joins us. It would give Gil and Wanda some time to themselves, especially if we invite all the children to go with us."

Pleased by Brant's suggestion, Marcy announced, "Looks like I'm overruled. How would all of you, except Gil and Wanda, like to go horseback riding?"

Both boys' eyes lit up.

"Can we, Mother?" Drake asked.

"Huh, Mother?" Kevin echoed.

Wanda looked at Gil, who nodded. "You sure can," she said.

"How about you, Elana?" Marcy questioned. "Do you want to go with us?"

"Yes, but I don't know how to ride."

"I'll teach you," Marcy promised, glad she and Amy were getting better acquainted with the Courtland children. They were happy, well-behaved children who could have a good effect on Amy. Marcy hoped they would be playing a much larger role in her Little Sister's life from now on.

"Erny isn't going to like having so many people at the ranch," Amy grumbled. "He said he liked it better when it was just him and the horses."

"Well," Kevin declared, "than means you can't go, either, because then it's not just him and the horses."

"I can go, too," Amy retorted, "because I know Erny and Daisy, and both of them like me."

Marcy leaned over and gave Amy a quick hug. "Well, Erny's going to have to accept all of us today. Besides, the horses need a workout, and this will be an opportunity to give all of them exercise at the same time."

Throughout the remainder of the meal, Amy was withdrawn. Everyone ignored her silence. Kevin and Drake kept up the flow of conversation with questions about the ranch and horses. After breakfast the children raced to the Bronco and were standing there waiting for Marcy and Brant, who lingered in front of the restaurant with Gil and Wanda.

"Thank you for taking the children with you," Wanda said to Marcy and Brant. "It's seldom Gil and I have an opportunity to be by ourselves unless we're working. Not that I'm complaining. I wouldn't exchange my children for the world. But dating is certainly more complicated when you've been married before and have children."

Brant twined his fingers through Marcy's. "That's what I figured. Besides, I want to impress Marcy with my ability to handle children. I learned last night that when Marcy marries, she expects to have a large family. At least four children. This should give us an idea of what we're dealing with."

"Brant!" Marcy's exclamation blended with soft laughter.

"Marcy!" Amy called. "We're ready."

"Yeah," Kevin chimed in, "we're ready."

Marcy and Brant said their goodbyes and went to the Bronco, leaving Gil and Wanda standing in front of Las Moras Inn.

"Who's going to drive?" Amy asked. She curled her hand through the door handle on the passenger side.

"Marcy," Brant answered, "since she knows the way and can get there without help."

"Well—" Amy opened the door "—I'll sit in front between you and Marcy, and Elana, Drake and Kevin can sit in the back."

"That's not a bad suggestion." Brant opened the back door. "But I have a better one—" he picked Amy up by the waist and swung her through the air "—one that's fairer for all of us. The adults will sit in the front seat, the children in the back. Right here."

He deposited her beside Elana. "Now, all of you buckle up for safety.

"I WISH I COULD GO with you." Erny pressed his hand against the small of his back and grimaced; then he reached up and adjusted the brim of his hat. "But I gotta get that fence up. Sure don't want them horses to get loose."

"Show me where the fence is down," Brant suggested, "and I'll put it up for you. I'll be better at that than riding a horse."

Marcy looked at him in surprise. She knew he could ride because he had told her so. When she opened her mouth to question him, he shook his head and continued to speak.

"Besides, Erny, you know the terrain and can make sure these city slickers don't get lost."

"Well," the older man drawled, "what you say makes sense, but putting up a fence is mighty hard work." He lowered his hands and again massaged his back.

"I earned my way through university doing mighty hard work." Brant glanced at Marcy. "Maybe it's time I returned to my roots. And I'd rather you were with Marcy and the children. I'd feel they were safer if you went along."

"Well—" his countenance brightening, Erny looked at Marcy "—it'll be pretty hard work, but if that's what you want—"

"It's what I want," Brant said.

Erny shoved his hat back on his head and scrutinized Brant. "Do you know how to use a posthole digger?"

Brant laughed. "I figure I do. By the time I was sixteen years old, Lonzo and Rubin Galvan had me working for the construction company. My first job was to sink postholes." He shook his head and smiled reminiscently. "At the time, I believed there must have been a hundred of them. I may be a little rusty to start with, but I have a feeling those skills will return real quick. Now, if you'll tell me which horse for which child, I'll help you and Marcy saddle them."

"Come on," Marcy called. "Let's go inside and pick out our horses."

Laughing and talking, the children skipped ahead of Marcy and Brant to look at the horses and to make their selections. Erny, moving at a slower pace, followed.

"You can't have that one or this one," Amy said. "That one is Bluebonnet, and she belongs to Marcy. This one is mine. Marcy let me ride her yesterday."

"I want this one," Kevin said. "I like gray horses."

"Good choice," Brant said, looking at Erny, who leaned against the stall.

The old man nodded. "Real good for a cowboy like this 'un. Brant, you and Marcy help the kids bring their mounts to me one at a time, and I'll show them how to saddle their own horses. If they're gonna ride 'em, they need to know how to take care of 'em."

Later under Erny's supervision, the children led the animals out of the barn.

"Now, since we're gonna hafta help Brant git that truck loaded so's he can dig them holes," the caretaker said. "We'll need to make sure the horses don't wander. We'll just tie the reins to this hitching post like this."

Marcy and Brant walked out of the barn together.

"You don't really have to mend the fence," Marcy said softly. "And neither does Erny. It's not nearly as bad as he's making out, and even if it were, he knows I'll hire someone to do it. He just putters around with things like this."

"I'll do it," Brant said. "It's a matter of pride with him, and this way, we've helped him save face. He's afraid you're going to think he's incapable of watching the place if he can't hold his own."

Marcy had always loved Brant; but now, that love rose to new heights as a result of his sensitivity and kindness to Erny.

With humor in his voice, Brant murmured, "I do have a confession to make. I haven't dug a posthole in nearly twenty years. I'm not really sure I know how anymore."

Marcy reached out and squeezed his biceps. "Or maybe it's that you don't have the strength to do it anymore. Too much easy living."

"That, too," he agreed.

"You'd better take some thick gloves."

"Tonight may be a Ben-Gay ointment night," Brant warned.

Marcy laughed with him, and they walked over to the pickup to join Erny. Following instructions, Brant loaded the equipment and fencing onto the truck. Erny also gave him a pair of work gloves and an old Stetson. Last, he handed him a map with directions clearly marked to indicate the area where the fence was down.

"Now, let's see if we can git these young'uns mounted, so's we can begin our ride. Amy," Erny said, "come here. Since you've already done this, I'll use you as an example. The rest of you watch real close how she holds her body, and I help her get her foot into the stirrup so she can swing that right leg over real smooth like.''

''Me next,'' Kevin shouted. ''Me, next.''

''Right,'' Brant said. ''I'll help you. Marcy you help Elana, and Erny can give Drake a hand.''

While Erny instructed them on how to hold and use the reins, Marcy gave Brant a quick goodbye kiss and swung into the saddle. Grinning, she said, ''You'll have to unhitch the horses.''

''I'll get you back later for this,'' he teased.

''We'll see you later.'' Erny slipped on his gloves, mounted his horse and led the young riders single file out of the corral. All the time he was calmly calling out instructions, reassuring the children and their mounts.

Marcy, riding in the rear, blew Brant a goodbye kiss. He stood beside the truck and waved until she was out of sight.

As they traveled, Erny pointed out landmarks. Although Marcy had heard Erny's tales of the Texas frontier during the 1920s and 1930s many times, she was as fascinated with this narration as she had been with the first. After about an hour, they reached a thick growth of underbrush—a mixture of cacti, mesquite bushes and trees, and scattered scrub oaks— sturdy but gnarled oaks that grew low to the ground. Then they entered a wooded area.

''What's that?'' Kevin shouted as a small animal scurried through the brush.

''Just a rabbit,'' Erny called over his shoulder. ''Keep calm. If you git scared, your horse will know and will git real scared too. Just keep an eye out. You may see more wild animals. Maybe some turkeys and deer. There's plenty of 'em out here.''

Excited, the children looked all around them, straining to see. Every rustle in the underbrush raised their expectations.

"Look!" Amy shouted and pointed. "Over here! I see something. What is it, Erny?"

"It's deer," Drake yelled. "It's a deer!"

Marcy peered into the underbrush and saw the small deer, its ears erect, twitching slightly, its head cocked, its golden brown eyes darting back and forth. As they neared, it darted to the side, stopped, and looked around. Clearly it was frightened; it snorted. Just then one of the horses stepped on a piece of dry wood and the crack resounded through the wooded area. The deer bolted through the brush and across the path immediately in front of Amy who was riding Daisy.

Frightened, Daisy reared. Amy screamed.

"Marcy!"

The terrified horse reared and the girl fell from the saddle, her foot caught in the stirrup.

"Marcy!" she screamed. "Help me! Somebody help me!"

"I'm coming, Amy." Marcy dug her heels into Bluebonnet's sides and rushed to Amy's side. "I'll see if I can grab the reins. The rest of you hold on to yours and stay here."

Marcy rode around the other children, who were watching in shocked silence. Amy screamed out in pain as the horse headed toward the thicket. Her shoulders and back brushed against the cacti and the prickly underbrush. She flailed her arms, reaching for the reins that dangled over the horse's back and neck. By this time, Erny was riding toward Amy from the other direction.

With the branches of the mesquite tree slapping her in the face, the prickly undergrowth catching and tugging at her jeans, Marcy veered off the path and moved to the side of Daisy, grabbing the reins and stopping the horse.

Kevin who was immediately behind Amy, now tumbled from his saddle to land beside her. He leaped to his feet.

"You're gonna be all right, Amy," he said. "I'm gonna take care of you. I'm not gonna let this horse hurt you." He began to untangle her shoe from the stirrup.

"Amy—" Marcy dismounted and passed the reins to Erny. "are you all right?"

Amy lay still on the ground. Her screaming had ccased, but the silence was even more terrifying. The child's eyes were open and she looked blankly at Marcy, who tenderly wiped blood and tears from her cheeks.

"Amy," Marcy said, gently touching the scratches on Amy's face. She examined her shoulders, looking at the torn material of her shirt. "Where are you hurting, darling?"

Amy only looked at Marcy; her eyes were vacant.

"She's not gonna die, is she?" Kevin asked, his face drained of color.

"No." Marcy's hands again quickly moved over Amy's body as she checked for breaks and lacerations. She pulled twigs out of Amy's hair and brushed dirt from her shoulders and legs.

Having dismounted by this time, Elana and Drake put their arms around Kevin and crowded around Marcy and Amy. Amy looked at each one of them, then began to sob convulsively. Marcy pulled her into her arms and hugged her tightly, reassuringly.

"Is she going to be all right?" Elana asked, her voice no more than a whisper. Her eyes were large and filled with fear.

"Sure, she is," Marcy responded with more conviction than she felt.

"Marcy—" Amy sobbed. "Oh, Marcy, Daisy hurt me!"

"Not on purpose, darling," Marcy soothed. "We frightened the deer, and the deer frightened Daisy."

"My shoulders hurt," Amy said. "And my head. My head hit the ground lots of times."

Marcy's hands examined Amy's head, and she found a small bump.

"How are we going to get her back?" Kevin questioned. "Is she gonna have to ride Daisy again?"

"No," Erny answered. "I don't think she should. We're not sure how bad she's hurt."

"What do you suggest?" Marcy asked quietly.

"Since I know the country better than y'all," Erny replied, "I'll ride back and get Brant. We can make better time in a car. Keep her still until I return."

"What about us?" Kevin demanded.

Erny put his hand on Kevin's shoulder. "Marcy may need some help and she certainly needs the company, so I want the three of you to stay with her."

Kevin straightened his shoulders. "All right. We'll stay here and take care of Marcy. You know, I'm the one who pulled Amy's foot from the stirrup."

Erny nodded. "You sure did."

"And I probably saved her life," the boy continued. "If Daisy had run away again, she would have drug Amy with her."

"That's right," Erny agreed. "You've really been a brave boy."

Soon Erny was gone, and Marcy and the children waited. It seemed to Marcy an interminable length of time passed before Brant and Erny returned in the Bronco. Brant leaned over Amy and examined her.

"No broken bones," he announced and Marcy nodded.

"Bruises and maybe a concussion," Marcy said.

"Amy," Brant warned gently. "I'm going to have to pick you up and put you in the Bronco. I'll be careful as I can, but it may hurt a little bit."

"Okay," she whispered. Dirt, mixed with dried blood and tears, streaked her face. "Does my daddy know?"

"Yes." Brant eased her into his arms and carried her to the Bronco. "Erny and I stopped by the cottage and called him. Your father will be waiting at the doctor's office for us."

Marcy sat in the back, letting Amy rest her head in her lap. The three Courtland children rode up front, and Erny was left to lead the horses back to the corral. Marcy promised to call him later to let him know how Amy was doing.

As the Bronco jostled over the dirt roads, Marcy thought they would never get to town. Occasionally Amy moaned, but for the most part she was a good patient. Marcy stroked Amy's head and kept reassuring her that everything was going to be all right. Finally Brant parked in front of the small building on the main street of Bracketville. The doors opened, and Gil and Wanda came rushing out.

"How is she?" Gil demanded.

"I don't think she's badly hurt," Brant replied. He opened the door and slid out.

By this time Gil had jerked open the back door and scooped Amy into his arms. Murmuring soothingly to her, he carried her inside the building.

"How did it happen?" Wanda asked.

"I saw it," Kevin broke in, following on Gil's heels. "A deer ran across the trail and scared her horse. He took off and she fell out of the saddle and her foot caught in the stirrup. He dragged her for miles and miles. We hoped she wasn't gonna die."

"It *seemed* like miles, Kevin," Elana said, "but it was only a few feet."

Kevin nodded. "Then I dug my heels into my horse and took off after her. I was right behind Marcy. I'm the one who rescued her, Mother. I pulled her foot out of the stirrup, and Erny said maybe the horse would have run away again, and if it had, she would have been drug with it. But I moved her foot, so she was all right. I did it like this." He demonstrated his grip several times. "It was hard to do, but I did it, and I saved her. That's what Erny said."

An elderly man came to the door. "Bring her in and let's see what we have here."

Gil laid Amy on the examining table.

"Hello, young lady," he said. "I'm Dr. Woods— you know, like furniture."

Amy smiled; Kevin and Drake giggled, causing the doctor to raise his head and look at them over his glasses that rested on the tip of his nose. His blue eyes twinkling, he looked at the crowd who stood in the doorway watching him. Then he turned back to Amy.

"I see I gotta be mighty careful here. We got a lot of people watching to see that I don't hurt you." He smiled gently. "What's your name, honey?"

"Amy."

"Well, I'll tell you what, we'll ask everybody but your parents to leave the room, so's I can examine you."

"I want my daddy." Tears flowed down Amy's cheeks.

"I'm here, baby," Gil reassured and reached out to clasp her hands in his. "I'm not going to leave you."

"Do you want me to stay with you?" Wanda asked.

Gil shook his head. "It'll probably be better for you to be with the kids. They're pretty uptight about the whole incident, I would imagine."

Putting his arms around Marcy and Wanda, Brant led them into the waiting room. Quietly they talked about what happened. Finally the door opened, and Amy and Gil walked out of the office. Dr. Woods followed.

"Good news," he announced. "Miss Amy sustained no permanent damage—merely superficial cuts and bruises. She's mostly shaken up. Because she's been such a good patient, I gave her some candy. Being the nice person she is, she asked me to give each of you some. And being the nice person I am, here it is." He held out the glass jar and passed it around. "Which one of you is Kevin?"

"Me." The youngest Courtland sank his hand in the goody jar and brought out two suckers. He deliberated on which one to choose.

"You did a fine job of getting her foot out of that stirrup, young man. It's a good thing you were there to help your sister. Take both of those suckers as a reward for your bravery.''

Kevin beamed, and his chest seemed to swell to several times its normal size. Marcy was surprised that Amy didn't correct the doctor about Kevin's being her brother.

''Thank you, Kevin,'' Amy said.

Marcy was proud of her Little Sister. She looked at Gil and saw that he was, too.

''It was nothing.'' Kevin shrugged the compliment aside, but his cheeks were flushed with pleasure.

''It was a daring rescue,'' Marcy declared. ''Remember, I saw it, Kevin. Without any thought for your own safety, you pulled Amy's foot loose from the stirrup.''

Gil put his arm around Wanda and squeezed; she laid her head against his shoulder. Now that the danger was over, everybody began to relax. The children scurried outside ahead of the adults.

''I'm sorry Amy had an accident,'' Gil remarked, ''but it seems to be working in our favor. The children have taken a big step toward becoming friends. Maybe toward becoming a family.'' He gave Wanda a smile.

''We'll gather up our group,'' Gil added, ''and head on back to the fort.''

''Brant and I will see you later,'' Marcy replied. ''I promised Erny I'd call to let him know how Amy was.''

From the doctor's office, Marcy called Erny to let him know Amy wasn't hurt; then she and Brant drove over to the hotel to check out.

While Brant settled their bills, Marcy went to Wanda's room to say goodbye. She was about to speak when, through the door, she heard Amy talking.

"I really didn't mean it when I said I didn't like you," the child confessed.

"I know," Wanda answered. "You disliked what you thought I was going to do to you. You were afraid I'd take your father away from you."

Amy nodded. "Will you forgive me?"

"It's forgiven and forgotten." Wanda looked up and saw Marcy standing in the doorway. "Come on in."

"Brant and I are leaving as soon as we get our luggage packed." She smiled at Amy. "I didn't want to leave without giving my Little Sister a big hug."

Amy ran to Marcy and embraced her.

"I'm proud of you," Marcy told her. "You've really been super today. You're growing up."

"Thanks," Amy murmured. "I love you, Marcy."

"I love you," Marcy said, "and I admire you. Admitting you've been wrong and asking someone to forgive you takes a lot of courage."

NONA FERGUSON SAT across the breakfast table from Gil and Wanda after they returned from Fort Clark Springs Sunday evening. "I put off talking to you about this until the children were in bed," she said. "I guess I was hoping I wouldn't have to go into the hospital to have these tests done, but the doctor insists. He called yesterday and wants me in the hospital next Monday morning. He said at my age, he'd rather be sure than second-guess."

"Of course, I'm not worried about the outcome," Nona continued, "but I am worried about who's going to take care of Amy. No one's had her since she was born but me."

"I don't know what I'm going to do," Gil replied. "That's when we have the managerial meeting, and there's no way I can get out of that, not if I expect more promotions. I've been entirely too lax with Amy recently, taking off days when it wasn't necessary and switching my agenda with Robin."

"I looked in the classifieds yesterday and started calling people who advertised to be maids, housekeepers, and nannies," Nona told him. "None of them sounded good to me." She paused. "Then there's the day-care centers, but my baby has never been in one before."

Gil laughed dryly. "I'm sure Amy could survive but I don't know much about the centers."

Wanda, who has been listening to the conversation interjected, "Gil, I could help. Maybe this happening during the first week of summer vacation is good. Next Friday is the last day of school for my children, too, and I have some 'comp' days. I could bring them and stay with Amy until Nona is out of hospital, or at least until someone else can be found to stay with Amy." Wanda asked Nona, "How long will your tests take?"

"He figures no more than a week, unless they find something."

"I have that much time," Wanda said. "If Nona should have to stay longer, this would give you time to line up a babysitter."

"Honey—" Gil took her hand and squeezed it gently "—I hate for you to spend your 'comp' time here baby-sitting, and I know your kids aren't going to like spending their vacation like this."

"They'll love being here!" Wanda countered. "We'll all have a great time. There's no place they would enjoy going that Amy wouldn't like too. Roller skating, movies, swimming, miniature golf—there're enough activities for all of them. They'll be happy all week."

"What about getting to them?" Gil asked.

"I'm familiar with San Antonio," she reminded him. "Remember, I worked here for five years, and you have a car I can use. Also, Gil, this would give Amy and me an opportunity to become better acquainted."

"Sounds like a good idea to me." Nona pushed back in her chair and rose. "While you're thinking about it, I'm going to check on the clothes in the dryer."

He nodded and was quiet, evidently in deep thought.

"Gil, are you worried about leaving Amy in my care?" Wanda finally asked.

"I'm just a little worried about leaving you to deal with Amy. I know you've made inroads, but we have so much further to go. She's just recently moved from dislike to tolerance."

"That's why it will be good for me to stay here with her. Amy will see what everyday living with the Courtlands is like. I want do it, Gil. If you don't object."

After a thoughtful hesitation, he smiled. "I don't. I'm grateful that you would want to. Thank you."

CHAPTER THIRTEEN

SUNDAY NIGHT AFTER Marcy and Brant returned from Fort Clark Springs, she lay in bed in Brant's arms. The blinds were raised, the drapes drawn, and the moonlight spilled into the room through the sheer curtains.

"Europe?" Marcy questioned.

"Mm-hmm," Brant murmured.

"How long are you going to be gone this time?"

"Two weeks," he answered. "I'd like to give you an engagement ring when I return."

"I'd like that, too," she said softly, "but I think it's rather premature. We love each other, but we have some basic differences we must reconcile before we make a commitment of marriage."

"Namely where we're going to live?"

"Namely more."

Marcy slipped off the bed and went into the kitchen, returning shortly with a large bowl of ice cream. She snuggled up beside him and offered him one of the two spoons that she had brought with her.

"What did you mean by 'more'?"

"It wouldn't really matter where we lived," she explained, "we'd still have a long-distance marriage. You're always on the go."

"You could travel with me."

Marcy set the bowl on the nightstand and turned to him. "That would be all right until the novelty wore off, but what about later, Brant? What's going to happen when we have a family? I want my children to have a father who's going to be home with them, who's going to take them to practice ball and to roller skate and to ballet lessons."

Brant caught a strand of hair in his hand and pulled it through his fingers. Shepherd had always accused him of being a workaholic and of being obsessed with the company to the point of not being able to delegate. While Brant had acknowledged this as the truth, the accusation had not bothered him in the past. He enjoyed traveling; he, himself, enjoyed being in control and pressing for the best deal.

"I don't want to stop traveling altogether," he told her. "But I can delegate some of the work so that I'm home most of the time."

"You can," Marcy pointed out. "But will you? For so long, Brant, you've kept a tight rein on your company. Can you begin to delegate now?"

"Yes," he declared. "I'm not going to lose you, Marcy."

MONDAY MORNING, a week later, Marcy was sitting behind her desk at the office working on the one, five, and ten-year company projections to give to Brant, so he would know the direction in which Marcy wanted to steer Galvan Construction in the future. After an hour of bending over her desk, meticulously going over the calculations and projections she and Joe had made, she put down her pencil and leaned back to look out the window.

Although Brant called every evening, she missed him. She marked off the days on her calender until he would return. Time seemed to fly when Brant was here with her and to drag in between those visits.

A cab drove up; the door opened and Amy climbed out, her suitcase in hand. Surprised, Marcy rose, walked out of the office and down the sidewalk to the parking lot. "What are you doing here?" she asked.

The driver opened her door, climbed out and leaned against the car, folding her hands on the top. "Your little sister was on Broadway when I picked her up. I wasn't sure whether to bring her here or take her to the police station. If I hadn't found you here, that's where I would have taken her. No good comes from a kid this little wandering the streets."

"You did the right thing," Marcy responded. "Thank you."

"She owes me fifteen bucks. She said you'd pay me."

"You'll have to pay her, Marcy," Amy said. "I don't have any money."

Marcy reached into her pocket and pulled out her wallet, handing a twenty-dollar bill to the driver. "Keep the change," she told her, "and thanks for bringing her here."

"You need to talk to her about taking these little jaunts," the woman admonished, shaking her head.

Marcy caught Amy by the hand and guided her into the office.

"What's the meaning of this?" she demanded. She was so frightened her voice sounded as if she was angry. "Don't you know better than to be out on your own like this? Amy, anything could have happened to you!"

"No, it couldn't," Amy said quietly. "When I called for a cab from the public phone I made sure I called a well-known company. They have only women drivers. I've seen the commercials on TV."

Flabbergasted, Marcy stared at the child. "Woman driver or not, Amy, it's not safe for you to be wandering around by yourself like this."

Ignoring Marcy's comment, Amy complained, "I didn't like my driver. She fussed at me all the way over here. She said my mama and daddy should punish me and make sure I didn't do this again."

"You're fortunate you got a cabdriver who cared about you," Marcy remarked.

Amy set her suitcase down. "I'm running away from home. I came here because I need to borrow some money."

Marcy moved to her desk, picked up the telephone and began to dial.

"Who are you calling?" Amy asked.

"Nona. To let her know you're safe and with me. This is absolutely the most idiotic thing you could have done." At about the same moment Wanda Courtland answered the phone. It took Marcy a second to regain her equilibrium. "Wanda, is that you?"

"Oh, yes," she replied. "Nona is in the hospital having some tests, and Gil had meetings he couldn't cancel or miss. I had the time off, so I agreed to stay with Amy. The children and I flew into San Antonio yesterday. We'll be here for the week."

"You sound rather harried," Marcy commented, her gaze straying to Amy who now sat in one of the wing chairs, thumbing through a magazine.

"I am," Wanda admitted. "I was up with Kevin all night, he had a sore throat and was running a temperature. The children are bored because they've had to spend the morning at the doctor's office. Right now, each of them is in a different room, and the house is quiet for the first time today."

"One of them is sitting in my office," Marcy informed her.

"Oh, my God!" Wanda exclaimed.

"It's all right," Marcy hastened to assure her. "Amy's fine."

"I had no idea," Wanda murmured, with tears in her voice. "She and Drake had a disagreement over one of her toys. When I chastised both of them, Amy shouted at me and refused to apologize. I sent her to her bedroom to think about the incident. If I hadn't been so tired, I would have handled the situation better. I had no idea she's slipped out of the house. Dear God, Marcy, whatever will Gil think of me? I can't even keep watch over his child. It's a miracle she's safe."

"She's fine," Marcy repeated. "She's sitting here in my office, looking through a magazine."

"I'll be right over to get her," Wanda said. "Give me time to get the children together, and tell me how to get to your office."

After Marcy gave Wanda the directions, she hung up the phone and turned to Amy.

"Why did you run away?"

"Mrs. Courtland was mean to me."

"She's worried about you."

"She doesn't care about me," Amy declared. "All she cares about is Daddy. Before he started dating her, Daddy paid attention to me. Now he calls her all the time and talks to her about things."

"What happened to make you change your mind about Wanda?" Marcy asked. "Sunday before last, when we left Fort Clark Springs, you and she were getting along fine."

"She got mad at me today because I wouldn't let Drake pick up my Barbie dolls, and then for no reason at all she punished me. She sent me to my room. She didn't do anything to Drake."

"Are you sure this is what happened?"

Nodding her head, Amy refused to look at Marcy. "She shouted at me." Tears began to flow down her cheeks, and she raised her head. "She shouted at me and made me go to my room, but she let Drake stay in the playroom and play with my dolls. He was playing with one of Mama's dolls."

Marcy took the child into her arms. "Did you shout at Wanda?"

"Maybe a little," Amy confessed.

"Well, that was wrong, Amy. She was trying to teach you that part of having a family is learning to live together and sharing."

"But I never wanted brothers," Amy said. "I only wanted a Big Sister. Brothers are mean."

"No, they're not," Marcy replied. "They can be mean sometimes, but so can sisters."

"If it wasn't for Drake, I would like Mrs. Courtland. He made her get angry at me. She punished me, but she didn't do anything to Drake. And she didn't make him put my dolls up."

"What did you do that made Wanda send you to your room?"

Again Amy lowered her head and mumbled, "I guess I yelled at her."

"Did Drake yell at his mother? Did he disobey her in any way?"

"No."

"Then Wanda was right in punishing you and not him," Marcy pointed out. "What if the scene had been reversed? Would you want her to punish you because she punished Drake?"

Amy shook her head and again mumbled, "No."

Marcy continued to talk to Amy as they waited for Wanda. When she finally arrived, her eyes were bruised and swollen from crying. Looking forlorn, Amy sat in the wing chair. Wanda rushed to where she sat, knelt down, and hugged her.

"I don't know what I would have done if something had happened to you." Fresh tears flowed down her cheeks. "I never dreamed you'd run away. I disciplined you because I love you, Amy. Because I care about you. I didn't mean to hurt you."

"You don't love me like you do Drake, and Kevin, and Elana."

"No," Wanda agreed, "I don't. I don't love Drake like I do Kevin or Elana. Each one of you is different, and I love you in a different way than I love any of them. If I didn't love you, though, I wouldn't be here taking care of you while your father is working and Nona is in the hospital."

"Where are the others?" Amy asked.

"You mean the children?" When Amy nodded, Wanda replied, "They're waiting in the car."

She stood and dragged the other chair closer to Amy. Sitting down, she extracted a tissue from her pocket, wiping her eyes and blowing her nose.

"You and Daddy are probably gonna get married, aren't you?"

"We're thinking about it," Wanda admitted. "Naturally, before we make a decision like that we'll have a family conference and talk it over with you guys. Your opinions are very important.''

Amy seemed to be considering what Wanda had said. Then she spoke: ''You let Drake play with my mama's Barbie doll.''

''Your mother's doll,'' Wanda murmured. ''I'm so sorry, Amy, but you didn't tell me. I wouldn't have allowed anyone to play with it had I known. I think we need to go through your games and toys and put away those you want to keep and don't wish to share with others. That way, other children will know which things are precious to you and they'll understand which toys are for sharing and which aren't. Does that sound like a good idea?''

Nodding, Amy stared at Wanda.

''You hurt Drake's feelings, too.''

''I did?'' Amy was surprised.

''He didn't know the doll belonged to your mother and that it was very special to you. He thought you just didn't want him to play with your toys. I had been making the children share their toys with you, but it seemed to him that you didn't want to share yours with him.''

''I just didn't want him to hurt mama's doll.''

''If your father and I marry,'' Wanda pointed out, ''or if he marries another woman who happens to have children, you're going to have to learn to get along with your stepbrothers and sisters. You're going to have to learn to cooperate. As for me, I won't tolerate any of my children running away every time something happens at the house that makes them unhappy. We have a standing rule that we follow.''

''What's a standing rule?''

"A rule that no one can break. It's a law," Wanda explained. "The rule is, that when somebody is unhappy, he or she will come to me and talk about it. Then we have a family conference to determine the best way of working out the problem."

The door opened, and Marcy turned to see Joe Alexander enter the office. His puzzled gaze moved around the circle of people, finally coming to rest on Marcy.

"Sorry. I didn't know you were having—" He paused as he saw the suitcase beside Marcy's desk. "—Having this," he finished.

Marcy laughed softly. "A family crisis. I'd like you to meet my Little Sister, Amy Calderon, and Wanda Courtland, a friend of Amy's father.

"Hello, Amy, Mrs. Courtland," Joe said and tipped his hard hat. He looked at Marcy. "When you get a few minutes, I want to talk with you. A question about Alamo Supermarket. It's not an emergency, but don't let it hang too long. Okay?"

Marcy rose. "If it's all right with you, Joe, we'll go in the other room and let Wanda and Amy have the office."

Joe nodded.

"Thanks, Marcy," Wanda said. "We won't take up your office much longer. Mr. Alexander, I'm glad to have met you."

"Glad to have met you," he responded, and then smiled.

After Marcy and Joe went into another office and closed the door, Amy spoke.

"Are you going to tell Daddy I ran away?"

Wanda nodded her head, but when she saw the tears running down Amy's cheeks, she hastened to add, "I have to, darling. You're his child. He has a right to know."

"He's going to be mad at me," Amy said. "So mad, he may never love me again."

"No," Wanda consoled her. "Your father will always love and forgive you. He'll even understand when I explain it resulted from a misunderstanding and you didn't know to come talk to me about the problem."

"You'll do that?" Amy asked.

"I will. I know your father will understand and not be angry this time."

Amy slid out of her chair and hugged Wanda. "Thank you, Mrs. Courtland."

Wanda gazed fondly at her little charge. "We're going to have to find some other name for you to call me. Mrs. Courtland sounds much too formal, doesn't it?"

Amy nodded.

"Are you ready to go home?"

Again Amy nodded. This time she walked to the desk and picked up her suitcase.

"I'm sorry I shouted at you," she murmured. "I didn't mean to."

"I know," Wanda answered gently. "I can understand how you felt when you saw Drake playing with a doll that had belonged to your mother. It is very special to you, and it shouldn't be played with. I didn't know that, or I wouldn't have insisted that you share it with him."

THE FOLLOWING THURSDAY night Marcy walked into Kyla's office for her second meeting since she had been matched with Amy. She was surprised to see Wanda sitting there. Smiling, Amy skipped to the door.

"When Wanda picked me up from ballet, she asked if she could come to the meeting with Daddy and me, and I said yes," Amy announced.

"Good for you," Marcy returned.

In charge of the meeting, as usual, Kyla sat in the chair behind her desk. "Well, now that we're all here, we'll begin."

This time Kyla relied less on notes and formalities, and soon Amy was occupying center stage. With great flourish she told Kyla about her many visits with Marcy, ending with her spill from the horse.

"Marcy stopped the horse," she said, "and it was Kevin who pulled my foot from the stirrup. He probably saved my life, 'cause if the horse had started running again, he would have drug me more. And Brant was the one who took me to the hospital." Hardly pausing to draw a breath, Amy declared, "Marcy's dating Brant, and he's my friend."

For a good while the conversation centered on Amy's ride and subsequent rescue. Then she began to talk about Nona and her visit to the hospital.

"Mrs. Courtland has been baby-sitting me this week," Amy explained, then quietly confessed to having run away. "But I promised Daddy I wouldn't ever do it again. We have a standing rule."

"Oh," Kyla remarked.

Amy nodded. "You can't go against a standing rule. It's law and has to obeyed."

Kyla nodded.

Amy, warming to her subject and speaking in a highly animated voice, which was made more dramatic by flowing hand gestures, began to talk nonstop about Elana, Drake and Kevin. Although Amy didn't talk as freely about Wanda, the fact that the child willingly allowed her to join them for the monthly meeting told Marcy that it was only a matter of time before Amy accepted her completely.

The meeting was a success. Afterward, when they were standing in the parking lot getting ready to leave, Marcy inquired about Nona.

"She's doing fine," Gil informed her. "The doctor found no signs of cancer, but at her age, the testing was rather stressful. He's putting her on a new medication for her arthritis and wanted her to take some time off. She should be able to return to work in a couple of weeks."

"Who's going to keep Amy?" Marcy asked.

"I'm staying through the weekend," Wanda answered. "Then Amy will fly to Dallas with me. Gil has agreed to let her stay with my stepmother. I've talked so much about Amy, Bebe wants to meet her."

Amy nodded her head. "And I've bought Bebe a new key ring. Daddy and I are going to have her name engraved on it. On the telephone she promised me that she'd hang it in her special cabinet." Amy quieted for a second, then asked, "You're still going to be my Big Sister when I get back, aren't you?"

"You bet I am," Marcy replied. "As long as we're matched, vacations and events will come along that will separate us for a while from time to time, as they do Brant and me, but we'll always be Sisters."

Marcy talked about it as, they made their way toward the cars in the parking lot.

"Daddy," Amy coaxed, "can we get an ice cream? Please?"

Gil smiled at his daughter, then looked at Wanda. "It's your decision. Your children are the ones who are being baby-sat."

"Debbie and Julie Burrows are staying with the children tonight," Wanda explained to Marcy. "The Burrowses were kind enough to let the girls stay, but they don't want them out later than eleven o'clock."

"We can be home by then, can't we?" Amy asked.

"Yes, we can," Wanda answered. "This is your night, and it's not that late."

"Oh, goody," Amy said. "Can I ride with Marcy?"

"You sure can," Gil agreed, "if Marcy doesn't mind."

"Not at all. This will be a good time for me and Amy to talk." She waved to Gil and Wanda. "We'll see y'all later."

Soon Marcy and Amy were buckled up and on their way across town.

"I'm so glad you're driving with me. I like to ride in your truck. What did you want to talk to me about?" Amy said, talking nonstop.

"I wanted to be the one to tell you that I'll be going to New York this summer for several weeks."

Amy was quiet for a second, then said, "To visit with Brant."

"That's right," Marcy said.

"It's—it's just a vacation, isn't it?" Amy asked. "You're not going to move there, are you?"

"Just a vacation," Marcy answered and clasped Amy's hand to give it a reassuring squeeze. "I'll be back just like you, and we'll have lots of fun during the summer."

"But if you and Brant . . . marry," Amy said, "you might move away from me. You won't be my Big Sister."

"Brant and I are thinking about getting married," Marcy admitted, "but I'm not planning to move. I'm going to be your Big Sister for a long time." Marcy released Amy's hand to make a turn.

"Marcy," Amy said after a while, "if either one of us moved, we could still be Big Sisters, couldn't we? I mean, maybe not with the program, but we could still be friends. We could write letters and call each other on the telephone."

Marcy stopped the car at the signal light and glanced down at the concerned little face. She brushed a tendril of hair from her cheek.

"With or without the program, no matter where we live," she promised, "we'll always be sisters and friends."

Amy's face burst into a huge grin. "Will you send me a card from New York?"

"I surely will." She smiled and winked. "What do you think about my buying you something to add to your Barbie collection while I'm there?"

"Oh, Marcy, will you!" Amy exclaimed.

"Of course," Marcy replied, "and you can help me think of gifts I can buy for Elana, Drake and Kevin."

"Yes." Amy giggled. "And we won't tell them. This will be our surprise, won't it, Marcy?"

Marcy nodded. "Yes, it will."

Later, as they sat in the ice-cream parlor, Gil told Marcy that he and Wanda were taking the children to Sea World on the following Sunday.

"We're not going on Saturday, Marcy," Amy explained, "because that's our first real softball game.

And I'm getting good at catching and batting. Drake has been helping me. He's going to come see my practice."

"All of us are," Gil added, then asked Marcy, "Why don't you and Brant join us on Sunday?"

"I can't make any plans for Brant," Marcy told him. "I never know when he's going to be in town, but thanks for asking."

"Where is he now?" Gil asked.

"In Europe," Marcy replied, wishing he were with her. "On his way from France to England."

"Brant's job is like Daddy's." Amy gave her ice cream a big lick. "He has to be out of town a lot, and you're lonely. You're really going to need me to keep you company." With an ice-cream-whiskered upper lip, she grinned. "And I will. I'm going to be the bestest Little Sister you can have."

SATURDAY WAS an excellent day for softball. The early summer weather was pleasant, and the sun was shining. Marcy was glad she was involved with the center's softball league. She would have been at loose ends had she stayed home. Brant had called last night to tell her he didn't know when he would be back.

When the practice game was over, Pete took Gil and Wanda for a tour of the center; Drake and Kevin joined several other boys, who were also visiting, in a game of tag; Elana lounged on the grounds with her cassette player and earphones. Amy helped Marcy collect the equipment.

When all of it was in the box, Amy declared, "I think Mrs. Courtland and Daddy are going to get married."

"What do you think about it?" Marcy asked.

"Well," Amy said thoughtfully, "it'll be different. I'll have two brothers and a sister—a Big Sister, too. Now I won't have to play make-believe any more. Elana will be a real big sister. I like Elana, but you'll always be my Big Sister, too, Marcy. No one will ever take your place."

"I know that," Marcy answered. "And it's fine for you to have other people in your life. You should. If your father does marry, Wanda, I think you're going to be very happy. She'll be a very good stepmother."

Again Amy was quiet for a long while before she spoke: "Mrs. Courtland was allowed to choose a special name for her stepmother." Not waiting for a response, she continued, "She's the one who decided she'd call her Bebe. Well, I've decided I'm going to have a special name for my stepmother."

"I take it you've been thinking of one."

Amy nodded. "I called my mother Mama, and Elana, Drake and Kevin call Mrs. Courtland Mother. I've been thinking it would be nice to call her Mother. Especially if her and Daddy should have any more babies. That way, we'll all be calling her the same thing, and the baby won't get confused."

"I think that's very nice and thoughtful of you," Marcy remarked. "Have you told Wanda?"

"No. I talked with Daddy about it, and he said he'd tell her."

"I think Wanda would like to hear it from you."

"Then maybe I'll tell her," Amy decided. "I also asked Daddy to tell me all about Mama."

Without Amy saying more, Marcy understood what she was talking about.

"He said Mama had always had a weak heart. She could have given up my little brother. The doctors could have performed an operation, but Mama felt that God wouldn't be pleased with her if she did. Daddy wanted her to let the doctors operate, but he told Mama she could decide. He promised her that if she died, he would take care of me. Now, she's in heaven."

"If your father and Wanda marry," Marcy asked, "are you worried about her having another baby?"

"No. Daddy said she was strong. He said she would be all right." They walked a little farther, then Amy questioned, "Do you miss Brant?"

"Very much," Marcy admitted.

"Do you want to marry him?"

"Yes," Marcy replied, "I do."

"I'm sorry about the way I acted in Fort Clark Springs. I really don't hate Brant, and I want you to marry him, Marcy. Even if you do marry him, you can still be my Big Sister, can't you?"

"Not only can I, but I will," Marcy declared.

"I'll always love you, Marcy, because you're my Big Sister. You don't have to spend all your time with me. You can spend some with Brant."

"Thank you for telling me this," responded Marcy. "It's a sign that you're growing up. But I'll always have time for you.

"Promise?" Amy asked.

"Promise," Marcy agreed.

THAT EVENING Clarice flung open the front door and smiled at Marcy. "I'm so glad you could make it," she said, then leaned over to kiss her sister-in-law on the cheek.

"How could I refuse? It was a summons rather than an invitation," Marcy teased, then asked, "Where are

Sarah and Diane? It's unusual for them not to be here giving me a warm welcome." She held up a decorator shopping bag. "I even brought them a gift."

"Josie's mother is keeping them for us tonight," Clarice explained. "We wanted this to be an adults-only party."

"What are we going to do?" Marcy asked mischievously. "Watch risqué movies?"

"Nothing that exciting," Clarice replied, leading the way into the spacious den at the back of the house. "The Galvan men wanted to have a family conference and since we have the biggest house, we were chosen to be the hosts. Actually, Ethan and I were outvoted four to two, and Mark and David even had the audacity to plan the menu for me."

"All of us here under one roof at the same time," Marcy remarked dryly. "This must be some conference."

Marcy repeated her comment when she saw her brothers and the other two sisters-in-law. After a great deal of laughter and talking, they sat down to dinner. It was a veritable feast, they all claimed unanimously. The conversation remained lively, but as soon as they finished eating, Clarice cleared off the table.

"I told you this was a family conference, and it is," she said to Marcy. "So we're going to leave the four of you alone."

Tammy and Josie rose with Clarice, and went walking into the living room.

Wondering what was happening, Marcy looked from one brother to the next. Ethan leaned forward.

"I only wish Papa and Mama could see you now, Marcy. They'd be proud of their only daughter, their baby."

"Even if she is a crusader?" Marcy teased.

"Yes," Ethan said. "You're the one who reminded us who we are. You're the one who continually reminds us where we came from."

Marcy blinked in surprise. She hadn't expected the seriousness of both his voice and his words.

"Mark, David and I have talked it over," he continued, "and while none of us wants to work at the company, we don't want it to leave the family. And we don't want you to have to sell the ranch so you can buy it yourself. You're the one who fought through the years to keep both. You deserve the ranch and you deserve the company."

"That's all been taken care of," Marcy began. "Brant is—"

"No. Brant isn't. Danny called late last night to let me know he had turned Brant's offer down."

"What?" Marcy exclaimed. "He can't."

"But he has. It seems that Danny's involved politically with Justis and owes him unwavering loyalty. In case you don't know, Justis Juarez is Colby Zacharias's silent partner."

"I knew it," Marcy said, as her earlier lightheartedness slipped away. "It looks like Zacharias will get the company, no matter what."

"No, he won't," David countered. "You have first option to buy. Uncle Lonzo guaranteed you that, and Danny can't change it even if he wanted to."

"But I don't have the money," she stated.

"We do," Ethan told her. As Marcy's gaze slid from one brother to the next, they all nodded their heads. "Among the three of us, we can borrow the money to buy Tío's share at the price Danny quoted you."

"Will this put you in a bind?" she asked, wanting to accept their offer but not wanting to be responsible for putting them in financial difficulty.

"It'll be the toughest on me," Mark admitted. "But Tammy and I agreed that this is something we want to do. As Ethan said, the company and the ranch are all we Galvans have left to show for our heritage. We want to keep them in the family."

"In our family," David emphasized.

"Each of us will have fifteen-percent interest," Ethan continued. "We're going to give you the leftover, five percent, so you'll always have controlling interest."

"But," David went on, "you'll have to promise us that you'll be solely responsible for running the place."

"Later," Mark said, "when you get the money, you can have the option of buying back our shares."

As tears ran freely down her cheeks, Marcy got up to hug each of her brothers.

Later that night, as Marcy was lying in bed, she thought about her brothers' sacrifice, and she realized with a start that although she wanted to keep the company, it no longer promised the same fulfillment it did for her before she'd fallen in love with Brant. He was the center of her life now.

The Center was still important, but she realized that it, too, could and would function without her. Fighting illiteracy was not a cause that was limited to one location or to one race of people; she could continue to support literacy programs wherever she lived.

Her only concern was Galvan Construction, but that concern had really diminished now that she was sure it would remain in the family with herself and her brothers forming its board of directors. Joe Alexander could easily run the company for them. If—*when* she was gone with Brant, her brothers could oversee the business. They could keep her informed.

Feeling lighter than she had in days, she went to sleep. Later the telephone rang and wakened her. Although the ringing continued to echo through the room, she lay there a moment before she moved; then she opened her eyes to peer through the darkness at the digital clock.

"Hello," she murmured when she lifted the receiver.

"Sweetheart." Brant's voice poured through the line to wash away her loneliness. "Do you look as sexy as you sound?"

Marcy laughed softly and pushed herself up on one elbow. "Hardly. Where are you?"

"London," he answered. "I'll be home next Sunday, but it'll be late. Real late."

"I don't care," she told him. "Be sure to call me. I want to come to the airport to meet you."

"No." He lowered his voice. "I'll rent a car and drive home. I want to find you in bed when I get there."

His words filled Marcy with pleasure.

"Honey, I had to call you." His tone changed to one of concern. "I just received word from Shepherd that Danny turned down my offer on the company. You're going to have to let me give you the money as a gift, so you can buy it outright."

"Thank you, darling," she replied with love for him rushing through her, "but we Galvans have it under control."

"You do?" He sounded genuinely surprised.

With pride Marcy related what her brothers were doing. "This way it truly remains in the family," she explained, "and I have controlling interest. It will be my company, Brant, and it will belong to the Galvans."

They talked longer, even to the point of repeating themselves, but neither noticed; certainly neither cared. They simply wanted to hear each other's voice. Finally, Brant rang off with the promise of seeing her the following Sunday.

Marcy returned the receiver to its cradle and snuggled under the sheet, but sleep was a long time coming. All she could think about was Brant coming home.

EPILOGUE

STANDING AT THE WINDOW of her office, Marcy surveyed the premises of Galvan Construction. It still belonged to the Galvans—to her brothers—and she had the controlling interest. In effect, it was her company. She had fought for it, and she had won. Had she won? She had everything she thought she wanted; yet she felt alone. Through an endowment, Brant had made it possible for POD to buy Estella Esteban Elementary School and surrounding property. She had her literacy center. But that was not enough to make her completely happy. Brant once told her success was a hollow victory if you had no one with whom to share it.

She saw the Lincoln Town Car pull into the parking lot. The door opened, and Brant slid out. He stood for a moment, looking around. Then, as if he knew she was watching him, he directed his gaze to the window.

His being here was no surprise. She had known he would be here to pick her up after work. But seeing him filled her with a an excitement and anticipation that time would never erase.

She picked up her purse and hurried through the office and out the front door. He held his arms open and she went into them, lifting her face for his kiss.

"Are you ready to go?" he asked.

"Yes," she said.

"Without knowing where I'm taking you?"

"Yes, I trust you. In the past your surprises have been wonderful, and worth the waiting and anticipation."

"I want always to be worthy of your trust." He brushed a strand of hair from her face. "You're the most important person in my life. Without you I would have no life."

She knew; she felt the same way about him. They walked to the car and soon were on their way to the Hill Country.

"The feasibility study came in last week," he told her. "I can open a branch office, here, Marcy, but it's not practical or feasible for me to work out of this office entirely."

She wasn't surprised. She had known this was coming.

"But I'm not going to give you up, Marcy. I'd like us to discuss a compromise."

"We *must* have one," she declared. "I don't intend to give you up, Brant. Before I lose you, I'd give up everything else in my life."

He quickly glanced at her and their eyes met.

"After the papers were signed and Galvan Construction belonged to me and my brothers," she confessed, "I was happy, but I realized it wasn't enough. Without you, my success was hollow, without meaning."

She took a deep breath. "Joe Alexander is the new manager of Galvan Construction, my brothers and I are the board of directors. I'll come to New York with you. I'll fit into your life-style, Brant. I'll even travel with you."

"You'll do this for me?" he asked.

"Yes. But when we decide to have our family, I want you home with me and the children."

He nodded. "I will be. Like you, I did a lot of serious thinking, sweetheart, and I determined that I wasn't going to lose you. I've already begun a major reform movement in my life. I've made Shepherd executive director of the company, and he'll be doing most of the traveling from now on. I'll be taking care of the home office, and of the home—*our* home."

As they drove, Brant talked about the changes he had effected in the organizational structure of his company. Marcy was so captivated, she didn't realize they were traveling to Chester Hudley's place until Brant turned off the asphalt onto a dirt road. She looked at him in puzzlement.

Brant smiled. "You said you loved this place, didn't you? And that you would love to own and decorate it?"

Slowly Marcy smiled. "Yes."

"Then I think you and I need to talk about whether we want to buy it or not."

"But... what about New York?"

"I was thinking that we could live there part of the year and here the other part. That way, you don't have to give up running your company completely, nor do I. We'll have the best of both worlds—if that's agreeable to you?"

"Most agreeable," she answered.

He parked the car in front of the house, and they strolled to the river. As they stood beneath the cypress trees, he reached into his pocket and pulled out a small package.

"I know it's rather presumptuous of me and I didn't discuss this with you beforehand, but when I saw it, I had to have it for you. I bought it with the guarantee, however, that I could return it if you weren't pleased with it for any reason."

"It," she teased. "What is this 'it'?"

"This is it."

He opened the package and withdrew a jeweler's box. He lifted the lid, and Marcy gazed at the diamond solitaire that sparkled in the sunlight.

"Brant," she murmured, "it's beautiful."

"Will you marry me?" he asked.

"Yes."

"When?"

"As soon as we can."

He took the ring out of the box and slipped it on her finger.

"I warn you," she said, "my family is going to want a big wedding with all the pomp and pageantry associated with one."

"As long as it's a wedding, I don't care if it's little or big. I'm eager for you to become Mrs. Brant Holland."

"I'm just as eager," she answered.

They sealed their engagement with a kiss.

LOOKING AT her reflection, Amy stood in front of the mirror backstage. Marcy combed her hair into a thick chignon and fastened the decorative barrette in place.

"How do I look?" Amy asked.

"You look beautiful," Marcy answered.

"I'm kind of scared," Amy confessed.

Marcy embraced her. "It's just the jitters, and those are natural. They'll go away as soon as you hear the music."

"Promise?" Amy asked.

"Promise," Marcy said. "Mrs. Eanes had special ballet classes all summer just for this recital, and you know your routines front and back, right?"

Amy nodded her head.

"Now you get out there and dance, Little Sister, dance."

In her purple tights and overskirt of lavender, Amy ran gracefully to center stage, and stood gazing at the curtain as it slowly rose. She listened to the music that swelled to fill the building.

"Welcome to the September Festival of Dance," Mrs. Eanes announced over the microphone, "Tonight I want to introduce our dancer for the quarter, Amelia Calderon. She's going to perform the..."

The ballet instructor continued to talk, but Amy was too excited to listen to her. The auditorium was full; one face blended into another. Then, on the second row, front and center, Amy saw her family. She smiled and in rhythm to the music began to dance. She swirled; she swayed; she danced and danced, feeling as if she were in the clouds. She closed her eyes and remembered when she used to make-believe that this was happening to her.

When the music finally stopped, the people clapped. The applause got louder and louder as the audience continued to applaud. Then they stood. Amy bowed— once, twice, three times. She blew kisses. Then she saw two boys walking up either aisle, their arms filled with flowers. Drake and Kevin.

Accepting them, she felt the tears burning her cheeks. She had never been this happy in her entire life. She smiled at her family—at Nona and Bebe, and Marcy and Brant, and Daddy and "Mother."

She looked at Elana—her big sister. Then her gaze went to Marcy, and she gave her a special smile. Amy no longer had to play make-believe: She had two big sisters.

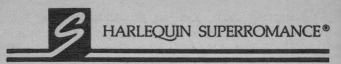

Books by Emma Merritt

BSEM

HARLEQUIN®

Temptation

Rebels & Rogues

Jared: He'd had the courage to fight in Vietnam. But did he have the courage to fight for the woman he loved?

THE SOLDIER OF FORTUNE
By Kelly Street
Temptation #421, December

All men are not created equal. Some are rough around the edges. Tough-minded but tenderhearted. Incredibly sexy. The tempting fulfillment of every woman's fantasy.

When it's time to fight for what they believe in, to win that special woman, our Rebels and Rogues are heroes at heart. Twelve Rebels and Rogues, one each month in 1992, only from Harlequin Temptation.

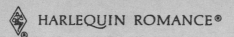

HARLEQUIN ROMANCE®

Some people have the spirit
of Christmas all year round...

People like Blake Connors
and Karin Palmer.

Meet them—and love them!—in
Eva Rutland's
ALWAYS CHRISTMAS.

Harlequin Romance #3240
Available in December wherever
Harlequin books are sold.

HRHX

HE CROSSED TIME FOR HER

Captain Richard Colter rode the high seas, brandished a sword and pillaged treasure ships. A swashbuckling privateer, he was a man with voracious appetites and a lust for living. And in the eighteenth century, any woman swooned at his feet for the favor of his wild passion. History had it that Captain Richard Colter went down with his ship, the *Black Cutter*, in a dazzling sea battle off the Florida coast in 1792.

Then what was he doing washed ashore on a Key West beach in 1992—alive?

MARGARET ST. GEORGE brings you an extraspecial love story this month, about an extraordinary man who would do anything for the woman he loved:

#462 THE PIRATE AND HIS LADY
by Margaret St. George

When love is meant to be, nothing can stand in its way . . . not even time.

Don't miss American Romance
#462 THE PIRATE AND HIS LADY.
It's a love story you'll never forget.

PAL-A